UNDER A VIOLET MOON

Wild and Free

Tara N Gabrys

To Elliott and Aria
You give me courage

CONTENTS

ONE

The sea is my soulmate. It has been since the day I first set eyes on its vast and ever-changing body. My mother gave birth to me in a storm, caught in an unforgiving riptide. She pulled me out with her own two hands and laid me right onto her heaving chest, slick with sweat and seawater. Since that day, I've had a connection to the sea, a magnetic pull. My body feeds off it in the same way a flower needs the sun to grow and flourish. If I didn't have it, I fear I might wither and die.

How fortunate that I live in Pearle Castle, named for its pearlescent walls, perched on the southern coast of Aqualasia Islands. Its steep stone tower walls jut straight from the sea, allowing the waves to lap at its sandstone base. Every night, I sleep with my balcony doors wide so the crash of the waves and the salty sea air can find their way to me, even in slumber.

I watch the sun move closer to the horizon through the canopy of the massive weeping willow I'm under and know my time is almost up. The vines of the willow sway in the wind, rustling the earth and the natural pool below. Its tendrils move, brushing the ground like delicate fingers. Without even glancing at my abalone pocket watch, a gift from my father, I know I need to get back to the palace. I look down at the crumpled portraits of the young women staring back at me and my stomach turns. I gather them together, leaving the mystery for another day, and shove them into my bag, preparing to head back home.

Tonight is another full moon, which means another party hosted by the king and queen of the islands, or, as I like to call them, Mother and Father. Every month, they throw another soiree to celebrate the Full Celestia. You would think a monthly lavish party with sparkling flutes and decadent pastries sounds dreamy, but it's anything but. It's all too much—faking pleasantries to strangers, honoring the moon simply because it's there. It gets old. The elaborate, seven-course dinners and dancing with acquaintances are overkill. The guests trying to worm their way into the royal family's good graces, feigning interest to see what they can leech from you is exhausting.

It drives me mad wondering why my parents are more concerned about the Full Celestia celebrations than the handful of portraits in my bag. Does it not bother them as it does me? Does it not keep them up at night wondering where these women have gone? I can't be the only one who sees this as more than just the age-old story of someone being lost at sea.

I can hear my mother's voice in my head. "We must honor the moon's cycles and energies beginning anew." But the full moon has never moved me like it does my mother. The only connection I've ever felt so strongly towards is the sea. Maybe that's how my mother feels about the moon.

As a child, I loved the monthly gatherings. The delicate dresses with all their sparkling adornments were something I looked forward to. I loved staying up late to watch the fireworks show and running through the halls with my cousins, sliding in our tights. Yet, as I grew older, I saw the soirees for what they really were: another way to keep the people of Aqualasia happy without doing much of anything but hosting a party.

Years from now, when I take the throne, these parties will be the first thing to go. No more spending time and resources planning and inviting strangers into our home to celebrate the moon and ignoring the fact that women are going missing.

I huff a breath as I sit up from the willow's limb, my violet-tinted brown curls dragging across the bark. If only I could spend the evening here, hidden under the canopy of the willow, stargazing with the sound of rustling leaves to comfort me.

This willow, surrounded by a lush, green forest, is easily my favorite place on the island. It's close enough to hear the roaring waves of the ocean break against the rocky cliff edges and near enough to the palace grounds that I won't be scolded for not using an escort. It's something about the wildlife here and the babbling of the stream flowing into the teal pond below that draws me in. Lilies, lizards, smooth stones that peek out from below the surface, and the lime-colored vines of the willow welcome me with open arms every visit. This beautiful tree is my sanctuary, the place I come to when the palace is too much when I need stillness and calm.

I slide down the trunk sloping right into the stream and welcome the cool water as my feet hit the pebbled sand. I pull up my skirts too late and curse myself as water drips from the soaked lace. I will never hear the end of it from Rose.

The pool is a small piece of the ocean that's somehow found its way into the island's forest. I sigh, taking one last moment before heading back, preparing myself for the evening ahead. I tilt my head towards the periwinkle sky, eyes shut as I fill my lungs with the earthy scent that can only be found here. When I exhale the last of the air in my lungs, I slip on my shoes, pull my dress up higher, and run home.

The trees and brush become a blur of greens and browns as I dash through the forest toward the Aqualasian flags flying high above the battlements of the castle. My mother will be waiting for me at the gates. If I'm lucky, she won't be too mad that I'm a little late and slightly wet. She takes the Full Celestia celebrations a little too seriously, in my opinion, pushing her beliefs onto everyone. The moon being fully visible to us roughly once a month is hardly a call for celebration, but to my mother, it's more than that. The death and rebirth of it all and the cycle beginning anew brings meaning to her in some way. I suspect my father leans toward my opinion on the subject, but mother is his queen, so the soirees continue, per tradition.

When the forest opens up to cobblestone roads and small shops teeming with people, I veer right toward the harbor, where I pass fishermen hauling in their catch of the day. A parchment flutters on the dock's wooden post; another flier for a missing person who probably won't be found. People are lost at sea more often than one might think—pirates, sunken ships, a quarrel on deck resulting in a man overboard. But this flier is of a woman, just like the others in my bag, which is why it catches my eye. It's rare to see a flier for a missing woman, as they don't often find themselves sailing the seas as men do. I grab the flier from the post and add it with the others. Maybe this one will offer some insight as to what is happening to these young women on our island.

The fishermen hauling in their catch look beat from the sun, their figures silhouetted against the glittering sea. Thick ropes wind around the dock posts; the boats line up in their rightful spots for the evening. Everybody is busy with one task or another, tending to their boats or loading supplies for the following day. Taking this way home allows me to enter through the kitchens and hopefully avoid the queen's wrath . . . at least until I'm in my room as I should have been hours ago.

In my hurry, I nearly run into the young fisherman with the sun-bleached hair hauling a crate of salmon from the docks. His blond locks are so striking, they almost appear white in the sun. He has been helping his father on the docks for as long as I can remember. But he's not just any fisherman. No, he was the first real friend I'd ever had. *Ezera.*

"Sorry!" I shout as I whirl past him. His muscled arms glimmer in the sunlight as he moves the heavy crate with ease. His wrinkled white shirt clings to his body with sweat or sea mist. Likely both.

When I was young, my father would sometimes take me down to the docks when he oversaw certain shipments. While he was busy being diplomatic, he would let me play with the boy on the docks, stringing nets along the pier. Ezera and I would see who could skip rocks the farthest, and he'd teach me how to tie sailors' knots. It's been nearly a decade since we've had any sort of interaction. Life has become more demanding as the years slipped by. It seems time has turned him into more of a man and less of the boy I remember.

"My apologies, princess." His husky reply is a mere echo as I round the corner of the castle wall leading to the kitchen's back door. Part of me wonders if he remembers those days on the docks when we were young. Or maybe it meant more to me than it did to him.

I slip through the kitchen door, panting, and slow my strides so I don't knock into the trays of food prepared for tonight.

"Good day, Cealene." The head chef drops a hefty lobster into a bubbling pot on the stove and chuckles as he watches me zigzag through the chaos of cooks preparing for the evening ahead. This isn't the first time I've attempted this strategy, entering through the kitchens, and it won't be the last.

"Don't tell the queen," I holler as I snag a powdered pastry from the stack before taking the stairs two at a time. When I hit the living quarters,

I slow my pace to a leisurely stroll so as to not attract any more attention, licking the sugared powder from my fingers as I go.

The sole upside of the evening's festivities is definitely the almond crescents. These delicate sweets aren't made often because my father doesn't fancy them. But tonight, I will be eating my weight in them.

When my bag slips from my shoulder, I clutch it in my hand crushing the papers within. The rustle brings my attention back to the newest flier among the rest. And I can't help but wonder who this woman is, or where she is.

But most importantly, why don't my parents care about her disappearance as much as I do?

Two

As I turn down the long hallway to my sleeping quarters, I nearly slam into my mother's slim, towering figure.

"Cealene," she scolds, arms crossed over her crimson gown.

"Hi, Mama." I smile as I kiss her cheek and continue to my room, hopeful she doesn't notice my haphazard state.

"Cealene, do not think for one second that I don't know what time it is," she calls to me as she follows me down the softly lit hallway and into my room. Rose is already at my vanity, waiting patiently for me to sit.

"Don't worry, Mama. I'm here now, and I am certain my tardiness won't interfere with tonight's events." As I drop into the velvet chair, I catch Rose's gaze in the mirror, amusement shining in her light brown eyes.

"And do not think for one second that I don't know where you've been. I told you, I detest the idea of you out in the forest by yourself. You are a princess, an easy target with a big reward if captured." At this point, she's crossed the room to where I sit, placing her delicate hands on my shoulders, looking at my reflection in the vanity mirror. "If anything ever happened to you, Cealene, I would never recover from it."

This is a dance we've danced before. She plays the guilt card, hoping I won't venture out again to keep her from worrying, and I try not to let it work. What she doesn't understand is that I need the solitude. I am more than capable of taking care of myself in the forest lining the western part of the palace grounds. I train in self-defense every spring with the royal guards, as required of any and all heirs to the throne. My beloved willow in the forest . . . is something just for me. Just me and nature, no palace nonsense complicating life any more than it already does.

"Mama, you do remember how old I am, right? I'm not a helpless child anymore."

She has her usual retort prepared. "You will always be my baby." She gently kisses the top of my head before her departure and I wonder if her worry comes from a fear that my face will one day be posted on a flier. Or maybe mothers are just in a constant state of worry for their children, no matter their age.

As my mother's flowing train follows her out the door, my cousin Angelina—already in an evening gown of glittering teal—replaces her.

"You look like hell. Really felt like making poor Rose work extra hard this evening, huh?" She plops down on my bed as if she isn't wearing finery of any kind. I try my hardest to throw a hairbrush at her without disrupting Rose's work.

"Shut up!" I joke. "I look superb."

On cue, Rose untangles a piece of bark from my hair, silently placing it in her skirt pocket with the extra hair pins. The laughs bubble out of all three of us unapologetically as I surrender the battle.

"Well now that you cleared the debris, I'll take over from here, Rose. Thank you." Angelina grabs the brush and replaces Rose at the back of my chair.

"Yes, Lady Angelina." Rose does a quick bow before leaving us to it. I mutter a thank you as she leaves, happy to have Angelina finish up my hair. She always knows just how to place the pins without scratching my scalp. When we were younger, we would braid our hair together weaving her golden strands through my dark ones. We would walk around side by side acting as twins. I smile at the silly imagination of my younger self.

Angelina pins my hair in a way that makes it cascade down my back, leaving tendrils to frame my face. She uses the pins with the pearls at the end, a stark contrast to my dark strands.

"Did you see the newest missing posters up around town?" I look at her in the mirror, waiting for her reaction. She lives at a manor near the palace but might have seen it on her way in.

"Not this again." She sets down the brush, twisting a lock of my hair. "Cea, we've talked about this. Let the authorities handle it." I resist the urge to huff in frustration, letting her finish. "I'm sure your father is on it."

"But that's just it, Ang. He's not on it. No one seems to care about these women who keep turning up missing!" I know that people are lost at sea more often than we'd like to think. It's the way of the world when you live on an island with pirates sailing the ocean. With shipwrecks and storms. But something is different with these. Something doesn't add up.

"Cea, you've got to relax. They have people out patrolling the waters all the time for that sort of thing. And if they're in Aqualasia, they'll be found." She pins a pearl into my curls. "Or they won't." She shrugs as if we aren't talking about people's lives.

"All I'm saying is that they could be doing more. They should be doing more. You should have seen everyone at the council meeting yesterday. The subject was visited and dismissed before my father could even take a sip of his morning tea." I don't know why exactly I feel so strongly about these women in particular, but something about them just doesn't sit well with me. It doesn't seem right. None of it does. "There is something bigger here that no one seems to care about or recognize but me."

"Well, you're fated to rule these islands one day. Propose a solution. Tell the council and your father what you think. Show your backbone." As she brushes the hair smooth just behind my ear, she smirks at me in the mirror. We've talked at length about me stepping up when it comes to ruling someday. About what changes I want to make. Angelina has always had my back, no matter the issue. Even one as fraught as this.

"Maybe I will," I say with vigor, puffing my chest out a bit.

"That's my girl!"

As Angelina pulls more locks back from my face, I wonder if she ever thinks of things as I do. Why she doesn't worry about the missing women like me? Is it just that I'm becoming too invested in something that isn't really there? Am I seeing a connection where none actually exists? I can't be sure of anything because I have no actual proof that this is any different than the other missing citizens of Aqualasia. But I do intend to find out.

"So, I hear there are some regal guests visiting the palace tonight. Something exciting to break up the monotony." I roll my eyes remembering that we are hosting the royal family of Tudeland this week, starting off with tonight's celebration.

"If I have to feign pleasantries to another bland potential suitor hand-picked by my parents, I'll combust." I huff a sigh when she finishes, knowing it's almost time to play pretend once again.

My look is complete with an aquamarine-encrusted tiara. The faint blue stones that shine atop my head were said to have been created from mermaid tears, a fairytale told to children still young enough to believe in such things. Still, it's one I revel in every time I wear it.

Tonight will be like any other Full Celestia celebration: dining with stuffy nobility who want only to see what we can offer them. Attending a celebration only to help themselves. I'll have to dance with gentlemen who are only interested in what a match with me can buy. It is no secret that as I get older, the king and queen have been inviting families with sons around my age, trying desperately to pair me up with someone of their choosing.

I know it's not only for the good of the kingdom but for my good as well. They do honestly care for my future. But something about them guiding my interests as opposed to allowing a natural course of events to take place doesn't sit well with me. I am capable of finding a husband all on my own. I know what to look for and when to steer clear.

"I heard the King and Queen of Tudeland have a few sons that will be in attendance tonight." Of course they do. "They might provide some much-needed entertainment." I laugh as Angelina's eyes sparkle with mischief. Leave it to Angelina to always find the silver lining.

Every month, when new families join the celebration, we rank how much fun can be had with the lot. Most of the time, it's a dull evening with the same old dances and the same swollen moon shining down on the island, illuminating everything in a soft pale light. Some nights though . . . some nights, Angelina and I get into trouble, make new friends, and escape the boredom of court politics.

One night, Angelina and I escaped from the party to the stables, taking two mares for a night ride along the beach. We covered our gowns with capes found hanging just inside the doors and set off into the night. We eventually made our way into town and ended up winning coin from unlucky men at the tavern who thought they could beat us in a round of dice. Little did they know, Angelina and I had spent many parties hustling almond crescents from the other children in attendance. If it weren't for those nights with Angelina, I would have never seen that part of Aqualasia as it truly is. I would have never fallen in love with our people so deeply. The kind, complex, compassionate beings that work alongside each other to make this land thrive. I would have never learned how humor can live in even the darkest of times when life doesn't play fair.

Granted, our kingdom isn't without its problems. We have pirate clans that dock at our shores and swarm into our towns, wreaking havoc wherever they go. We have poverty and land issues that will never truly be remedied, no matter how hard we try. Still, we *try*, which is more than I can say for other lands facing tyranny and unrest.

Unfortunately, those issues sometimes bleed onto our islands, finding their way to the palace gates. That's why visiting the villages and spending time in the taverns is important to me. That's why I take the risk. I want to know the people of Aqualasia, *truly* know them. I want to know their fears, their wants, their hopes for a better life here on the islands.

Having a little fun with Angelina is an added bonus. And we always leave a hefty tip on the slick wooden bar, brightening the night of the lucky individual who is serving drinks that evening.

I slip into my violet evening gown as Angelina helps me with the buttons, fastening me in like a swaddled newborn. The gown hugs my hips before draping to the floor. The sheer sleeves dip off my shoulders and end at my fingertips. I turn to her for approval and she says, "Well Cea, once again I've outdone myself." She gives me a quick wink.

I lace my arm through Angelina's and we head down the hall together to honor the moon once again. Something that happens so often, you can't help but wonder why it needs an elaborate celebration.

The moon, it seems, is quite vain.

THREE

After we make our way down the black velvet-draped staircase, Angelina snags us a couple of bubbling flutes, and we zigzag our way through the guests chattering about how lovely the moon looks tonight. As if it looks any different than it does any other full moon.

The women compliment one another's gowns. The great chandelier in the center of the room dazzles with light. Its various shades of blue and green polished sea glass allow the light to bend and refract, bouncing in every direction, creating an illusion of being under the sea. Iridescent shells accent each tier like a cake turned upside down. Everything here is made or decorated with some part of the sea. Between each paned window, conch shell wall sconces illuminate the room. Soft yellow light shoots from above and below it, creating a pink glow from within. Even the ballroom floor is bejeweled with bone-white seashells set into a lotus-shaped mosaic beneath our feet. The tables are already set and my mouth waters as I watch the steam rise from the fresh bread that adorns each long table.

As I look around the room, I see a few faces I recognize, but a good number that I don't. The King of Tudeland Angelina mentioned stands out because of his dazzling uniform, but it's more than that. Something about his posture demands to be seen, like a lighthouse standing tall in a sea of waves. It seems Angelina's intel was quite accurate.

Idling beside the King and Queen of Tudeland are three young men, all cut from the same cloth—sandy brown hair, muscled builds, and stiff postures. Their faces are all severe, even the youngest of them who must be around twelve years of age. I can't imagine they would be any fun if this is how they appear at a party. Tudeland is known as a kingdom with a strong militia that is nearly impenetrable. I'm sure my father opening his home to them is nothing but strategic.

Angelina and I take our places at the back of the room near the kitchen's entrance. This way, we get the first and freshest of the starters. As guests filter into the room, the chattering conversations become a constant buzz.

Too soon, my father finds me leaning against a pillar with Angelina and waltzes over with my uncle, Lord Gunell. Trailing behind them are our little cousins, Lily and Magnolia. I watch as their matching pink hairbows sway with their steps.

"Cealene, Angelina, look who was able to make it this month. You remember Lily and Magnolia." They curtsy in unison, and I return the gesture.

"I do. You two look dazzling." We embrace them each, crouching down to their level. "Are you two excited to celebrate the Full Celestia tonight?" They nod excitedly. "I heard that the chef made almond crescents for dessert," I whisper to them, giving a wink. They exchange a look and grin as if I have just told them the best of news. Sweets are an easy way to most females' hearts.

Once the girls wander through the party and are out of earshot, I broach the subject that has been gnawing at me since I saw it.

"I saw another flier at the docks today, Father."

"You mean when you were out when you shouldn't have been?" he scolds, and I silently curse myself. I walked right into that one. Before I can retort, he continues, "Yes, well that brings me to what I wanted to speak with you about. I was actually just talking to your uncle about it before we saw you." My uncle nods in agreement.

"When the King of Tudeland's eldest son approaches you, please be gracious." I try not to look appalled at my father for thinking I would be anything but gracious to our royal guests like I'm some kind of flippant child and not the heiress he raised me to be.

"Aren't I always? And shouldn't we be more concerned with the missing civilians piling up?" I've barely finished my sentence when I see the wrath creep into my father's eyes, the vein in his forehead bulging. Once again, I've overstepped. The disapproving look on his face says it all. He is the king and I am not.

"Sometimes, the best we can do in a situation such as this is to provide our people with hope. Even if that hope looks a lot like a false sense of security. Now please, enough of this tonight." My father's tone is damning and I know I cannot retort. That he forbids it. I feel the absence of Angelina from behind me and scowl. *Coward.*

"Of course." I look over the crowd, trying to find that guppy when my father releases me from his invisible hold.

"You and Angelina have a good time tonight."

I nod as my father pulls my uncle along into the crowd, but I hear my uncle turn back and add, "And behave!" I can't help but laugh at his assumption that the command was necessary when Angelina and I are together. He knows us too well.

My mother clinks her crystal flute from her spot atop the grand staircase to gather everyone's attention. "Good evening, family and friends. Thank you for coming to celebrate another beautiful Full Celestia." Her glittering crown of diamonds, gold, and emeralds sits atop her head as if she was born with it, a regal corona of elegance. My mother is poised and beautiful with her high cheekbones, cupid's bow pout, and silky skin. Like mine, curls sit atop her head, but where my locks are a deep violet-brown, hers are a rich caramel, making her green eyes shine bright. Looking at her now, I wonder if there was ever a time in her life when she wasn't so poised and perfect.

"I can't tell you what it means to me to fill this room with love and life to celebrate the waking of another celestial cycle. I want to take a moment to welcome our honored guests of the night, the royal family of Tudeland. Thank you for joining us this evening. If everyone would please find your seat, dinner will be served momentarily. Enjoy!"

The chatter is replaced with the sound of rustling fabric as everyone finds their seats, and the second part of our evening begins.

As music filters through the air and empty plates are swept away, the ballroom is opened for dancing. The lights are dimmed, allowing the full glory of the moon to filter through the wall of windows in the ballroom. It truly is a breathtaking sight. The glowing moon hanging above the water, glittering with reflected light. The sapphire horizon meets the darkness of the sea in an infinite line. Maybe the moon has a right to be vain. Something that can shine so much light on a sea of darkness really should be appreciated.

I look to my left to find Angelina already up on her feet, ready to dance the night away. Although I am not required to dance with anyone, per se, I have always been given the strong suggestion to welcome all who offer a dance. Except, of course, tonight, when my father has a deal on the line. So when I see the eldest son of the King of Tudeland walk my way, I drain the rest of my wine, knowing I will soon be twirling around with this handsome stranger. It certainly could be worse.

"Care to dance, Princess?" He bows, offering his chestnut palm. His voice is husky and deep, shocking me to almost stunned silence.

"I would love to." I grasp his rough hand and rise from my seat, sweeping my violet dress aside, and realize I have yet to learn his name. To say he was taller than me would be a gross understatement. He towers over my small frame as we enter the dance floor and I catch a whiff of his cologne, something woodsy and strong. Couples make space for us and we blend into the flow in step with the beats. I let the rhythm take over, guiding my movements.

"We haven't been introduced," he murmurs as he twirls me around, flaring my skirts like a flower opening its petals. "I'm Prince Markos Hawksen." I twirl back in, light on my feet as he pulls me close with a firm grasp. "And of course, you are Princess Cealene Tirulia," he continues.

"The one and only." I smile at him, not entirely trusting his charm.

"You look radiant." His compliment strikes me as sincere, even though I am no fool for flattery. People often send compliments my way, hoping for something in return because of who I am. Very rarely do they come from a place of sincerity. But in this case, what could a prince want from me? He already has everything he needs.

"And you, a dashing gentleman." He smiles, revealing a perfect set of teeth. He truly is striking. Not a hair out of place, lashes for days, and a jawline that could cut stone. Something tells me he knows exactly how handsome he is.

"Tell me, do you ever tire of it? The monthly celebrations?"

I check myself at his question, wondering if boredom shows on my face. How could he know that I would prefer to forgo these frequent soirees? Before I can answer, he continues, "I mean, the exquisite food, dancing in finery under a full moon—it sounds like a dream you wouldn't want to end." He twirls me again, before dipping me low and ever so slowly bringing me back to an upright position, and I truly cannot tell if I am unnerved by him leading or impressed. I'm about to ask him about his own royal gatherings back in Tudeland, but instead, I stop myself and answer honestly.

"Actually, I do tire of it." We sweep through the sea of people, as I twirl on the balls of my feet. "Without sounding ungrateful, sometimes it just feels . . ."

"Like it's all a bit much?"

"Exactly." I find myself genuinely smiling at him. Oh, he's good. Before we have a chance to continue, the song changes and the dance has ended.

When a new one begins, a tap on the shoulder has me turning around to face the youngest of the brothers, bowing. Hand extended.

"Princess, may I have this dance?" Like a smaller version of his brother, this one didn't want to miss out despite his age. It seems all the Hawksen men are good at this game.

"I would be honored, Prince . . . "

I take his hand in mine as he says, "Finnick, but you may call me Finn."

"A pleasure to meet you, Finn."

"I feared if I didn't save you from my dull older brother, you might whither from boredom." Laughter escapes me as we begin the next dance. *Oh, they are all very good.*

After what feels like an eternity of dances, my feet beg for a break, taking me to one of the lounge areas in the far corner of the room. I pour myself a glass of minted water from the crystal pitcher and nearly gulp down an entire glass. I haven't taken a dance break since dinner ended. I roll the soreness from my ankles beneath my dress and decide to head out onto the balcony for some fresh air. Try as I might, I cannot get the image of that missing woman out of my head.

As soon as I step onto the marble floor of the balcony, the cool sea air kisses my warm cheeks and I exhale in relief. It's easy for a ballroom of dancing people to become stuffy. Even easier when they have stuffed themselves with food and drink. I walk to the edge of the railing, resting my elbows on the smooth iron, and lean into the rolling winds coming from the waves of the ocean. The sound is music in my ears. The absence of all that noise already lightening my spirits.

"Enjoying the evening?"

Startled, I turn to find Markos walking towards the railing, hands in his pockets.

"I am." I lean my hip into the railing. "Just . . . needed a break from all of the dancing."

He settles next to me, resting his hands on the smooth metal of the railing. "The cool breeze does feel wonderful."

"It does." I look up at the night sky. Millions of stars freckle the vast atmosphere. "A perfectly clear night's sky."

"It really is beautiful." With that, I feel him move behind me, placing one hand on my shoulder, the other pointing up into the sky. "You see that there? Just to the right of the moon? That's Piskos. It is said that it symbolizes the two fish who helped great gods from another world. Their tails are tied together so they never lose one another."

The story is one I know well, but with each word, I can feel his hot breath against my ear. His chest presses against my back and my spirits plummet as he pins me in place. I do not want this attention and I do not appreciate being confined. I try to separate from him but the railing is already against my chest. There is no room for me to escape his presence. He has me trapped. Unsure of how to explain that his attention is unwelcome, I gently remove his hand from my shoulder and try to put some more distance between us. Try to keep my cool.

"I'm actually quite familiar with the story of the goddess and her son. My father used to tell me the tale before bed when I was a child." I make a good attempt at keeping the mood light and give him the benefit of the doubt. Maybe I gave him the wrong impression. Maybe he read a signal wrong. But my instincts scream at me to get away.

As if in response, he presses his hips into my bottom, pinning me against the railing. "Speaking of bed," he growls placing his hands on the railing on either side of me. Alarms go off in my head. This handsome, highly noble man thinks he is entitled to whatever he pleases. I push my hands against the railing, forcing my back into his chest to give me room to escape.

"Prince Markos, I believe you may have gotten the wrong idea, here." I push him away and spin around to face him directly.

"Come on, Princess. I know what you want. You came out here for some privacy." My heart hammers in my chest, and beads of sweat slick my brow. My tongue turns metallic in my mouth.

"You may be entitled to whatever you desire in your own kingdom, Prince, but that is not the case here." My words come out venomous as I stare him down, seeing the arrogance in his posture.

"On the contrary, I believe our betrothal makes that untrue, Princess." He spits my title back at me, although the rest of his words are soft. My heart nearly stops at the word. *Betrothal.*

No. My father never discussed anything of the sort with me. He would never do such a thing without my permission or at the very least my knowledge of it. Is this why he invited them here? Or is this prince narcissistic enough to believe this arrangement was all for him? He reaches for my waist, but I push his hand away. "Stop."

"That's not what you want," he coos. He thinks this betrothal means that he owns me. That I no longer belong to myself, but to him. My blood boils within my veins as I think of my father. How could he?

Not wanting to further this conversation a moment longer, I turn to head back inside and hear him curse as I bolt around the siren statue that sits at the far end of the balcony, as if eying the events taking place, leaving him out on the balcony, alone. The heat from his proximity is replaced with brisk air and I welcome the change. Sliding the tall glass door open, I head inside as quickly as I can before I give myself the chance to turn around and knock his teeth in.

Sickened by the night, I walk back to the lounge area of the ballroom searching for Angelina, but before I get very far, I spot her heading over with two full glasses of deep-colored wine. I plop down on a tufted velvet chaise, letting my gown drape over the edge. It takes everything in me to calm my nerves and not blurt out what happened as she sits across from me. It's better to wait until we're somewhere more private. I school my face into neutrality so she doesn't pick up on my frayed nerves.

"Tiring already?" Angelina eyes me with amusement. "Boy, how the mighty have fallen," she jokes, handing me the glass. I take a large sip, savoring the flavors as they present themselves. Deep berry and a floral earthiness. I want to tell Angelina what happened as soon as I see her but

I need to get my bearings. I need to collect myself enough to figure out the best way to handle this.

"Meet you at our spot?" I ask. She nods with a grin and scans the room before we make our escape. Most nights of the Full Celestia celebrations, Angelina and I end up lounging on my balcony with snacks, gossiping about the evening, or talking about anything and nothing at all. And right now, I need that more than anything.

"I'll grab the provisions," I reply and we both leave the lounge area, heading separate ways. Her, to the stairs. Me, to the wine cellar.

FOUR

Before anyone can come find me for another dance, I walk down the short hall to the kitchens bustling with activity, and out the back entrance. When the palace was first built, there wasn't a wine cellar, but when the sixth king had one installed, he wanted it separate from the palace, near the ocean. He claimed that the sea and the moon would penetrate the bottles and charge the wine with the natural magics of the earth. It should also be mentioned that the sixth king was known to be a bit off his rocker. I push away the urge to look over my shoulder for any signs of Markos, and continue ahead to the small hut with a wide moon roof to let the energy in, or whatever the king had hoped for. The back of my head throbs where it connected with Markos's stupidly perfect nose. I hope I did lasting damage. And I hope he fumbles with his words when asked what caused the injury.

After opening the heavy stone door, I head over to the wine selection near the top of the beehive structure. Maybe the crazy old king was right and there is something in these bottles that will erase the memory of today. I don't spend time searching for a perfect one, settling for a dark green bottle at the center of the moon roof's opening.

Angelina is going to lose it when I tell her what happened.

When I jump down from the shelving, bottle, and skirts in hand, I hear someone just outside the cellar and stop mid-step. Boots scuff the stone steps in quick swipes and I hear heaving breaths. My first thought is that it's Markos, completely losing his mind and following me out here, but when I open the door to the outside, I see Ezera.

Bloodied and in distress, he runs a hand through his hair as he paces the private beach of the palace. An area that is off-limits to the public. I see a boat docked at our private docks, next to the royal boats and my mind spins. He's hurt or in trouble. What else would he be doing here? Normally, if it weren't for the party, a few guards would be stationed here in the unlikely event that someone would have the ludicrous idea to enter the palace grounds here. But truth be told, the guards do tend to get a little lax during a Full Celestia celebration.

It's been years since I've interacted with the fisherman and now I see him twice in one day. *Strange.* His eyes search around the kitchen frantically as he makes his way closer to me.

With three small steps, I walk out from the cellar and then I see it. Blood has stained his ivory tunic, seeping through like watercolors. It's not just his hands like I first suspected. My heartbeat quickens again because I know he's in some kind of trouble. There's no way he would end up here if it weren't a last resort. I know this boy . . . at least I used to. No one would risk getting caught here if it weren't their only option left.

I step towards him, my gown sweeping the stone steps as I walk down the sandy beach, "Ezera?" My voice comes out watery, much more timid than I intended. He startles at the sound, relief filling his eyes.

"Princess." He bows. "I'm sorry to be here," his voice cracks with emotion. "My father . . . he's hurt. *Badly.* I can't seem to free him on my own." My heart pounds a little harder in my chest at the look in his eyes, like he's caught in a memory. Maybe he *does* remember me.

"I know these are palace grounds and I would have never docked here otherwise, but I—" Before he can finish, I drop the bottle into the sand and rush past him towards the sea, but when I only hear my own footsteps sinking into the sand, I stop and turn around.

"You coming?" I stand at the far end of the beach as I watch his features change from worry to surprise.

"You're going to help me?" My eyes snag on the scar on his chin, the one shaped like a crescent moon that I'd asked him about when we were young. He got it the first time he threw out a line. The fishing hook caught him right as he was casting.

"Of course I am." He jogs towards me and takes the lead as we venture out into the night.

"I'm sorry to take you away from the party tonight." He turns to look back at me as we jog to the docks. Gathering my gown in my hands, I pick up my pace careful not to tangle my feet as I jog ahead.

"Oh, please. I loathe these things. You've been to one, you've been to them all."

I hurry past him towards the dock when I see their boat bobbing in the water. What were they even doing out here so late? It is highly discouraged to sail the seas at night.

"I can't thank you enough for this." His voice sounds harried and I can hear the panic within.

"Nonsense. I owe you for teaching me how to tie sailors' knots." Something that I would practice with the vines of my willow, creating a swing to sway on. He nods once and passes me, taking the lead onto the wooden dock.

I immediately hear the groaning of someone in pain, the sound sending a cold sensation down my spine. My stomach flips at the thought of what kind of condition I will find this man in. But I can't spot him in the dark amongst the bobbing boats. It can't be good if Ezera came here. I follow his hulking figure as he leads me down the small dock, farther out to sea and that's when I see him. Ezera's father is impaled with a serrated harpoon, blood flowing from the wound as he hangs from the side of the boat, tangled in thick braided rope. Blood dribbles from his mouth as he feebly attempts to untangle himself with his free arm, fingers intertwined with the rope.

I can see now why Ezera wasn't able to help his father alone. Everything about his entrapment appears deliberate, like someone did this to him. His breath comes in short wheezes, and he tries to say something as we approach. His blood is a black slick shine in the night. Dimly lit lanterns line the dock, not nearly enough light for what we need to see. I look around to see if the possible culprit lingers near, but, of course, we are the only ones occupying the private beach tonight.

"Dad, I'm here. Just hold on." Ezera takes no time in stepping onto their fishing boat. He crouches down on one knee at the edge and tries to pry his father free. Without direction, I kneel on the wooden slats and begin to untangle the rope. Ezera hands me a dagger, hilt first. Now that I am upon him and can really see how he is trapped, it is clear now why Ezera was willing to risk docking here. If he were out at sea, he would have needed to get to shore immediately so that when he did free his father, he didn't drop down into the open ocean. There is no way he could have done this on his own. As I work on the rope, Ezera begins to cut off the speared end of the harpoon so he can ease the shaft from his father. With another blade, Ezera saws away at the sharp tip of the harpoon, his muscles swollen with force. The strength it must take to cut through that harpoon is not lost on me.

I look down at his father, pain lacing his pale face. I know enough of blood loss to know he doesn't have much time. His blood is flowing too freely from his wounds and the lapping waves aren't helping as his lower half dangles into the water.

His father attempts to speak again, "Ezera, listen to me," his voice barely audible amongst the waves of the sea. "Your mother and I . . . you changed our world. And I am so proud to call you my son—"

"No. No, Dad. Don't do that. Don't you dare do that. You are not dying tonight. Don't even think about it." Ezera snaps the tip of the harpoon off the shaft and tosses it into the water. Without missing a beat, he slowly pulls the rest of the foreign object from his father's chest, and groans fill the air. I gasp as a rush of blood spills onto my arms and look up at Ezera.

"You ready? I'm going to hold him up while you finish with the rope. When he's free, I'll pull him onto the deck."

I only nod, not trusting my voice. Ezera keeps his composure so well and I'm fraying apart over here. He should be the one crumbling over his father and I should be the one keeping it together. Tears sting my eyes as I cut away the final pieces of rope. With his arms linked under his father's shoulders, Ezera pulls him from the side of the boat. His muscles strain and his veins bulge underneath his skin as he groans from the effort. His sweat glistens in the moonlight.

"I've got you, Dad." His voice is barely audible over his father's screams as they fall back onto the deck of the boat. The screams pierce the air and I'm shocked no one has come to check on the commotion. But the noise from the celebration is deafening enough to swallow sounds whole.

Ezera's strength is astounding, and I wonder if the love for his father fuels his fire.

The bond they share is deeper than an average connection between a father and his son. They share their days together on the water, relying on each other. And right now, something is threatening that bond. The reaper has come to try and steal it away. But I see the determination in Ezera's eyes.

Tears sting my eyes as I stand from the dock, my legs wobbly and weak. What was he doing out here so late? Regardless of why, this was not a mere accident. Somebody did this to this poor man.

Once I know he's got it under control, I leap across the narrow gap between the boat and the dock to help Ezera with the wound. My muscles quiver as I use every bit of strength to help pull his wet body away from the edge of the boat, blood streaking the hull. When we lay him onto the deck, we pack the wound.

As I watch Ezera care for a wound of this magnitude, I wonder how many of these men deal with these injuries in this business. The only reason I know much of anything when it comes to healing is thanks to my mother who was determined to teach basic healing skills in case I find myself "in peril."

I tear the bottom of my dress and wrap his chest tightly, trying desperately to stop any more blood from spilling out. My fingers, slick with sticky blood, shake as I tie the knot, a temporary fix until he can be properly taken care of.

Ezera prepares the boat and begins unbinding the rope from the docks.

"Where will you take him?" I ask as I bring a water canister to his father's lips.

"There's a healer near our home. She will know what to do." His confidence in this healer eases my nerves a bit, but I worry about how long it will take to get him there. He kneels down next to his father. "Dad, hang on just a little longer. We're going to make it." His hand holds onto his father's tight. His piercing blue-green eyes are filled with anguish and . . . rage.

"Surely I can get the royal physician to come down. Then you wouldn't have to travel for help." I'm sure if I explained the situation to Father, he would send aid. He's a fairly reasonable man.

"Oh no, you have helped so much already. Really, we'll be okay." He places his fingers to his father's wrist, checking his pulse, and sighs with relief. "His pulse is stronger already."

Something about his reluctance to accept my help has me curious as to the true situation these two find themselves in. It makes me worry for their safety. If someone was willing to leave this man within an inch of his life, what's stopping them from finishing the job next time?

"You know . . . your father's injuries, they don't appear accidental." I fold my arms over my middle as the cool breeze steals my heat. He gives me a measuring look as he fusses with his father's bandaged wounds. Finally, he stands and extends a hand to me.

"Thank you, Princess. I am forever indebted to you." I take his blood-ied hand and squeeze, feeling the warmth spread into my palm. I hate his polite formalities as if we didn't spend our childhood together.

"Please, call me Cealene."

His eyes reach mine and my heart nearly stops. Even in the darkness, the swirls of blue and green are almost unnaturally bright like the southern beach on the sunniest of days. Like the aquamarine stones that line my tiara.

"Cealene." My name on his lips sounds like a secret, a promise. He gestures towards his father propped up against a barrel. "My father, Harrison." He introduces me as he begins readying the boat for departure, adjusting rigging and tying rope.

"I remember, Ezera." As my words reach his ears, his brows shoot up in surprise.

"You do?"

"Of course I do." The wooden pier groans beneath my feet as I shift my weight. "If it weren't for you and your father, I would have never learned how to tie such intricate knots into my hair for these evening balls." I wave my hand towards the glowing palace. He chuckles in response as he secures the front sail.

"I'm surprised the heiress of Aqualasia remembers someone like me from all those years ago." He continues to ready the boat as he converses with me, and I feel reluctance to let them go.

"On the contrary, I wasn't sure if you remembered me."

"Oh Cealene, as if I could ever forget you." He finishes winding the rope around the notch at the side of the boat.

At that, I'm speechless. Is he flirting with me? Heat creeps into my face when his smirk reveals a slight dimple.

"If there were ever a way we could repay you for your kindness—"

"Something tells me you would have done the same for me." I leave it at that and step back from the edge of the dock, knowing that they must be going. Saltwater can only do so much to stave off infection.

"Maybe I will run into you again," he calls out, as the boat begins to glide through the water.

A smile tugs at my lips, knowing he refers to our earlier encounter from today when I ran into him carrying the crates. "Maybe you will."

Covered in blood and sweat, I begin my short journey back to the palace, my ripped dress brushing my legs. My parents are going to lose it. As I walk along the small cobblestone path to the back entrance of the kitchens, I watch as the moon follows me home.

Angelina must be wondering where I am by now. Maybe she's gone down to look for me, or maybe she has fallen asleep in my bed. It wouldn't be the first time we ended the night asleep atop the covers, shoeless but still in our gowns. I look down at my dress covered in blood and seawater. Pieces of frayed rope have entwined in the sleeves. I look up at the moon, and it looks back down at me. I can almost feel its light illuminating my face in the darkness. The moonlight glitters and bounces off the ocean ahead, and for a moment, it feels like I am the only witness to its beauty. This is how I would prefer to honor the moon. Quietly.

A siren songbird calls in the distance, it's melody ethereal.

As the sea calls to me, I throw logic to the wind and turn, rushing up the grassy hill to the cliff's edge preparing to jump in and wash off the sick feeling of Markos's breath on my skin and the blood from Ezera's father. Carefully, I remove my tiara and place it atop the shoes. My parents would kill me if they knew I was about to jump into the sea at night in my evening gown. But they don't know the night I've had. And even if I wanted to change my mind, it's too late. There's no going back now. The water is calling to me, inviting me into its abyss and every cell in my body begs for it. The instinct to dive into the black waters overwhelms me the closer I get to the edge. A soft hum fills my ears, and I can feel it in my bones like my body has come alive. Maybe it's my body coming down from the shock of the night, or maybe I'm just tired. Or maybe I've had too much to drink. But in this moment, I've never felt more alive.

I step up to the edge of the rocky cliff, looking out into the distance. I take a deep breath of the crisp night air rolling in from the waves, and I jump.

FIVE

As I free fall into the ocean, my dress flutters around my legs waiting for the water to kiss my skin. Fear grabs me by the throat as the wind tears through, thinking of the endless number of dangerous creatures that linger below. Something about the darkness makes sea monsters a little more believable than when the sun is up.

I plunge into the cold abyss as tiny bubbles release around me, floating up to the surface. I can feel them creep up my prickling skin as the cool water shocks my system. My hair loosens as I descend farther down, gravity from the jump still pulling me under. When I begin to feel the tug of buoyancy, I scissor kick my legs and watch the watery moon from below the surface. Its edges blur and move with the overflowing sea, bringing it to life. Somehow from under the cool water, it seems to glow even brighter, as if a halo shines around its edges, sparkling.

A tingling begins beneath my skin as I kick my legs, which quickly turns to immense pain, burning, searing all over my body. White and hot. I look down to see what's causing the heat, but the water is too dark and my legs are mere shadows in the night, leaving me with only feeling. It's like my skin is tearing apart, exposed to the saltwater. My gown shreds around me and I kick harder now, trying to swim up for air but my legs won't work. I will them to move, to send me up to the surface, but it feels like they're tied together by a rope, bound as one. I try to kick and kick, but no matter how hard I try, I do not ascend higher. Instead, I idle below floundering about. My lungs ache and just when I'm positive they are going to burst inside my chest, my ribs sting like a knife slice from within. I bring my hands to my side to feel the tender part between the cage of bone and almost gag when my fingers slide into the thin slits that have formed. The ache in my lungs subsides as water filters through, like second nature.

Fearful of what I'm pretty certain I might see, I look down at my fused legs and see a tail covered with glistening teal scales. *And fins.* They flutter in the water like gossamer or silk chiffon in the wind. The length of my tail is nearly double what my legs were. Panic rises in my chest. With my dress fallen away, completely torn to shreds now, I look down at my stomach where scales appear along my skin, becoming more concentrated at the waist before turning completely to a scaled tail, no skin in sight.

My vision is sharper now, allowing me to see more clearly in the night. Even in the dark, the deep blue-green scales catch the light of the moon through the water. Floating beneath the surface I reach my hand to my torso, feeling the smooth scales along my skin when I see my hands webbed and clawed like a monstrous predator. I shriek, horrified at what I see, and wonder if my mind is playing a trick. Some kind of hallucination brought on by the stress of tonight. Or maybe it's some kind of dream.

But something in me knows. Everything is too acute to be a farce. Too sharp.

I know this is real. I am real. The pull that was drawing me into the water was real.

What just happened?

I am trapped here, under the sea. I cannot go home.

I want to cry, scream, run, pull my hair out, tear my skin off. Anything to release this feeling that is trapped inside me. The silence down here is deafening.

Mermaids have been extinct for thousands of years, thought to be killed off long ago by pirates and sailors alike. They are basically an ancient myth with little proof of their existence. They are a fairytale story told to children at bedtime. A fable passed down through generations. Only children believe that such creatures still exist in our waters. I have lived my entire life near the sea, and never once have I ever encountered such a creature. No stories of fishermen out at sea coming across a half-human half-fish. A maiden with a tail. Not since the great Sea Wars. As I recall the well-known stories, I watch my tail sway forward and back of its own accord, keeping me in place. I watch as the iridescent scales glisten and move like lava.

Mermaids are sung about in songs, and painted or sculpted in artwork. But most believe mermaids are the result of too many nights spent at sea coupled with bad moonshine. Angelina and I would often swim along the private beach of the palace with our legs moving as one, playing pretend as children do, our imaginations running wild with blissful ignorance. Never did I imagine I would see such an ancient creature in my lifetime, let alone become one.

The pain has finally subsided and I turn around, my hair dragging through the water, to look at my surroundings. I can see much farther and clearer than I could only moments ago, developing some kind of underwater night vision. All sound is muffled and subdued. I watch iridescent fish glide through the water, never getting too close, and then I notice someone hovering between the plunging rock walls. A female.

Her silver hair splays around her, floating in the water. Her onyx tail is black as the night. A predatory instinct has all of my senses on high alert. But another part of me, the human part, is fascinated that she . . . we . . . even exist. Not only are mermaids as real as the moon, but I am one of them. Somehow, against all logic, against all beliefs, I am a maiden of the sea.

I swallow down my fear and stand my ground when she approaches, slowly. Her tail sends her forward lazily. When she's about twenty feet away, she straightens and points back towards where she came from, her clawed nail like a talon. She wants me to follow her.

So fast I almost miss it, she turns and swims back through the rock walls. The need for answers outweighs the lingering fear, and I follow her as best I can. Curiosity has gotten the best of me, winning the battle against my fear. The mermaid is fast. Faster than any fish of her size, and I worry I might lose her in the darkness. Her onyx tail is a blur of motion, moving through the water.

My tail propels me forward so quickly I nearly give myself whiplash from the shock, much faster than my human legs ever could, and move with much less effort. On land, I've been raised to be graceful, but down here, in this form, I am unnervingly aware of my tail. It's as long as my entire body is in my human form and so powerful. Just the smallest effort and my movements propel me through the water, and I can't quite seem to get the hang of it. I feel unmatched.

But in my attempt to keep up, I glide through the sea with ease as I follow this female into the dark trench. She stops abruptly, turning back towards me, and points up. Towards the surface. I look into her emerald eyes and nod once, following her cue, scared as ever. I follow her as we swim up to the surface and note that we are surrounded by a rock outcropping near the palace.

When we emerge, I can see her more clearly. She's much older than I am, but still impossibly beautiful with full lips and silver hair like silk.

"I've been waiting for you for a very long time." Her voice is like syrup. The wind whistles through the rock as I look into her eyes.

"You've been waiting . . . for me." It's not a question, but more of a confirmation that I am hearing her correctly. My own voice sounds foreign to my ears, like echoed chimes. How could this . . . creature have been waiting for me? She circles around me once swimming backwards, tail trailing lazily behind her. Everything about her is enchanting, from the way she glides in the water to the way her voice carries through the wind.

"Every Full Celestia since you were born."

"Wha—" I don't even know which question to ask first. But before I even have the chance, she stops, turns to me again, and says, "Come, I'll show you around," and dives below the surface. Her shimmering onyx fluke is the last thing I see before plunging in after her.

I dive down beneath the surface following her wake and find that in just a few moments we are several meters below sea level, the pressure caressing me like an embrace. It would have taken me much longer and with much more effort to swim the distance with only a pair of legs. Before I know it, we are deep down near the ocean floor, swimming through an underwater forest. Thick seaweed reaches towards the sky, shadowed to black in the night like a haunting dream as the plants sway with the water, creating shadows and figures. I follow as closely as I can, but this mermaid is fast, quickly turning corners and switching directions. It takes everything in me to keep up, especially in the dark unfamiliar waters.

If I were fully human right now, I wouldn't be able to see anything down here. But now, in this form, I can actually see the sea life up close. I can see the landmarks and reefs and it's incredible. Like a lantern guides the way, illuminating everything in my path. We catch a small current that carries us along at an unusually fast pace. I feel it as soon as we hit it, pulling me along, propelling my fins forward. We must have swum miles already. Further away from my home.

The mermaid makes a turn into a series of caves, openings of all sizes in mountainous rock. The water gets cloudier the further we go. Something about being in this form allows me to *feel* the water around me. It bends around the objects within it, allowing space for the rock and coral, expanding and contracting as creatures pass through. It's like I have a spatial awareness of the water that wasn't there before. I was never as acutely aware of the water when I swam at the palace's private beach. I never knew what was lurking below without seeing it.

Now I can *feel* the change in the water's pattern.

I follow the mermaid's glittering tail through a tight tunnel, as tiny fish with neon stripes scurry out of our path. Not once does she look back to make sure I am still following or keeping up with her pace. She either doesn't care to know or already knows I am. And from her comment earlier, about waiting for me, I believe it's the latter. She feels my presence tailing her.

Finally, without warning, she begins to ascend, swimming towards the surface. As I follow, I see more figures coming into focus, as light filters through the darkness. But it isn't moonlight. No, this light isn't the bright natural glow of the moon. This light is vibrant and warm, a soft pink. A low roar muffles through the water and as I look up I notice the rushing water pouring into the surface from above at several spots. Various plants line the walls of the cave, all luscious and beautiful. Some drape over the rock and some grow right through it. Intricately carved stones guide our way through the maze as I follow her up. I nearly gasp when I see other mermaids begin to appear, each beautiful and alluring in their own way. Their tails vary in size and color as they swim past us. Some glance our way, others swim by without a care.

When we break the surface, I see we're in a large cave of coral and rock that opens up to the sky above. Slabs of stone jut out from the water like chaise lounges for merfolk. Some braid their long locks while others chat. And some eat shellfish or create jeweled weaponry. An actual community of merpeople live here and it's like I've walked right into a dream.

I see now where the muffled roaring came from when I was below the surface. Multiple waterfalls cascade down the cave walls throughout. Some are just a mere trickle while others are a rush of pure white flowing down into the sea below. Their sound coupled with the sound of the merfolk brings the space to life.

It takes everything in me not to balk when I see a pair of females manipulating water with their hands, shaping the liquid into figures floating in the air between them. Absolutely incredible. Absently, I wonder if I, too, have the power to control water as they do. If it is possible for me to hold a bit of the sea in the palm of my hand and bend it to my will.

The silver-haired mermaid swims up to an open rock lounge, the water lapping against it as she perches atop, fins still floating in the sea. The water ripples back down the angled rock, gliding over her smooth tail before draining back into the ocean. I mimic her movements and swim up onto the one beside her, nervous and silent. I feel a bit like a newborn doe in my sea form, uncertain of how my bottom half works. Awkward and .

But I'm more concerned with getting answers than anything else right now. I need to know what happened. How this community exists without our knowledge.

I'm surrounded by a world I never knew existed. A world of wonder and magic. A stark contrast to the stories surrounding darkness and death. I look around at these creatures and cannot believe what I see. I brush my hand down my hip and feel the unfamiliar smoothness of glistening scales of the most mesmerizing teal. Blues and greens exchanging space along my tail. After eighteen years of living as a human, why in the world did this happen to me tonight? How is any of this real?

"My name is Calypso." Again, her voice is enchanting to my ears, and I yearn to hear more. "And I would like to tell you a story." My ears perk at that, wondering where she is going with this, hoping she answers the hurricane of questions swirling in my head.

"Long ago, before our kind became the subject of fairy tales and folklore, mermaids were not a secret to the world. We were not a fable whispered in the night. We lived wild and free, among the humans above with no fear of being spotted by anyone on land. We would often visit the mainland and lived in peace with the humans. But that was ages ago, long before your ancestors became rulers of Aqualasia." I look at her flawless skin and see no sign of the years. My family has been ruling the people of Aqualasia for dozens of decades. I can picture each regal portrait lining the great hall of the palace. This creature in front of me has been around for quite some time, indeed.

"When I was young, I would often help the people who would sail the seas. I enjoyed navigating their ships through rough currents and storms. I learned the customs of the people on land and was fascinated by their way of life. It was so much more complex than the lives of sea creatures below. So many familial relations and celebrations. So many objects of finery. Some nights, music would pour from ships and the people would dance and sing through the night, laughing together in harmony. It was incredible to see the complexity of their lives made simple by something as easy as music.

"You see, below the surface, most merfolk prefer to live simply. We don't require as much as humans do. We prefer not to burden ourselves with extravagance and materials. Out in the deep blue, it is kill or be killed. There are no laws protecting us or holding us back. And for that reason, our values align much differently than that of humans. Our pods are sacred to us, and we will always protect our own but we don't bother with human status and rules as is typical on land.

"There is something beautiful about the simplicity of it, living a life of your own. No status to uphold or connections to others holding you back or weighing you down. *Wild and free.* But for me, I yearned for personal connections to others with the complexities that came with a society. I was intrigued by what drove the humans to structure their lives in such a way." She pauses, looking around the room.

The neon glow of the cave makes her silver hair shine bright like it's electric. I am so enthralled in her story—in *her*—that I've barely moved since she began. To live a life that is free from the confines of what I know. To live a life that is wild and untamed. It sounds like a dream to simply wake and explore the world around you, become one with the sea. To simply live unaltered. I can't help but yearn for the life these creatures live. So very different from the one I am accustomed to. Nothing about my life is wild or free.

Her eyes twinkle as she begins again.

"I met him when I was a young sea maiden. Many, many years ago. The ship was called *The Moon Chaser,* and she sailed these seas endlessly. I used to follow in her wake, riding the waves alongside her belly. Music always played on deck, alerting me of her whereabouts, luring me closer. Her huge ivory sails billowed in the wind like puffed clouds.

"One night, the ship was caught in a relentless storm, spinning and tipping her into the sea. Rope and sail tore through the waves, barely hanging on. The male tumbled overboard and crashed into the sea, sinking like an anchor as bubbles escaped his lips. Of course I was there, trying to tame the waves. But sometimes even mermaids are no match for Mother Nature. I linked my arms through his and carried him back to the surface while trying to calm the seas surrounding the ship.

"When the storm finally faded, I placed him on the deck with a soft wave of water, and he thanked me with a string of pearls. We were inseparable after that, spending every possible moment together, swimming in the ocean, lying on the beach. We were two kids in love, and the world was our playground. He made everything brighter for me. Everything he touched, everything he did was like pure magic. I loved him with every cell of my being.

"We wanted to spend our lives together. To marry. But not everyone was as in love with the idea of us being together as we were. The villagers from where he resided did not like that I was taking what wasn't mine. Even when I had spent time among them on land, walking through the streets as they did. Even though I had only ever shown them kindness and grace, they viewed me as a thief. As a siren who put a spell on one of their own.

"They wouldn't hear reason or see our love for what it truly was. They only saw hate. A problem that needed to be stopped. The morning that we planned to elope with a matrimony of the sea, the humans devised a devious plan to trap me, luring me to the ship with their music. When I swam closer, only to see that he wasn't there, they captured me and hauled me onto their ship like I was some prized catch. My call to my sisters was barely enough to save me before I was slaughtered. But before they could turn me to sea foam, my sisters came, saving my life, just in time . . . but not soon enough. Not before they stole the little life that grew inside of me, a product of our love. They stole not only my soulmate, but my child. The one thing a female can never recover from. I can still hear her cries when they tore her from me. I hear them in my sleep."

I watch in horror as she brushes the jagged scar across her belly, remembering the pain. A sick feeling coats my skin at the vile act committed against this female.

"They left me bloodied and barren. Empty and broken. If it weren't for my sisters, I would be nothing but a memory. Loyalty is a virtue ingrained in our souls. We protect our own. If only they came sooner . . . things might have been different." Her words are like ice, spoken from a dark corner of her heart.

"But you see, because of this fierce loyalty, my sea sisters would not stop at saving me. They needed retribution. They wanted revenge for stealing one of our own, infantile or not. And I wanted it too. I wanted them to burn for what they did. For stealing what was mine. For taking a part of me. For defiling my body in immeasurable ways. It was the last straw for our kind." Her shoulders relax as if the hardest part of her story has passed.

"War broke out on land and sea between the villagers and the seafolk. It was brutal and it was ugly, and the love of my life died because of it, leaving my child to be raised by strangers. All because I had the gall to fall in love—to take something they thought wasn't mine to have. As a result, merpeople have not been welcome on the shores of Aqualasia. As if we ever desired to interact with such monsters ever again," she says the last part like it tastes foul in her mouth, needing to spit it out.

"And for a time, we were hunted. The kingdom wanted to end us for good. Nets. Spears. Flames. So we learned to hide within the depths of the ocean to hide from their wrath. After years and years, we have become nothing more than ill-documented history." She pauses to gaze down at the waters below. She stops, and then dives her hand down into the ocean, pulling out a small fish skewered on her claws, flailing. She rips the head off with her razor-sharp teeth, the flesh tearing like thin tissue, and begins to eat the meat inside. I try not to gawk. Not to stare. To act as if this is a completely normal thing that I see every day.

"I tell you this story, not for your pity, but so you know the histories of your past. So that you understand why you never knew we existed right outside your palace walls. And so you understand that for all of the talk of our kind resembling evil incarnate, humans can surprise you with what they are capable of."

Though I've never been in love or lost someone so essential to my being, I feel for her. To lose someone like that, in that manner, must be devastating. But she doesn't want my pity or my condolences so I move away from apologies as I try and find my voice. "You said you've been waiting for me . . . every Full Celestia. Why?"

Her tail moves lazily in the water as she tosses the fish carcass away from us. "On nights where the moon is full and the stars are brightest, creatures like us have the ability to shift from fins to feet or feet to fins. Tonight, you have finally transformed into your true identity: a mermaid. For years, I have patiently waited for you to discover your heritage. And tonight, at last, you have."

I try to make sense of what she is telling me. A whole other identity lived within my bones that I was blind to. If only I decided to take a night swim or walk along the beach on an evening when the moon was full. But then suddenly I realize it like it hit me square in the face.

The parties.

Those wretched, extravagant parties said to be in celebration of the Full Celestia. What a load of rubbish. Those parties were a distraction to keep me busy. To keep me from discovering who I am. I think back to all of the conversations where my mother made it clear that the celebrations were a top priority and were non-negotiable, how important it was that I attend every one of them. I spent so many nights under their watchful eyes, and it was just an elaborate ploy to keep me from ever wandering too close to the sea.

But why?

Why would my parents keep this from me? Why lie about something like this? On top of the alleged betrothal, now this? The lengths that they went to keep this part of me a secret is outrageous. I think of the guest lists, the dining, the fireworks display. All just to keep me blind to my truth.

Did they not believe I could handle it? Are they ashamed of who I am? Worried I would be hunted as the other creatures were years ago?

A part of me wants to dive off this rock and swim far, far away. Back to my willow. Back to the life I had only hours ago. *If only I could swim back in time.*

There is no doubt in my mind that my mother knew what I was for she must be the same. They must think that this glimmering fishtail won't fit well on the heir of Aqualasia Islands. Being a mermaid surely would not be tolerated if I were to claim the throne one day, especially if they were once hated creatures that were hunted to near extinction. Not to mention that most don't even believe mermaids to have ever truly existed at all.

Do I believe what this sea maiden claims to be true?

Something about her, about her tone when she told her story, about the look in her eyes tells me it is not a farce. The pain that lingers cannot be faked.

Before mermaids were a forgotten species, they were hated creatures. Things to be despised or feared. I look around the cave at the magnificence that surrounds me as sorrow fills my chest. How could anyone want to destroy something so beautiful?

I look to Calypso, hoping for more answers to questions I can't put into words. "All my life, I felt like the sea was always calling to me, so real and present that I could hear it like a song. When I was near it, I felt better. Complete, almost. This is why." The realization hits me like a tidal wave—so hard, that it takes everything in me not to cry.

This changes everything. The most fundamental relationship in my life has been a lie. My parents withheld this truth from me because they didn't like what I was. Because it didn't fit with their plans. Their vision. The part of me that they were ashamed of, they tried to hide. As if it wasn't there at all. As if secrets could stay hidden forever. The reality tastes bitter in my mouth.

I look around the cave once more, surveying all of the merfolk amongst us, and wonder why Calypso waited so long just for me.

"Why me? There are plenty of others like us that live below the surface with you. Why was it so important for me to discover what lived in my blood?"

Her eyes turn sinister as she smiles at me, baring all of her teeth, "Because, great-granddaughter, you are the answer to our salvation. You are the key to our immortality."

Six

I'm not sure which to address first, the fact that Calypso told me I am the key to their survival or the fact that she claims to be my great-grandmother. Either way, I find it difficult to form words. I look around again at these self-sufficient creatures living in this cave and wonder what they could possibly need me for. They are predators in every sense of the word, from their talon-like claws to their razor-sharp teeth. Their speed and agility alone could defeat any human. As I say this to myself, I look down at my own webbed hands and realize it's not *they*, it's *we*. I am as much of a predator as they are. I just never knew it. So I decide to go with the issue of my ancestry.

"Did you say. . .granddaughter?" Her raptorial smile softens as if I'm as naive as a newborn.

"I have been on this earth a very long time, but yes, you are a descendant of my lineage. My blood runs through your veins. Your mother, and her mother, and hers...they all have merblood in their veins. I am your ancestor. Your family."

Family. She has my blood. Or rather, I have hers. And my mother's. As far as I know, my mother is an only child. She never talked much about her parents. They died before I was born. Was my grandmother a mermaid too? Did she know it?

Somewhere down Calypso's bloodline, someone must have decided to hide their true identity, allowing for the secret of our lineage to die off. Probably sometime after the Sea Wars ended, and merfolk were being hunted and slaughtered. My ancestors were having children of their own who never knew the truth. Or maybe they knew enough to keep it quiet for the sake of their own survival.

I think of all the ways my parents kept this huge part of my life hidden, and I wonder if they even knew. I wasn't so sheltered because I was heiress to the throne, but because I had something more dangerous in my blood, something even I wouldn't believe.

The look in Calypso's eyes tells me there's more. These sea creatures don't strike me as sentimental so she wasn't just waiting for me because she wanted to make some memories. She probably couldn't care less that I am her descendant. If she waited for me every month for the past eighteen years, there is a reason. A reason beyond wanting me to know my history. Fear grips my insides like a vice but I ask the question anyways.

"What do you want from me?"

Her dark lips tug at the corner with a smirk, "Clever girl." She knows I'm no fool, believing she has my best interest in mind. "When the Sea Wars had ended, the mermaids discovered they could no longer bear younglings. It took our kind years to discover that we'd been cursed with barrenness. You see, when the Sea Wars ended, a witch from the lands cursed our kind, rendering our species unable to procreate, so we could no longer steal what wasn't ours. She wanted to rid the earth of what humans viewed as evil. Lucky for me, a seed was already planted in my womb."

"There is an orb that reveals itself in the sea on nights when the violet moon appears, foretelling prophecies to the merpeople. Sometimes it warns us of brutal storms, sometimes of newcomers in our midst."

The violet moon, separate from the one we see every night, doesn't come around often. I've only seen a few in my lifetime. My mother said I was born under a violet moon.

"When you were born, the prophecy orb revealed itself while I was hunting with a group from my pod and showed a vision of your arrival into the world. It was the first time I had ever witnessed a prophecy foretold and it is a day I will never forget," she pauses, closing her lids as if remembering back to that day.

"Under a moon of violet hue, the curse will fracture a hair.

A child born of the sea will alter fates aware

With merblood in her veins, she will be the only key."

Me. She's talking about me. How can I be the one to break this curse? I don't have strength or power. The only special quality I own is my destiny to the crown. There must be some kind of mistake. If I truly am the one to break the curse, wouldn't I feel it? Wouldn't I have some kind of sixth sense or marking labeling me as such? Or is it really just as simple as what runs through my blood and my birth? It all just seems too bizarre to be real.

"A merbaby hasn't been born in years. Mine might have been one of the last. Half-bloods on land have kept our family lineage alive thus far, but a true merchild of the sea. . .I can barely remember their tiny delicate fins flipping through these waters." Her emerald eyes pierce me into place, swirling with a vengeance that frightens me to my core.

What she claims, about her kind being unable to conceive. . .it's devastating. My aunt from my father's side struggled with having children for years and it nearly broke her. Even as a child, I could see my dear aunt hollowed out with despair.

To think that such a beautiful and alluring creature could die off and truly someday become just a bedtime story is a tragedy. Despite the predatory and lethal nature of mermaids, there is something beautiful about them. As Calypso said, they are creatures who live a life so much simpler than humans do, at peace with the earth and with nature.

There is a reason mermaids were given the gift to control and manipulate water itself and humans weren't. Maybe humans couldn't be trusted with controlling a core element. Maybe the Mother knew the overwhelming power of controlling the elements and felt humankind could not handle the weight of that power. Only few creatures are able to wield magic like mermaids can, and a witch is one of them. Few and far between, witches are very similar to mermaids as they are born and not made.

"So I ask you, Cealene, will you help restore our species? Will you claim your destiny?"

My ancestor's words lure me into a trance. Something about her voice makes me want to please her.

"You only have tonight to decide. When the sun begins to rise above the sea, whatever form you're in, you will remain in until the next Full Celestia, when you can once again have the chance to shift."

My heart beats in my chest, banging against its cage like a wild animal. I can feel my fate tilting on its axis as she says the words. I have a choice to make. Do I stay here, beneath the ocean where my soul belongs? Or do I go back home, to what I know?

My answer lies in front of me before I even need to contemplate it.

The sea is my soulmate. It always has been. When I am near it, my body sings with rapture, like I am truly alive. The days I would spend under my beloved willow weren't just for the solidarity. Her long tendrils of vine dipped into the seawater below connected me to her with the life I never knew I needed. The small amount of ocean that crept into the forest, into my sanctuary, carried so much more than just water. It carried life. It carried my destiny, my blood. It carried an essence of *me*.

A fleeting thought of my parents bursts to the forefront of my mind and gives me a slight pause, but only slight enough to boil my blood with rage for lying to me my entire life. For betrothing me to another without so much as my knowledge of it and for withholding who I really am—my history. The parties they knew I dreaded were all just an elaborate farce to keep me caged in. To keep me in the dark.

Well, the darkness has finally given way to the light of the truth tonight. I look at my ancestor with her mystic tail as dark as night and a dorsal fin sharp enough to cut diamond and I smile, "I'm in."

After all, she is family.

Stories of mermaids have been told for as long as I can remember. Mostly legends of sea goddesses conquering an armada of ships or falling in love with a human. Everybody knows about the dangerous mythical creatures that once lurked below the sea millennia ago, luring humans to their demise, drowning men with the kiss of death. Some even believe that mermaids were the first humans and that we evolved from merfolk into human form over time.

But now, to call someone a mermaid or a siren would be a grave insult to their character. It is equivalent to calling them evil, slippery, or manipulative. Not something anyone would want to be referred to as. But to think that the term once meant something different, something majestic, reminds me how important perspective can be.

Nothing seems real anymore.

After our history lesson last night, Calypso told me to get some rest. The stone lounges are for anyone, along with woven nets that drape into the water, which is where most of the merfolk sleep. A few shells are sprinkled around the caves for anyone who prefers one. Sea moss and barnacles crust the exterior edges. One petite sea maiden with violet scales curls up in a classic giant clamshell, like something straight out of a fairytale, while a dark-muscled male tucks his tail into a Queen Conch.

Calypso has assured me of my safety, and the only reason I choose to believe it is because if the stories are to be believed, they need me. However, I do wonder how, exactly, I will be utilized to break this curse. Suspicion stalls in my outright compliance as I wonder what I will need to do. So I try not to think about the fact that I don't have legs or where I am and I let sleep take over. It isn't hard when the exhaustion from the day hits me like a barge.

I wake to a seagull's call echoing throughout the cave and when I lift myself from the stone lounge I notice Calypso is gone. Her lounge is empty except for an aquamarine gem lying in a small shell. I grab it with my clawed hand, which is a startling reminder of how much my body has changed, and hold it up to the sunray that shines through the very top of the cave and watch as the light bends and scatters throughout the damp interior, staining the rock walls with color. Its brilliance reminds me of the stones in the ballroom at Pearle Palace and I wonder if the sayings are true—if aquamarine is really made from the tears of mermaids.

A dark-skinned male with deep maroon scales swims past me but stops to say, "She left that for you. As a thank you for your help."

"Oh." I nod holding the gem in my palm, watching it roll to the creases in my webbed hand. "Here, let me," he takes the gem from my hand and puts it to my now-pointed ear.

"Aquamarine stones are a sacred gift when given to someone of our kind." I feel a sharp sting as he anchors it into my ear. "Sorry. We wear them with honor and gratitude." He turns his head to the side to show off the four shiny stones embedded in his pointed ear with surrounding scales. "The scales will grow around it to hold it in place."

I reach up to touch my jeweled ear and wince at the tenderness. When I pull my hand back down, dark red blood stains my fingertips. "Thank you. . ." I pause, not knowing his name, feeling silly for not asking earlier.

"Okiro." His wide smile is warm and welcoming, and I find myself smiling back.

"Cealene." I press my hand to my chest in greeting.

"It's good to make your acquaintance, Cealene." The handsome male bows in return and swims off through one of the dark, narrow tunnels. My body slides down the stone lounge and into the water, coming alive with invigoration, my skin drinking it in. I dive deep to wash the blood from my ear and feel the gills at my sides begin to move, exchanging saltwater through my ribs. I begin to look around for Calypso, but I don't have to look far.

Below, I find her hunting and swim closer. Not wanting to startle her prey, I wait at a distance. A giant lobster hides beneath a flat rock as she approaches from above. Slowly, she stalks it. The crustacean's antennae searching, as if it senses danger from above.

Before I can even register the movement, Calypso strikes with her claws, pulling it out from beneath the rock, but the lobster's shell is stronger than her talons. It shoots away from her by flicking its tail, swimming farther and farther from the rock.

Calypso swims past the crustacean and whips her tail into it, slamming it into some nearby rock. The lobster stills and she grabs her prey, tearing it in half. Admiration and astonishment fight for a place in my mind as she lazily swims towards me and hands me the tail. I take it with gratitude and disgust as she swims back up to the cave and breaks the surface. I follow behind, wanting to talk.

I break the surface and find her on the large platform of the cave, her tail curled around herself as she breaks apart the lobster shell with nothing more than her bare hands. I toss my half of the crustacean onto the platform and haul myself up, using my tail for momentum. I slither near her and begin to tear the white meat from inside, not wanting to appear ungrateful. My mouth waters as I bring the shellfish to my lips, uncertain if it is from nausea or hunger. Either way, I eat the food that has been offered to me, and find it to be perfect. Definitely the freshest seafood I've ever eaten.

In the palace, we are no strangers to eating food from the sea. From grilled octopus to seaweed salad. I've had it all. But something about eating something that was alive only moments ago gives me pause. Hard for me to admit, but my privileged lifestyle might have something to do with it. Never really knowing hunger like a creature of the wild might.

"I see you received my gift," She nods towards my pointed ear now bejeweled with the stone.

I caress the point absently, "Yes. It's beautiful. Thank you." My words are heavy with gratitude. There's nothing I want more than to belong here, where my soul feels complete. When I look at her, her smile is soft for the first time since we met. Everything about Calypso screams severe, from her serious predatory stare to her dark tail. Her very essence commands respect and maybe even fear. But that smile—it softens her face a bit. Curving the edges of her severity.

"So, I'm sure you have questions."

Questions. Ha. Sure, you could say that. But where to start?

"You said it's been prophesied that I have the ability to break this curse of infertility. How? How do I unlock a curse that affects every mermaid in the sea?"

Her eyes crinkle with amusement. "Let's start with something simpler."

Something tells me Calypso is not someone you question, so I hold my tongue for now. I can wait until she deems it's time to relinquish that bit of information. Part of me worries that she won't discuss the curse breaking because it is dangerous or trickier than assumed. The other part of me wonders if Calypso just likes control.

"How about we begin with the history of mermaids? It is important to know your past. Then I will take you around to hunt. Certain places should be avoided due to the dangers that lurk below, or the paths the ships take to and from different ports. You want to steer clear of those."

I nod as she tosses the empty shell into the water and I watch as it sinks below, until the darkness swallows it up completely.

"It is said mermaids were created by the goddess of the sea, Aphrodita. She was born from nothing but pale green sea foam frothing on a day when the sun was the highest in the sky. The foam was formed from the cusps of waves, created by sailors passing through. Each tiny bubble that formed the sea foam held a sailor's prayer for safe passage across the waters. It is from these prayers that Aphrodita was created." She leans forward on the rock and her long silver hair dips into the water, tiny braids sporadic throughout.

"Creating more mercreatures is a bit different."

I stare at her dubiously, wondering if I'm about to get a sex talk from my ancestor.

"It is a female's choice whether she prefers to mate with a human male or a male of our kind. The result of which will be a half-blooded or pure-blooded child. No matter the amount of merblood, the child will have merblood in their veins and will always be viewed as one of us and will have the ability to transform their body to accommodate their surrounding."

I watch as the undulating waves in the cave lap up onto the rock platform, bathing our tails in saltwater every so often, and I wonder how long one can stay on land before needing to meet the sea once again. I don't dare ask as she continues with more information about this life. I'm too hungry for answers.

"As you may have already noticed, we all possess the ability to manipulate water. We can control it easily enough in small amounts, but only the most powerful of merfolk can bend entire waves to their will. Practice can improve your ability, but practice can only take you so far. Mother Nature is the true goddess of our world and can overpower any of our abilities if hard pressed. Even the strongest of us cannot battle against the Mother during a hurricane. So I wouldn't waste time in trying. Everything has its limits."

I follow along as she leaves the platform and drops into the water, swimming on her back. We float on the surface, and I watch her glittering tail lazily slap the water as she goes. When we pass others, I can't help but take in their beauty—each one uniquely alluring in its own way. Different shades of scales and skin. Hair like silk and eyes that can pierce one's soul. They flutter and flow with such ease, at one with the water.

"Although we are one of the top predators in the ocean, we aren't the only. There are other species as quick as we are, and just as hungry.

Always be on alert when swimming outside of our caves. Think like a predator, or you will become prey. If you like your body parts as they are, don't get spotted by humans. And do not get trapped in a net. Stay away from the ships. It's easier that way. We can't afford to lose any more of us."

I wonder if my parents have search parties out on the waters, scouring the sea for me. But something tells me they know exactly where I am and what has happened. They know I haven't been kidnapped or taken for ransom. It's too much of a coincidence that I disappeared on the night of a Full Celestia. They must know I discovered the truth. Of what they've hidden from me my entire life. The timing of my disappearance is too obvious.

Let them worry. They deserve to be kept in the dark for a while, just as I was.

The thought reminds me of the missing posters lying in my room somewhere, abandoned. If only anyone took their absences as seriously as I have. Guilt fills my insides at the thought of my abandonment. In all of the excitement from last night, I didn't even think of my mission to find the missing women of our island. There is no way I can do them any good from out here. It will be a month before I can even shift onto land again and by then, who knows what will come of them.

I make a silent promise to myself that I will not give up on them. I won't allow this to continue on our island any longer, no matter what life throws my way—*even if it's a tail.*

Calypso takes me through a series of tunnels that run through the caves and then open up to the open sea. Miles and miles of blue. We swim through thick sea forests teeming with wildlife that pays us no mind. I follow close behind her, keeping up with her swift speed. Her onyx tail glistens as the sunrays pierce the water. Seahorses bounce around the tall stalks of seaweed and tiny colorful fish dart through the lush reefs. The sea floor is filled with life as we swim by. The abundance of undiscovered territory is intoxicating. My heart feels full in my chest with the weight of pure delight—like I've finally come home.

When we get to another patch of open ocean, she turns her direction up toward the sky and swims vertically—her fins dancing as she goes. Her speed picks up as her arms reach above her head, toward the surface. Without pause, she breaks the surface, her entire body leaving the water and she's gone. A moment later, she dives back down into the sea and swims towards me—unfiltered bliss rippling through her face.

She nods at me to try it like it's now my turn to breach from the water and experience the true life of a sea maiden. Without hesitation, I swim a little deeper towards the ocean floor, giving myself plenty of space to work with. The sun filters through the water in this part of the ocean, which is clear as glass. Unlike the deeper parts of the open ocean that hold a fog to it, its color is a deep blue. The water here is light and airy. In the distance, sea turtles ride a current.

I stop and right my position, looking at Calypso. She gives me a nod as a smirk tugs at her lips, as if to say "Go ahead, let's see what you got. Entertain me."

I begin to pump my tail, undulating as it curves through the water, sending me upward. Propelling my body higher and higher. I feel my loose tendrils being pulled back through the water, trailing behind me, mimicking my motions. I pick up speed as I near the surface and feel the blood beneath my skin become alive again, pumping lightning through my veins.

I break the surface and continue higher, completely breaching into the air. For a moment I'm flying. Weightless. Wind in my face and sun on my skin. I shout with untamed abandon as I arc my body through the atmosphere and dive back down into the sea. As I descend back down towards Calypso, my body sings with bliss, life-altering bliss. I look to her as if to say, "I could get used to this," and her smile widens, emerald eyes aglow.

She lets me take a few more shots at it, and each time I push myself to see how high I can get, before gravity greedily pulls me back down. My heart is nearly pumping through my chest, and I feel like I am on a high that I never want to come down from.

Eventually, she pulls me back to reality so she can teach me a few pointers on how to hunt for myself. Most of which was allowing my predatory instinct to take over. Once I let go of my human tendencies and really allowed the other animalistic part of me to take over, it came much more easily as if I was shedding a skin to reveal another layer of myself underneath, like second nature.

Calypso is a beast in the water, relentless and swift. Once her eyes are set on her prey, nothing escapes her. I follow her lead and learn from her experience enough to hunt for myself. Pride swells in my chest when I snatch a fish of my own, skewering it with my claws. Knowing I can depend on myself for food and not need to rely on anyone else is a feeling of freedom and independence I've never known.

Growing up in the palace, things were always readily available to me. I never wanted for anything—not food or shelter or warmth. Although I was grateful to have them, I think I took the ease of having them for granted. But now in this form, following my ancestor's path and learning as they all have, I can't help but feel elated by the freedom that comes with it.

After hunting for enough food to fill our bellies for the day, Calypso tells me that she will be gone for about a week on an annual hunting trip with a few others from neighboring pods. She tells me to use this time and space to breathe in my own body and to direct any of my questions to the other merfolk of the pod, specifically Marina. Something tells me she's hoping I fall in love enough with this life that I never plan to leave it for land. I can't say that I'm certain she'll be wrong. At every turn, I am falling more in love with the sea than ever before. For all of the lessons I sit in on at the palace, none of them could ever teach me this.

We plan to meet back at the caves at dusk, but she leaves me to my own devices for the rest of the day, which leaves me feeling equal parts excited and embarrassed for feeling scared to swim the sea alone. I feel like I've been given more freedom just now by Calypso, than in my entire life. An entire ocean at my disposal. An entire day to discover myself and what the sea has to offer. And I am barely equipped enough to keep myself fed. She must assume I won't get myself lost or eaten. Meanwhile, Calypso said she had a few things to go over to learn how to break this curse. None of which she explained to me in any detail.

Before we part, a few others have come to collect her. Their tails splashing hurriedly through the waves alerting us that her presence is needed elsewhere. Of the short time I have known my ancestor, it seems that she is the monarch of this pod of merfolk. Although she has never said it, she doesn't have to. It shines through her like an aura. Her presence commands respect and I can see that she has earned it every time she enters a space. The others treat her as their leader, confiding in her and alerting her of any news. In the short time we've spent together, I've seen more mermaids and males come to her with one thing or another eager to have her attention.

She mentioned being around quite a long time, which could contribute to her superiority, but it's something more than that. Her pod admires her in a way that I've always strived for when I someday rule. Observing my father lead the islands has taught me that respect is earned and does not last forever. You must constantly continue to earn the admiration and respect of your people in order to keep it.

Once Calypso and her clan leave, their colored flukes the last thing I see, I take in a shaky breath wondering if this ocean is too big for me. In the palace, I was almost never alone, always surrounded by family or staff or courtiers. But here, without all of the bustle and noise, I suddenly feel very, very small. Overwhelmed by the weight of the prophecy, I dive deep below the surface, worried if I am truly the one to unlock these creatures from this punishment.

SEVEN

Somehow, I have found myself swimming towards the palace, and though it is the only home I've ever known, that's not what draws me to it now. I think the familiarity of the island is only part of my pull towards the rocky coast. A bigger part of what drives me forward is the people who reside on the island. My people. Despite everything that has happened the last day and a half, I can't help but think about those missing women and where they could be. Whether anyone knows it or not, I have a duty to them to figure out the mystery of their disappearances.

As I swim along the coast of Aqualasia, keeping low enough to be undetected, I think of the last time I was in the castle, which feels like decades ago. The party, the balcony, Ezera and his father. The blood. The painful transformation. I shudder at the memory of feeling like my skin was burning off, like every nerve ending was being split in two with agonizing precision. I wonder if every transformation feels as painful. A month from now, when the next Full Celestia occurs and I shift back into human form, will the pain be so severe? So unbearable? My stomach clenches at the thought of being on dry land again. Despite my duty, I haven't fully convinced myself that I want to.

I spin through the water like a porpoise and swim closer to the surface with my face to the sky. The sunlight dazzles through the water's surface, like a pattern in motion, and I feel the rays hit my face through the waves. I don't plan to make my presence known when I arrive at the private water gates of the palace. I just want to be near it, to feel something familiar. I peer up through the surface and see the palace just as it always appears, regal and strong. Its pearl pillars shine bright, and its architecture is sweeping and intricate against the clear sky.

On a typical day, my father would be busy with meetings and my mother would be planning another event, but today might look different if I walked into the castle now. I wonder if they've sent guards out in search of me or if they are just waiting for my return from the sea. I wonder if Angelina knows. She must have come to my parents once she discovered I wasn't going to arrive in my room to meet her that night. Did they tell her what they'd been hiding from me? Does everyone in the palace know where I've gone? Or have my parents come up with a clever lie to hide my whereabouts?

Maybe that's what they're doing now. Working on a clever coverup for their missing daughter.

The stone steps that descend directly into the sea are patched with algae and moss. I've only used them a handful of times in my life, preferring to enter the ocean from the private beach, but from this angle, the steps seem ethereal, like they might lead to another world. I almost laugh to myself when I realize *they do.* These stone steps lead to a world on land with laws and structure, so different from the one I'm currently living in. My thoughts have been so scattered lately with where my life will lead that I just need something stable and comfortable. Something familiar to anchor me. As angry as I am at my parents for keeping our history from me, I still love them.

I've always thought my parents and I had a close relationship. Maybe it's because I am their only heir. Or maybe it's because they view me as a peer and not a child. We would spend nights together before the roaring fire in the great room, enjoying mulled cider and discussing the outrageous attire of the lords and ladies from the various festivals we would host, laughing at the lengths people will go to for the attention of others. To not blend in. We often shared our hopes and dreams with each other dining over a roasted turkey. My relationship with my mother and father has always been an open and honest one. At least I thought it was. *Until recently.*

As of late, I'm not sure what was real and what was staged.

When I near the edge of the city, I can already hear the commotion of people and ships sailing through the sea. I turn and dive deeper below the surface as I spot the wide belly of a fishing boat up ahead. A manatee bobs in the kelp forest nearby, and I stop to observe its behavior. The gentle giant seems to be in distress, pacing back and forth throughout the towering kelp stalks. Her whine is like a beacon for help. Cautiously, I drift closer to see if she's hurt.

When I near her vicinity, her sweet deep eyes are filled with sorrow. I can practically see the worry rolling off of her. I right my position as I ease towards her with my hands out in front of me. Slowly, ever so slowly, I place my hands on her whiskered cheek, assessing for any injury. But everything seems to be in order. She seems healthy, aside from her obvious distress.

She nudges her snout under my webbed hand, towards the boat. I turn and see a dark figure idling below in the foggy blue sea. As soon as I begin to swim towards the fishing boat, I already know what I'll find when I near. I know what the dark round figure is hovering below the boat, and my heart cracks right down the center for this helpless mother.

When I near the belly of the boat, the plump little calf comes into focus. Its skin is nearly flawless, not yet weathered by life under the sea. It is caught in the net, part of its flipper immobilized by the rope. I reach my hand out tentatively hoping the calf can see that I am not a threat, but before I can begin untangling it, broad hands reach down into the water grabbing the net. I duck down deeper below the belly of the boat as I watch the net tug the calf through the water to the back of the fishing boat. Two bare feet dip into the water, dangling off of a platform.

"It's alright, little fella. I'll get you out of this mess so you can swim back to your mama." I hear the words so clearly despite being under the water. His voice is sweet and light as if the calf can truly understand what the fisherman is telling it. I know that voice. It's the voice from the night of the Full Celestia. The one from my childhood.

Ezera.

I swim out towards the small sea stack rising out from the water just a few dozen feet away and watch from above the water, through a small crack in the stacked rock. His sun-bleached hair almost glows in the daylight. White and gold locks dangle over his face as he leans into the water, working through the tangled rope carefully. The sun glistens off his tanned jaw as he continues to talk to the calf.

"I'm sure she's worried about you." His hands are gentle and meticulous as he maneuvers around the calf's little flipper with such care. "You will have to extend my apologies to her. I truly am sorry that our nets got in your way." He untangles the rest of the netting from the calf, freeing it from its hold and the calf's head bobs on the surface of the water, whiskers poking out like fuzz on a peach.

"Wait up." He places his hand on the calf's slate head, "I've got something for you. A treat for the inconvenience." Ezera jumps up from the platform and rushes into the cockpit. After a moment he emerges with a bushel of thick leafy greens, bending down on the platform and offers it to the manatee. The calf takes it greedily, whiskers dancing about. The smile that emerges on Ezera's face lights him from within. I can see in his eyes that freeing this young creature has brought him delight.

When he wipes his wet hands onto his rolled pants, I see a discolored gnarled marking on his calf where the hair no longer grows like a scar of a symbol marked into his flesh—a branding. My stomach drops as I wonder where it could be from and what the symbol means. It's too meticulous to be a result from a fishing accident and it's not a symbol that I recognize from Aqualasia either. To wear a brand like that cannot be voluntary. The pain one must endure to get one sounds paralyzing.

As the calf disappears below the water, presumably to return back to its mother, Ezera folds his arms across his chest and watches the dark blob beneath the surface go, presumably checking the flipper for any injury from the net.

Not many men would treat an animal with such respect and care. Not many fishermen would take the time to rescue an innocent creature from the foreign objects they dropped into someone else's home. Being in a business such as this, one must become immune to the violence it has on creatures of the sea. Day in and day out they must see dozens of small deaths in the ocean. But no deaths are small, and I think Ezera knows that. He doesn't seem to be like most men, showing empathy and grace even if the creature does not recognize it. His kindness had no ulterior motive. It was not a show displayed to impress anyone, but a moral code he must live by.

Although the manatee is long gone now, probably shadowing its mother through the kelp forest, I haven't moved from behind the rock, unable to tear my eyes away from Ezera. I watch as he moves about the boat, running his broad hands through his hair, attempting to free his face from the locks veiling his view. Roped muscles contract under his bronzed skin as he cranks the handle for the fishing net, dragging it out of the water. The net spools onto the boat, dripping seawater onto the deck.

"Dad, I'm pulling the net in. Once it's secure, we'll move to the west and drop there." Pleasant shock runs through my body when he addresses his father. *He is alive.* He survived. I can still feel the stickiness of his blood on my hands from that night. I can still remember the pained expression contorting his features as we freed him. I wait for a response from his father but never hear one. He's not on the back of the boat from what I can see.

Ezera secures the net and continues to move around the stern, rolling barrels, and adjusting sails. As the wind begins to take them away, he jumps onto a barrel and swings his body around the small mast, leaning into the wind, into the sea. His hair catches in the breeze as he closes his eyes, soaking in the sun, the sea, the world. After only a moment's peace, he swings down from the ledge and hurries into the wooden cockpit. As the sails catch the wind and the boat slowly turns west, I see his father sitting at the bow, pale but alive. My heart swells with relief to see him in one piece. If Ezera didn't come to find me that night, I don't know if his father would be sitting there with him today.

It is clear that Ezera has taken on the work of two men while his father recovers from the accident. A fishing crew of only two is nearly too much work to stay afloat, but to take on the responsibility all on your own? It's impossible. When we were young, Ezera's father had a crew of about five men while Ezera slowly grew old enough to become an official member. But as the years went on, it seemed they preferred to work with only each other. I always remember Harrison as being friendly and kind. I can't imagine what made them decide to work with a skeleton crew. The upkeep of sailing the boat alone is a full-time job, and then there is the actual fishing itself. Catching enough in a day to bring to the island is no small task.

I have no idea how Ezera will ever keep this up while his father recovers, but I hope for both their sakes he recovers quickly. Despite the circumstances, Ezera's face doesn't show an ounce of defeat or exhaustion. He's a workhorse who still makes time to free an innocent creature from a net. I watch as they sail into the distance, the boat shrinking from sight as it goes.

Four days have passed since Calypso left on her hunting trip, and I have been spending every single day exploring the sea and becoming more acquainted with my new body. Life in the pod is a refreshing change from life at the palace. There are no hidden agendas or ploys to manipulate. The merfolk just *are*. Most are friendly enough but seem to prefer the quiet—such a stark contrast to life at the palace. On any given day at Pearle Castle, people are always visiting for one reason or another. I understand the palace is more than just a home for my family, but sometimes I just want to enjoy my family and our home without having to play hostess all day. The connections between these creatures, though quiet, are strong and honorable.

I've found a few favorite places near the pod where I like to hunt, and I'm getting better at my techniques when hunger strikes. The key is to listen to your intuition and strike fast. There's no room for hesitation. Swimming along the reef is the best place to hunt if you like variety. But today I swim along the rocky cliff of the main island of Aqualasia, marking the terrain and wildlife that reside here. I thought about sneaking near the docks to see if I could glimpse any new missing posters, but was too scared of getting caught. I can't ignore the nagging sensation to figure this mystery out. It feels like no one is taking it as seriously as I am.

The cool water feels good on my skin after being exposed to the sun from lounging on the rock earlier, studying the cliffside. The cool temperature of the ocean doesn't affect my body like it would as a human, but I'm much more sensitive to direct exposure to the sun and air like I'm a dried-out sponge, in need of misting. I swim through the kelp forest and past a school of striped fish when I see the tunnel leading into the island from the cliffside. It takes only a moment for me to wonder where it leads before I realize there is only one place it can be.

My willow.

It is the only place on this side of the island that has a water inlet from the sea. I never knew how, exactly, it filtered into the island and created a pool of water beneath the willow, but this must be it.

I place my hands on the edges of the opening and peer inside, feeling my hair floating around me in a cloud. The tunnel is dark. Really dark. Hesitation grasps my arms, holding me in place, while I contemplate the unknown. There's no way to be completely sure where this will lead, or if there are several tunnels that branch off from this one. It's entirely possible that this could just be a dead end. Or that an electric eel will kill me before I even get the chance to find out. As I idle at the opening, I nearly jump out of my skin when a sea snake slithers out. When it sees me, it reveals razor-sharp teeth before quickly swimming away, and I feel the instinct to attack creep into my senses. I try to push it down now that I know when surprised, my immediate defensive response is to harm. This change in instinct may be necessary for a creature of the sea, but it isn't me.

I push the instinct away and tell myself to calm down. The creature is gone and was probably more alarmed to see me hovering over its only exit to the ocean.

The thought of seeing my beloved willow again drives me to enter the darkness. I need to see if I'm right about where this tunnel will take me. If my memory is correct, it can't be too far into the island from here. And if I'm wrong, the tunnel should be wide enough for me to turn around. I muster up as much courage as possible before I let go of the edge and enter the dark unknown.

Eight

As I travel down the dark tunnel, tiny specs glow in the rounded walls, illuminating my path just enough that I can see. If it weren't for the faint little light creeping in from a crack in the rock above, the tiny glowing specs would be disorienting, like tiny moving stars. Neon pinks and yellows oscillate ever so slightly as I pass by. Small fish swim past, but the darkness reveals nothing more than the movement of tiny fins. The fear loosens its grip on my chest as the tunnel brightens and widens out, like the reverse of a funnel. I pick up speed, working my tail against the water to drive me farther in, toward the light.

When the passage takes me higher, more and more light filters in, and almost immediately I can feel a change in the water here. Less salt, more warmth. I spill out into a pool of warm light and I nearly cry out as I see the canopy of my willow appear beyond the water, her trunk dancing in the ripples. The pool is thick with sea grass and vegetation near the bottom, creeping up around the edges. My willow's so much more beautiful than I ever noticed from above, reminding me that perspective is everything. I feel like I'm seeing this place with a new set of eyes. An entire ecosystem was living right below me all of this time without ever realizing it.

I break the surface of the pool and breathe in the fresh forest air.

"Hello, Willow," I greet her as I push myself onto the small bank of sea grass. I feel like it's been ages since I was last here, lounging in the crook of her arm. My entire world has been turned upside down since then. *I may not be able to climb your limbs, but I'm still me.* I'm not sure if the comment is more to assure myself or the tree. In response, the willow's vines sweep around my shoulders, caressing my body. The feather-light breeze sends goosebumps up my spine. I can hear a faint melody carry on the wind like a song whispered in a single breath. The air around me suddenly feels charged. *Electric.*

A powerful presence is here.

I sense movement in the water before I hear it. The light splash of water parting way for something. Or someone. I shimmy back into the pool as quickly as I can while scanning the perimeters, my eyes just above the surface. Not that my hiding will do any good. Whoever is here has either already spotted me or will see me idling in the clear pool soon enough. The only reason I risked coming here was because this part of the forest is always empty of visitors due to the proximity to the palace grounds, no one wanting to be caught trespassing on royal grounds by mistake.

A strange female appears from the other end of the pool, pale and beautiful.

"You have nothing to fear from me." Her voice is almost ethereal. Like tiny bells chiming through a gust of wind. She approaches me slowly with the sun beaming off of her, creating a soft golden glow. "I know who you are."

Her porcelain skin is as pale as the moon, and her eyes are an ice blue so pale that they're nearly colorless. The faintest hint of pink graces her lips and cheeks. She looks like she just dropped down from heaven with her pale yellow hair braided in a crown atop her head. She continues to move closer until she is mere feet away. Her generous lashes are the length of spider legs, fluttering as drops of water fall from the tips. An obvious reaction to this stranger should be fear, but I can't feel anything but awe. This female is absolutely breathtaking in an unfamiliar way. With my guard down, I dare to move closer. My self-preservation clearly needs a priority check as of late.

The female is draped in jewels of gold and pearl and gems. Her braided crown sparkles, as well as her pointed ears and neck. Beads of pearls and boldly colored gems adorn her chest, layered like amour. Finally, I find my voice again after taking her in. "A pleasure to meet you . . . ?" I wait for her to supply me with a name.

In answer, she rises from the pool, water pushing her higher, like a fountain, defying gravity and revealing the rest of her scaled body. Unlike the other merfolk I've encountered, this creature is covered in scales starting just below her necklaces. Rather than a single tail ending in a fluttering fin, this sea maiden has two tails that branch off at thigh level. The scales that make up most of her body are pale blue, almost iridescent, capturing the light and turning it into magic.

"Most refer to me as the Lady of the Lake, but I prefer my given name, Alana."

The rush of water bubbles behind her voice as it settles her back down into the pool. Something tells me this one has an affinity for the theatrics.

"And you are Princess Cealene, of course. Heiress to Aqualasia and the key to breaking our curse, if Calypso is to be believed."

She knows Calypso? I want to ask her how but skepticism laces her words when she says the last part. It's clear she's suspicious about the prophecy Calypso claims to have seen. I don't comment on my own doubts about breaking this never-ending curse.

"You don't believe the prophecy?" The words leave my mouth before I can even be sure I want the answer. The tightness in her jaw tells me tension surrounds the topic. But what makes her so skeptical of Calypso? Is she known for being unreliable? Or do these two have a tangled past?

"That has yet to be determined. I am reluctant to believe most things these days." Her tails spin and flutter beneath her as she glides around the pool, almost as if they have a mind of their own, swimming and moving through the water, as the top half of her is engaging in something entirely different. I wait for her to continue, learning that the less I say, the more information I receive when it comes to creatures of the sea.

"Before I was chained to this small, misplaced piece of the ocean, I lived freely in the sea just as the others. Until I was summoned to the land by the king himself. He required my services to create an enchanted sword for him from the sea to defeat his enemies. You see, not many mermaids can do what I can. So he sought me out, hearing the tales of my magic.

"I was as surprised as any to discover my love for him ran deeper than any ocean. I begged and pleaded for the merfolk to let me live on land with the king, as I was bound to serve the sea by duty. But since the Sea Wars, they couldn't understand how I could have any affection for a human. It was a rarity for the king to even reach out to our kind after the blood had settled from the Sea Wars. I saw his request as an opportunity to create a connection, but my sisters did not. They took my feelings for the king as a betrayal of our kind and cursed me with these tails to mock my desire for permanent legs and exiled me to this small pond so that I may never live on land nor in the ocean." Her eyes glisten with unshed tears. "Sometimes I wonder who holds the prize for the cruelest of beings."

My throat tightens with emotion feeling the pain from her story. What a cruel thing to do to a mermaid. What a hurtful way to mock someone's dreams. I watch as the sorrow spreads from her eyes to her entire face and curse myself for feeling any gravitation towards the fisherman. Another mermaid who fell in love with a human. Another life ruined from loving the wrong species.

It occurs to me that Alana has been here for quite some time . . . yet I have never noticed her during all of my visits to the willow. "I've never seen you here before."

"Oh, but I've seen you. Many times. I've watched you grow over the years as you've visited this part of the forest. Always so eager to run away from the palace."

How could I have never noticed such a presence in what I'd always considered my part of the island?

She answers me like she can hear my thoughts. "You never saw me because I didn't want to be seen." Her sorrow-filled eyes turn cold and hard. "I choose to stay in the shadows of life now. It's easier this way. Simpler. When you've been turned into a mockery of a creature, there is really no place in the world for you. Not that I have much of a choice now.

"And if I'm truly being honest, between you and me, I'm not quite sure what would happen if I unleashed my fury onto the merfolk for what they've done. Burn me once, I turn to ash. Burn me twice, I will rise in flame."

Something dark simmers beneath her ice-blue eyes, such darkness in contrast to all of that light, ethereal grace. The chills return to my skin. I look at the pool and, as lovely as it is with its vibrant colors and mystical atmosphere, to be trapped in such a small space for the rest of your days, is torture. *I would know.* There were days when the walls of the castle threatened to crush me. My advisor who planned my daily lessons and meetings constantly breathed down my neck, demanding more of me, and critiquing my every move and every word. That need to be free, to get out was almost unbearable. Those are the days that I would end up here. Under the willow, where the breeze flows as free as the vines of the tree.

My paradise in the forest was a beautiful prison to her. The exact opposite of what it means to me. A sea creature versus a land creature. Two completely different worlds, colliding in one place.

Although we might have opposing views on this place, we yearn for the same thing. We understand the suffocating feeling of being trapped within the walls that someone else built for us. Alana and I may come from different worlds, but in this, I know her sorrow. I feel her anguish intimately.

I look to the Lady of the Lake and see her despair beneath her jewels and glow. Her own people made a mockery of her. For the merpeople to do such a thing to their own kind is quite telling for how much the Sea Wars must have wreaked havoc on everyone, even after it was over. I didn't need to experience war to know it had a lasting impression.

"I'm so sorry for what they've done to you." My apology sticks in my throat like I've swallowed too much at once. Her long lashes flutter closed as she bows her head in appreciation.

"Don't ever forget that even roses have thorns." With that, she turns away from me and sinks down under the surface as a cold wind sweeps through the pond. I swim towards the tunnel that leads back out to the ocean and leave the Lady of the Lake in peace but turn towards my willow one last time.

I will see you again, old friend. I nod toward the willow's trunk before diving deep into the crystal pool to find the tunnel hidden below.

When I reach the ocean, I try to swim off the eerie feeling I was left with after meeting the Lady of the Lake, like the water surrounding me was filled with a heaviness, clinging to my scales and pulling me down. I swim through the kelp forest and find myself in a narrow strip of mangroves outcropping the western sea, their roots like spider legs digging into the sea floor. Wildlife rushes throughout the maze of roots, creating a flurry of motion as I pass.

I wonder about the power of the merfolk and how foolish I would be if I wholeheartedly trusted them with my life. I think back to the few mermaids and males that I've met thus far and couldn't detect any ill will from them. They all seem to present themselves with none of the hidden agendas that I'm used to encountering on land. Calypso is much too complex a creature to truly get a read on, but then I remember the aquamarine gem anchored into my ear and think about her words. Mermaids were born to live wild and free. She wanted only that—a simple life of freedom . . . and love. Plus, she's family. That has to count for something. I am her descendant and the one who can bring fertility back to her people. There has to be enough value in that to keep me relatively safe for now. At least safe enough not to end up like Alana.

As strange as our meeting was, I feel a deep connection to her, to her story. Maybe, under different circumstances, we could be friends. She could probably use a friend, despite her wanting to hide what she's become. Even in this different form, she is still beautiful.

Alana's final comment snags in my mind, bringing questions to the curse breaking. *Even roses have thorns.* Was she alluding to merpeople as a whole or Calypso specifically? My mind hovers over my great-grandmother and how she hasn't told me how to break this curse. Something tells me it's because it is a lot more complicated than she wants to admit. I have to imagine that for a witch to place such a curse on an entire species, it can't be simple to break. I shudder at the thought of what breaking the curse could entail. The notion that snags in my mind is that the price could be my life. *Am I willing to pay it?*

As the sun begins to set, a shadow casts along the mangrove trunks, alerting me of the time. I need to head back. When I make my way through the caves back to the pod, I see the male from earlier who anchored the gem to my ear with another male. His copper-colored hair flows through the water as he moves. Robin egg blue scales shimmer in contrast to the deep maroon tail of Okiro's. They swim together in tandem; their bodies move freely in the water and their fins follow their pattern, extending their movements like a graceful trail. Their fluidity is enticing, like a dance between two lovers, and I wonder if they are. Trying not to stare as I pass them by, I remember what Calypso said about our kind mostly keeping to themselves.

Anxious to meet with Calypso and hear about her discoveries on how to break this curse, I search the caves above and below for her onyx tail. Before I get very far, I feel a webbed hand tug at my arm, pulling my body through the water. Not hard, but enough to startle me.

Without even thinking, I bare my teeth and turn to face whoever has a hold of me. Immediately I calm when I see one of Calypso's right-hand sea maidens stare back at me with amusement, as if I could ever take her on. Her hair is black as night, billowing around her petite face. She nods for me to follow, the same way Calypso did the night we first met. I follow her amethyst tail as it gleams through the tunnel, catching light where it can. The color is so saturated and bold, that I can make out the vibrancy even in the darkness of the ocean at dusk.

We swim up when we hit an open cave, and I can already see the pink glow from the unusual sea life, lighting up the room. We glide onto the stone surface crusted with algae and crystallized salt. Calypso sits in a pool of seawater that dips into the cave floor, like a natural divot was carved out from years and years of the rushing water wearing away at the rock. A tiny waterfall trickles behind her, filling and spilling over the pool, making the cave wall glisten. Her onyx tail curls around her like a snake. Two other mermaids accompany her in smaller water pools as we approach. Each one lovelier than the next.

"I'm Marina, by the way. Nice to make your acquaintance, curse breaker." My stomach drops as the purple-tailed mermaid addresses me. The weight of this expectation is starting to become quite heavy.

"Cealene," I introduce myself, already knowing she knows exactly who I am. It seems everybody does.

"Cealene, my dear, how did the waters treat you today?" Calypso asks in that honey-coated voice. Marina glides on her belly under the trickling waterfall, arching her back and letting it shower her black locks down her spine.

"Quite well. I don't think I could ever get enough of it." I mean every word. The ocean is a beautiful beast with wonders at every corner. But I don't wish to delve into my love for the sea right now. I want to know what is required of me to break this damn curse. Because I have a feeling it might be more than I'm willing to give.

"I'm anxious to hear what you've discovered today." It takes everything in me to ask this without sounding as frightened as I feel, pushing the subject to someone who seemingly never does anything she doesn't want to.

"So eager, my dear. Come, sit. Lyla's bringing us her famous clam medley." I bite my tongue as I swim through the shallow water and prop myself up on a ledge, letting the water trickle over my tail. Sure enough, a copper-haired mermaid who must be Lyla appears carrying a large clamshell filled with various colors of white and pink meats, careful to keep it above water. Sea greens garnish the edges and it almost looks like something that would be served at the palace. For a moment, my heart tugs at the memory of my home, of Chef sneaking me morsels of the day's meal when I chassé through the kitchens.

She places the shell on the stone surface before hoisting herself onto the platform. She slaps her silvery tail onto the surface and waits for Calypso to take the first piece. Not sure if this is out of respect for Calypso, who is clearly the leader of this pod, or if it is a sacred rule of the merpeople. I wait to see how sharing a meal among this species unfolds. Without hesitation, Calypso stabs a piece of meat with her taloned nail and the rest follow suit in a relaxed and civilized manner. I grab a piece of my own but can barely wait a moment longer for Calypso to spill the information I so desperately crave.

"Lyla, you've outdone yourself yet again," Marina says between bites, her canines sharp as knives.

"The lagoon always has the best pick of shellfish this time of year," Lyla counters, modestly. The tight curls of her hair spring up as they begin to dry. She looks strikingly similar to the copper-haired male who was with Okiro earlier. I wonder if they're siblings.

"How do you prepare it?" I ask, hoping my question doesn't sound rude.

"A magician never tells her secrets." Lyla eyes me playfully before serving herself onto a small open-faced shell. "If you're asking where we make all of our meals, there's a ledge behind the draped vines over there where we keep our tools and dried herbs. They call it Lyla's Ledge, but truly anyone is free to use it."

Before I can thank her for the meal, Calypso grabs my attention. "Sweet descendant of mine, today I had my sea sisters visit an old friend of ours to confirm a few details on how to reverse this spell. As you can probably imagine, it has been years since we discovered how, exactly, to break the curse. If and when the time came around, we wanted to be prepared.

"As suspected, the ring of the Dark Witch who cursed us is required for this to work. Fortunately for us, she died years ago. Unfortunately, she was buried on the Island of Bones. The ring was buried along with her body."

Never hearing of such a place, I can only assume it is some sort of resting place for the dead. Witches don't typically frequent our islands, preferring life in the mountains of larger lands, but they've visited the islands in the past on occasion. Personally, I've never met one, having never left Aqualasia before. But after meeting this pod, I wouldn't mind coming across a witch, if they weren't as threatening as they seem.

"The Island of Bones is a tricky place to get to by ship or by fin. For us, we will need to wait until high tide before the storm hits in two days' time, so we can reach the center of the island without getting our tails shredded by the viper vines. They have thorns so sharp, they'll tear you to ribbons if you aren't careful." Her brows raise in a knowing way, as if to warn me of the risk. If she's trying to instill fear, it's working. I can't help but feel out of my element here, still so new to this life. Despite my connection to the sea, I still have a lot to learn.

"No creature ever escapes their hooked claws. Once you're in, you never get out," Marina comments, now lying on her back under the waterfall, swaying her tail through the flowing stream. I note the trail of aquamarine stones lining her left ear and wonder about the story that each holds. I've come to associate one's character with how many stones adorn their ears, knowing how rare and sacred they are to our kind. Most don't have any at all, their ears bejeweled with other treasures of the sea: pearls, shells, sea glass, various stones, and my favorite, a fishing hook. Merfolk can be quite ironic it seems.

"Can't you cut through the vines? So you don't need to enter during a storm?" My voice quivers with uncertainty, knowing I must be missing something.

"The vines were designed to protect. So not only are they very strong, stronger than most metals, if burned or cut away, they will grow back within seconds, fusing the opening created." To my appreciation, Calypso's voice holds no irritation at my question and my lack of knowledge on the subject. I'm shocked to find she is happy to enlighten me. Calypso seems like someone who doesn't take kindly to her time being wasted.

"But don't worry, dear. You won't be going anywhere near the Island of Bones. It's simply too much of a risk to send you in with no experience on the unique nature of the island." My stomach tightens at the thought of such a place. "Luckily, my second and third have extensive experience with places of this nature. I will send Marina and Brea to fetch the ring, as they are my most trusted subjects with the highest agility and strength. This won't be their first tangle with the viper vines in a manner of speaking."

I look toward the dark-haired sea maiden with thousands of tiny braids trailing down her back, jeweled with tiny gold ornaments at the tips, and wonder if she was given the choice to say no to such a dangerous journey.

Calypso turns to Marina and Brea. "You two have proven yourselves time and time again. With every battle and breach, you both come out as victors." Both mermaids nod and mutter their gratitude for the opportunity. But I still have so many questions.

"If mermaids have the ability to manipulate water, can't you summon a wave large enough to carry you safely over the viper vines?" I hate how my voice sounds. Hesitant and weak. But if there were a way around the risk of the viper vines, I would much prefer they take it.

"We do have the power to bend water to our will, but so does the Mother. If a storm of this size is brewing, her powers will outweigh our own. As good as I am with water wielding, I won't risk Marina's safety in the possibility that I am not strong enough to get us over safely," Brea explains, her voice as quiet as a lullaby.

"But what if . . . I mean . . . Isn't it dangerous?" I don't know how I feel about having someone else do the dirty work while I sit around swimming in the ocean. I've never been one to sit in the background while someone else gets their hands dirty. As my father says, I'm a doer, just like him.

"No need to worry about us, Cealene. We're pretty deadly, ourselves. Plus," Marina turns her body towards me, getting my full attention, "we want this curse broken as much as any mermaid. And we're willing to face danger if that's what it takes."

Her direct candor is a welcome change to this conversation that seems charged with dangerous plans but no outward emotional response whatsoever. I don't doubt that Marina and Brea are intimately invested in ending this curse. I'm sure they or someone they know would jump at the opportunity to bear a child. But I still can't just sit back and wait, and if I'm being perfectly honest with myself, I want to go. I want to see this forbidden island with a deadly barrier. For too long I've been sheltered from life, and I've just begun really living. I'm going.

I just need to figure out how to get Calypso's approval.

"What is the ring needed for, exactly?" I try to calm my breathing, excited to get some answers on what lies ahead.

"The ring will need to be worn by the curse breaker for the incantation to work." Calypso's emerald eyes simmer with steadfast power. This creature is not one to mess with.

I wonder if breaking the curse will directly change her life, and if she desires to procreate again after all she endured the first time. After all of these years with the curse in place, it seems only half-bloods can reproduce on land in human form, and it seems even they might not know what they truly are anymore. Not after the Sea Wars caused panic amongst the half-bloods. It wouldn't surprise me if most were like me, not even aware of another part of them lying dormant their entire lives.

Maybe Calypso's time to create a family has expired altogether. I never asked if mermaids have an infinite number of years to reproduce or if their childbearing years are as limited as humans are. If their lifespans are much longer than that of humans, I would guess their childbearing years would be too.

Imagining how hard it must have been for Calypso to live with such a loss, to know her child was being raised by humans, a species she despises for so many reasons, must be unbearable. It must have felt like she was living a nightmare to have someone physically tear her apart. Like the arteries and muscles snapping in two, severing the connection of life. To then go on living with a piece of you missing for eternity. I never asked how old Calypso is but it is clear she has been around much longer than the average human. To live so long with that loss, I wouldn't wish that on my worst enemy. She may just be the strongest being I've ever encountered.

Admiration swells in my chest for this fierce female who sacrificed so much. If it weren't for her, I wouldn't be here today. My mother nor her mother before her. If the birth of her child had gone a different way, my life may have looked much different than it does now.

I want to be a part of this journey. Of this change in history. "I want to come to the Island of Bones." My request comes out surprisingly strong and is not how I intended to broach the subject, but I continue, not wanting to lose this chance to persuade her. Calypso respects confidence, that much is clear. She responds to dignity. "I need to be a part of this. I can't just wait around while someone else journeys for what I was made to do." I try and sit up straighter, puffing out my chest. I want her to know the severity of my request.

She scrutinizes me, debating, and I try not to shrink under her crushing gaze. I swear ages pass as I wait for her to say no, to tell me it's out of the question, that I am too much of a liability. But Calypso seems to know how trapped I felt at the palace. She seems to understand what it means to live with the same freedom as they do in the sea. Would that be enough for her to say yes? To let me travel the seas with her most trusted mermaids? I continue to hold my breath as I wait for her reply, and it seems I'm not the only one. The cave is silent, save for the rushing waterfall.

"Very well," she says, her voice clipped. "But you will not enter the island itself. It is too much a risk for you to set fin on the island. You can accompany them on the journey, for the sole reason that I refuse to deny you a chance to live as you always should have. You've had too many years to live in the sea stolen away from you as it is." Heat spreads in my chest as her words hit me. "But you will not go anywhere near the viper vines.

If you are compromised, our kind will face absolute extinction." She pauses, and I wait, knowing there's more. "There is a fine line between protection and captivity."

"Understood." I smile at my victory, but feel the dread closing in with every second that passes. Because although I successfully compromised with Calypso, I also just volunteered myself to travel to an island of the dead.

NINE

After our meeting, my mind reels with talk of tides and residual powers. The mermaids explained to me why, exactly, we needed to wait until high tide at night right before the big upcoming hail storm. Marina said the Island of Bones was specifically chosen as the resting place of beings like the witch who cursed them due to its unique features.

"Viper vines act as a barricade surrounding the land, preventing anyone from visiting to disturb the unstable dead." Her tone is enough to tell me that she respects the lay of the land, but not enough to forgo the mission. "Beings like the witch can still hold unstable magic that has settled into the body upon death. It lingers there, with no place to go, and can be very unpredictable if disturbed."

"Like an old stick of dynamite," Brea comments.

"You know what dynamite is?" The words fly out of my mouth of their own volition. I don't even have a chance to apologize before Brea explains.

"Just because we don't dwell on land, doesn't mean we are naive to the world, girl—"

"What Brea is trying to say is that our species is an intelligent and perceptive kind. We know plenty of the human world." Marina's soft-spoken words dull Brea's sharp tongue.

"Also . . . I take a liking to observing the human realm on occasion." As Brea talks, I mark the intricate weaving of her braids. Her smirk tells me she is something of a spy, a mermaid observing humans without detection. Sneaky. Before we can say anything more, Calypso hisses at us. Our attention snaps to the silver-haired mermaid.

"Some have ventured to the Island of Bones seeking the power that lingers there, but not knowing the dangers that accompany it," Calypso continues. "The fate of those who have ventured there wasn't one to be desired. The hail storm will provide enough leverage for Brea and Marina to venture towards the center of the island without getting tangled in the barbed vines." Calypso explains this security system with a lethal tongue.

"The trick will be swimming so close to the surface during a hail storm," Brea explains. "Ice pellets pierce through the water like bullets. It can tear through anything in its wake." Marina nods in agreement.

"We've fastened together armor made of the strongest turtle shell. That combined with mollusk shells will line their dorsal spines to prevent injury from the hail." Calypso's eyes glimmer with wit when she explains the logistics. "But carrying the weight of the armor will create strain when maneuvering around the vines. It will require agility and precision to succeed." She looks to both Brea and Marina, a hard stare telling each of them to be prepared. There is no room for error. But their confidence is something to be admired. Each of them seems more than up for the challenge, already preparing for the journey ahead.

Which is why this morning is a flurry of activity with talk of the curse being broken soon. It's like a hive with its worker bees darting through tunnels and Calypso as their queen. It seems some of the merfolk have begun to dream and hope for the first time in a very, very long time.

As I pass by others, they look to me with wonder and awe and I can't help but want to reject it, not having done anything to deserve it yet. But I understand that feeling of longing for something. Feeling like a final piece of the puzzle is going to be put into place. Like everything is coming together as it should, after years and years of feeling off-kilter. There is talk of bravery over morning meals when discussing Brea and Marina's upcoming journey. I try to keep to myself, avoiding unwanted attention, and decide to venture out of the caves early.

I swim back to the mangroves, yearning for the slowness of the water there and to glide through the roots and contemplate what lies ahead. Alone.

As I pass the bright colors and textures of the sea, I wonder if my future will hold this unique and breathtaking environment, or if it will include ballgowns and court politics . . . and a heavy crown. Calypso only alluded to having to choose which life I want to live. One of land or one of sea. I couldn't very well just show up at the palace one month and disappear the next. I can't be half a queen and half a creature of the sea. Especially when people might not take too kindly to the news that mermaids are, in fact, very much real—and very much alive. Who's to say that the hostility that was felt all of those years ago isn't still present at the mere mention of our kind. That must be why my parents kept this from me all these years. Or they know that breaking this curse could affect their daughter in a less-than-desirable way. Either way, I refuse to believe that it's because they don't want more mermaids swimming the seas.

I think of the story the Lady of the Lake told me, shuddering at what they did to her. Beings of land and sea were so busy hating one another, that they never even noticed how similar they can be. Their tendencies mirror one another.

I should visit her again. See if I can get some more information out of her about the curse and about Calypso. She might be more willing to share with me if the stakes don't affect her directly. Also, she might enjoy the company of someone who doesn't see her as defiled. Someone who understands her pain of being trapped.

I break the surface and search the horizon for anyone on the water but see no one. The coast is clear.

The sun is high today. Clouds streak the sky like ripples of white paint. The airy blue bleeds through the sheer ribbons creating a sorbet of colors. I drift on my back as I watch the gulls soar above the mangroves, catching the air beneath their wings and searching for an easy catch from below. My tail guides me through the maze of the groves as I let the sun warm my skin, and my face. The gills at my sides idle as I breathe in the salty sea air.

I hear the sails before I spot them coming around the bend and quickly dive below the surface, hiding in the tangle of roots that branch out from the sea floor like spider legs doming through the water. The belly of the boat glides through the trail of mangroves from below and as it nears, I see that familiar sun-bleached mane through the rippled surface of the water.

Ezera

My heart begins to thunder. What is he doing out here at this hour? Surely he should be prepping for a day of fishing with his father.

I slink back into the thick of the foliage as he passes through the winding water trail between the trees. The shadows of the round waxy leaves darken the water where I wait, blocking the sunrays from reflecting off of my blue-green scales. I dare to peek above the water, just enough to see him more clearly. His white shirt ripples across his broad chest in the morning breeze, as he pushes his wild cornsilk-colored hair away from his face. He lowers the sails, slowing his boat down in the lush forest.

To maneuver such a thing through here has got to be no small task, with all of the unexpected angles of the trail and the rising and falling water levels. Roots and branches jut out at random, making for a maze of a journey. I can barely maneuver my own tail in this part of the sea, let alone an entire boat.

As the boat lazily passes me by, I notice the looping script along the side. Calligraphy in a deep blue color.

Juliette

The name of his boat. A woman's name. For reasons I can't identify, my heart constricts, wondering who the woman might be. As he nears a shoal in the water when the trail narrows, he takes a few long strides to the back of his boat and begins tugging the rope, adjusting the sail. As he quickly handles the rigging, I watch as the frayed rope gets caught in the metal pulley, snagging.

With the slightest breeze, the rope snaps and he grabs on quickly, but the sail pulls the rope through his hands and I watch as the blood trails down his arm, dripping from his elbow into the water. He lunges back to hold the sail in place as he tries desperately to grab the other frayed end of the rope. I duck down below, ready to manipulate the water around him and guide him through the narrows and into the open ocean, but when I slither through the roots towards the belly of the boat, I see them coming. Three lethal striped sharks glide through the roots of the mangroves, aiming right toward the swirling cloud of blood that Ezera has left in the water. I know the exact moment he spots their dorsal fins slicing through the water because a colorful curse breaks from his lips. If the sailboat had higher sides on it to protect him, the threat might not be as dire, but as it is, a motivated shark could easily breach the deck.

He is stuck and surrounded by hungry predators.

Without a second to waste, I recall my lessons with Calypso, learning to manipulate water and hold it to my will. I gather my power from within just as she taught me, pulling it all to my center and focusing it into a concentrated ball of energy. I take a steadying, watery breath through my sides and direct my gathered power to the water surrounding us, letting it spread.

Wrapping my power around each and every drop claiming it as mine for the taking. Calypso has only had enough time to teach me to control small amounts, but I can feel the weight of the swell as I prepare to transfer the tons and tons of water surrounding the boat. Bending it to my will, it's nearly crippling. Quickly I move the water in a calculated direction to push the boat through. My concentration is so acute it feels like pushing syrup through a tiny tube. But when my efforts turn to action, I nearly lose my control with excitement.

A wave pushes Ezera through the narrow gap among the mangrove roots, unexpectedly knocking him off balance. He catches himself on the ledge and his eyes go wide with surprise as the wave carries the sailboat through the mangroves and into the open ocean. But with his main sail compromised, it will be a slow trip home, and the sharks are still trailing him, his blood causing a frenzy amongst the three sea beasts. Their teeth are like razors as they turn the corner and follow the rush of water created by my wave.

I trail them through the water, becoming the predator and making them my prey. Heat rises through my veins as I pump my tail, gaining speed. Claws out, I make a wide turn below them and emerge ahead of the boat, floating in the middle of the open ocean. Only deep blue surrounds me on all sides. Nowhere to hide. I bare my teeth and they stall once they see me. One shark peels away and scurries below, leaving me to face the two black and gray-striped beasts. We are so deep beneath the surface now, that I pray Ezera has assumed the sharks have left. Leaving him to return home in peace, with the remaining sail intact.

My body sings to life with a feral calm as I face the two sharks ahead. Refusing to let my human senses push the fear through to the front of my mind, I grab onto that predatory instinct and don't let it go as I bare my teeth to them again. Claws ready to strike. The dorsal spikes that line my back prick to attention with anticipation of an attack, and I'm ready. These two *fish* don't stand a chance.

Before they gain any ground on me, I charge ahead into the deep blue, heading straight for them. My tail pulses at full speed as I advance on them. They watch me approach and bare their layers and layers of pointed teeth, not budging an inch. Their black soulless eyes focus on me. At the last second before either of us can strike, I turn my body and knock the smaller of the two beasts out with my tail. Blood puffs from the side of its head as it drifts down to the depths of the open ocean. Mother Nature drags down her dead.

I don't allow myself the victory because the last shark is triple my size and a tail whip might be just enough to agitate it. I turn my body to face my opponent but before I can get my bearings, the massive shark catches the back of my arm in its large mouth, leaving my skin in ribbons as I pull away before its jaw can clamp down, crushing my bones. My blood is now flowing freely in the water, clouding around us in a purple haze. Pain floods my senses as I grit my teeth, trying to shake off the burning and focus despite the blood loss and pain slowing me down. I swipe with my good arm at its pitted inky eye, clawing the side of its face, hopefully obscuring its vision. But as soon as I do, I am knocked back by its massive tail, my head spinning and disoriented. Immediately, I lose all sense of direction as I spin through the water, my hair tangling around my face. I squeeze my eyes shut for a moment and shake my head, trying to get my senses back before the next attack.

As I right myself in the water, leaving space between me and the striped beast, I sense movement from below and my stomach sinks, fearing the other shark will come back to finish me off. But instead, an amethyst tail spins at lightning speed as Marina barrels through the water, right into the shark. Before the creature knows what hit it, Marina digs her claws into the shark's head, sinking her nails deep into the leathery skin like anchors, and bites between its eyes. When she pulls away, blood, tissue, and brain matter cloud the space between her and the shark. The bite was small yet deep enough to do damage.

Marina turns her head to the side and spits out chunks of shark into the deep blue. Pushing the body away, she dislodges her claws from its twitching corpse. My mouth agape, I watch as the beast floats lifelessly in a cloud of its own blood. I draw my attention back up to Marina and see her picking shark bits from her nail. The look in her honeyed eyes is one that says *What the hell were you thinking?*

Abashed shame heats my face when I realize what it must have looked like when she came across this scene. Before I can react, she motions for me to follow her, presumably to the surface, to talk. I follow her blue-tipped fins through the water after searching for the belly of the *Juliette* gliding on the surface, unaware of the massacre that took place below. We swim towards a small cropping of islands just south of Aqualasia, where huge rock formations jut out of the sea, forming a blue grotto that glows from within.

My muscles ache as we finally arrive under the dome of black rock and slow our pace. Various tails bob on the surface with sheer fins of green and pink. From below they sway through the water like curtains. I follow Marina's lead as she breaks the surface in the center of the dome and stares me down with eyes of fire.

"What the *hell* were you doing taking on a tiger shark?" Miraculously, her white teeth gleam in the glow of the grotto, no shark remnants to be found.

"You did what?" Brea appears from the small cluster of mermaids lounging on a few nearby rocks.

"Actually, it was three . . . tiger sharks." My voice is a mere whisper among the chatter.

Marina's eyes widen to saucers, brows raised as if to ask if I have some self-destructive tendencies.

"Do you have some kind of death wish?" Brea yelps. I try not to laugh at her implication but one look at Marina's stone face and my smile fades to a wince.

"I didn't set out to battle with a few sharks on purpose. It just sort of . . . happened," I explain, not wanting to include why, exactly, I was in the situation in the first place. I can't tell them that I was lured by a human, and then felt compelled to save him from a gruesome death.

"It just sort of happened. Hmph," Marina muses. "Well, whatever the reason, I hope it was worth it. I nearly ruined my freshly sharpened claws." At this, her face softens into feigned amusement, and I know that she will drop any further investigation.

Brea grabs Marina's hand and checks her daggered nails. "Mmm. You're lucky it was Marina who found you. I would have let you become shark chum to save my manicured claws." They giggle to themselves, unashamed of their vanity.

"Thank you for coming to my rescue." I will my face into neutrality as I say the words aloud, hating that I needed aid in the first place.

Marina brushes me off, not missing a cue. "Please, we protect our own." The compassion in her words tugs at something deep within my chest. "Plus, I've been looking for a fight ever since Kai ruined my kill last week."

"Marina, Kai did not ruin your kill, you wretched fish. He was being chivalrous. Most sea maidens like when a male can provide an entire squid for them. Take on the dirty work," Brea scolds in bold amusement, splashing Marina with the back of her hand.

"Then he obviously doesn't know me very well if he doesn't understand that takes all of the fun out of it." Marina winks at me as she begins to sharpen her claws on the barnacled edge of a rock. I chuckle at the brazenness of these creatures. So very different from the people on the island, and yet, not. There's something about mermaids that aren't afraid to stand in their truth. They're unashamed and bold. What you see is what you get. They wear no masks in the sea.

I fall into a pattern of easy listening amongst the group, finding it easier than I ever did in the castle. Back home, it felt like every conversation was laced with lies. Small talk amongst courtiers often came with a hidden motive. Always feigning interest in the hopes of getting something in return. Most of the girls my age were only interested in the latest fashion trends or which males were attending the upcoming Full Celestia celebration. Never having an original thought of anything substantial to discuss. I never felt a true connection to any of them. That's why I never had many friends at the palace besides Angelina. No one ever cared enough to want a true friendship, only a bridge to get where they want to be.

Here, in the sea, these creatures have grit. Despite their animalistic tendencies, they are intelligent beings. And they are loyal, looking out for each other without question. They allowed me into their circle without hesitation. Unlike humans who would rather play games with words and politics, these creatures would battle out their issues honorably if there were a quarrel amongst the pod. There are no hidden motives, no veil draped over words.

Talk of procreation swirls amongst the mermaids. Who has an interest and who would make a good mate. These maidens compare males like they would be a good catch of the day. Comparing their size and appearance to one another. It is clear from the conversation that Kai has every intention of mating with Marina. Although she seems to be a bit less inclined than he. It sounds like most mermaids are thrilled for the mere option to reproduce, having it stripped away from them for years. It makes me wonder how old these sea creatures are if none have been born in years, and I suddenly feel very, very immature and naive to the world in comparison.

I must admit, the idea of a merbaby amongst the pod brings me joy. The thought of new life being introduced to a group that hasn't seen the brightness of change in too long makes me giddy. These fierce and beautiful creatures deserve that. They deserve the joys and challenges that come with raising their young. Before I even realize it, I notice that I have pictured myself being here, amongst the pod, when the time comes for them to raise their young. And I see now that I want nothing more than to see a fresh new life grow into a beautiful, fully grown mermaid. Or male. To watch the light in their eyes sparkle when they see the magnificent wonders of the sea for the very first time. To not be tainted by humans and their greed.

Remembering Marina's instinct to protect me today tells me that she has what it takes to be a great mother in the wild. Which leaves me wondering . . . would I? Do I see my young being raised in the castle or in the sea?

TEN

When Calypso returns from a visit with a neighboring pod, I make it my sole purpose to speak with her about the rules around transforming from land to sea and about the truth behind breaking this curse. I can't stand the uncertainty of my future any longer. I can feel my mind beginning to fray at the edges, trying to unravel everything without all of the pieces. I know in my heart that I belong to the sea, that she is a part of me as much as my arms are, but I can't forget that I have a responsibility to the people of Aqualasia. People whom I love dearly and have a duty to protect and lead, even if it comes with an unwanted betrothal.

As dreamy as this transformation has been, as breathtaking as the sea can be, I need to know what lies ahead. To give up the throne and let down my parents—my kingdom—is a huge decision to make. And I don't intend to make it lightly. The clock is ticking until the next Full Celestia, and I am no closer to knowing what lies ahead. My parents undoubtedly know exactly where I am, but the rest of the island? How have the king and queen explained my absence thus far? A vengeful voice reminds me that it is a problem they created when they hid the truth from me. But how will I explain my absence if I decide to stay here longer than a month and return much later?

It's all too messy. Too uncertain. The people of Aqualasia need a leader they can trust and depend on. Not one who vanishes into thin air. Despite how I feel about my parents, the people of Aqualasia deserve better.

So I need to decide. I need to have a plan. But before I can make such a monumental commitment, I need information. I need all of the cards on the table to assess what is to come. Which requires a chat with Calypso. As soon as I can get a minute to speak with her. It seems I am not the only one who was anxious for her return. Mermaids and males have been swarming her bejeweled alcove since her return, badgering her with questions of the curse breaking, reporting on movements from other pods, and hoping to stay in her good graces with goods and prizes. I've only known my ancestor for a few weeks and even I know it would be a death sentence to ever get on her bad side.

So I wait, as patiently as I can. But by afternoon, when my body begins to crave the waves of the open sea, I toss my patience aside and swim through the cave tunnels, needing to stretch my fins. The need to glide through the ocean is almost like a physical ache in my bones. Like an itch demanding a scratch. I know now why our kind prefers to stay here in the sea and not on land, amongst other reasons, I'm sure. The need for this life grows stronger and stronger within me every day. The peace of the water, it's everywhere. It's in the muffled sounds that echo deep below the surface, in the easy ebb and flow of the waves. It's in the crisp beauty of the wildlife. It's even in the absence of the hurry and bustle of the court life I've grown so familiar with. This life down here is addicting.

It fulfills me so much more, by physically giving so much less.

Wild and free. Calypso's words ring true in my ears. It's the way life was intended to be.

I swim along the bottom of the ocean, careful to steer clear of the crevasses and black holes that scatter the sea floor. I watch the sea life below as my figure casts a dark shadow over the clusters of coral I pass. But some creatures dart into hiding as I approach, wary of what I am, a predatory animal at the top of the food chain. But I've already eaten and have no plans to attack these creatures right now.

Hunting has become second nature to me these past weeks, mostly surviving from shellfish and small catches. Never in my wildest dreams would I think that I would not only be preparing food for myself but catching it too.

The thought pulls Ezera to the forefront of my mind—of the first time I saw him all those years later, in the kitchens of the castle. Wait—no. That's not actually true. I ran into him, quite literally, that day at the docks, when I was hurrying home for the party. There's something about him that tugs at my curiosity. Maybe it's a coincidence that our paths have crossed multiple times now, on land and sea. But . . . maybe it's not. Maybe the Mother keeps entwining our paths for a reason.

I try not to laugh at my own foolish thoughts as I come across a massive shipwreck, decaying into the ocean floor. Its masts shoot up from the sand at a sharp angle. Dark holes in the belly telling me it's been down here for quite some time. This territory is new to me, never having ventured this far north before. The setting sun is causing the scene below to seem more ominous than it should be. It's just an old ship withering away from the elements, but the algae and sea moss drooping from its limbs is giving me haunting vibes. I shake it off as I near the massive vessel cautiously, curiosity getting the best of me. I've never been one to deny my curious tendencies. Mermaids are not the only vicious things that live below the surface, and I'm no fool to forget that dangerous creatures lurk in the dark, but I can't seem to just swim on by without a look. Thoughts of adventure and discovery swirl in my head as I hover above the deck.

If the ship's decay wasn't enough to tell me it's resided here for years, the make of the helm does—or what's left of it. The handles of the wheel curve in a way that you don't see much of anymore. Maybe in old history books from when Aqualasia Islands was a trading post for pirates and sailors before the islands had a structured society.

When mermaids still coexisted with humans.

In the histories, pirates would claim multiple sightings or encounters with sea maidens, blaming them for shipwrecks or mishaps with a trade. Obviously, children of the island have been taught that these stories were fabricated by deceitful pirates and lowly sailors to get them out of a jam or draw the attention of people seeking a good story of adventure. Since mermaids were believed to be extinct well before trade routes were established, the stories were never believed.

The names of old famous ships have always fascinated me. It was my favorite part of lectures, learning about the celebrated ships that crossed the seas to discover new lands. I marveled at how each one got its name and its history, so I swim around the sides of this beast searching for any curved lettering marking its wooden panes. But the algae and sea moss have grown thick over the years, creating a layer of green that moves with the water when I pass by. I hover over the side of the ship that angles up towards the surface and scrape my claws along weathered wood, removing as much algae as I can, but the ship is large and the name could be anywhere along the wooden panes if it were a ship for pirates.

I'm scrubbing along the bow when a gaping hole disrupts my pattern. I peer inside the darkness, my vision straining to see the shadowed structures, when I see a dark figure of movement darting through the interior.

Dark scales reflect the small amount of light that has filtered down from above. I jump back, pushing off of the boat with my hands, shaking with adrenaline. My instincts kick in as I wait for an attack. I'm thinking a conger eel, barracuda, or reaper shark. Something deadly and vicious.

When I sense more movement in the belly of the ship, I anticipate a quick attack, but flounder when dark wavy hair emerges through the opening followed by a purple tail.

Marina.

What is she doing way out here?

My arms drop to my sides when she approaches, the rush of adrenaline leaving my body in waves. She smirks, knowing that her presence nearly scared the living daylight out of me. Knowing I was waiting for a fight to the death with whatever emerged from that ship. I cross my arms not wanting to admit she's right but follow her inside when she invites me with a wave.

The hole in the top of the ship allows a view of the open ocean above. All of the ship's finery has been lost to time, but the real beauty inside this vessel swirls at its center. Where the bottom of the ship once was, a bed of coral glows, thriving in the cracks and illuminating a small section of the ship. Tiny glowing jellies pulse through the water like fireflies, reminding me of my precious willow at night.

My eyes dart to her when an echo of chimes rings through the water. Marina has begun to sing—no, not just sing. That is too small a word for what she's doing. Her voice is like a siren, pulling anyone in her path toward her. Unlike typical voices spoken underwater, this one doesn't sound muffled or muted. It sounds perfect. Crystal clear and strong. The sound is so surreal I almost wonder if the tune comes from her or my own imagination.

The water around us begins to shake with vibration as water sprites appear in the dark cavern. Their tiny golden lights glow as they zoom around the belly of the ship. Their tiny delicate fins flutter through the water like silk. They're mesmerizing—like small flames come to life.

Figurines of all kinds scatter every surface of the ship. Barely visible in the water against the dark backdrop of worn wood. There are tiny mermaids of glass with various tail shapes, fins, and claws. All so unique in their own way. I even find objects from land in her collection. One tall structure swirls in a funnel like a tornado paused in time. I reach out to touch one of the clear figurines and am shocked to find it cold. Like ice. Never melting or changing shape. It's *incredible.*

Marina changes the pitch in her song bringing her voice higher and higher while she moves her hands in a dance, swirling and manipulating the water in front of her. The water begins to take shape before my very eyes and suddenly stops. Marina's song is low now, causing the figurine to stop moving, no longer flowing like the currents around it. A statue of ice.

Before I can begin to wonder how it doesn't change over time, the water sprites come together around Marina's work and simply touch it causing it to glow for only a moment before it begins to drift down to the ocean's floor.

Before it hits the bottom, Marina grabs it with her hand and places it on a shelf nearby that's covered with others.

Marina is an artist and this is her studio—a hidden wonder and her very own sanctuary. I can tell by her movements and the hesitation on her face that this place means a great deal to her. My insides warm at her wide-eyed anticipation as she shares a part of herself with me. She trusts me with her art. I am in complete awe of her creations as I continue to follow the path of frozen figures along the way, admiring the detail of each statue. Each piece is like a moment from Marina's life.

Before I'm ready, she pulls me up through a break in the deck towards the surface but we make a sharp turn and head east, towards the Blue Grotto.

We break the surface and the stars come to life in the early night sky, crisp and clear without the blur of the water obscuring them from view. They mark the sky by the thousands, speckling the violet night. The moon is a perfect crescent hanging above us, causing a strip of the sea to glow with reflection.

"They are incredible, Marina," I say, resting on a smooth rock hidden just below the surface.

"Thanks." She blushes, and I almost can't believe that this is the same female who dismembered a beastly shark three times her size. "I visit the ship as often as I can. I used to go there to get away and explore, but a few years ago I discovered what my song can do. And with the help of the water sprites, it can last forever. It centers me." Her words strike true as her face fills with passion.

"You've found your gift, and it's beautiful." The cool night breeze blows through the grotto, dragging my damp curls across my freckles.

"You know . . . that ship was named after my mother," her eyes drop from mine as if she doesn't want me to recognize her sorrow. "The captain fell in love with her before the Sea Wars. And when she became pregnant, he had her name sketched across the only other thing that held his heart. Once she had me, she told him that she lost the baby and vowed to spend the rest of her life on land with my father." The words sting as I realize what she's telling me. Her father never even knew she was born, never even met his child, and her mother abandoned her.

How could any mother do such a despicable thing? My stomach roils at the thought.

"The ship sank during one of the bloody battles, speared with harpoons wielded by the merfolk. It had so many holes in it by the time it hit the bottom of the ocean, it looked like a sea sponge." She looks down at the water. "At least that's what the stories say." She sighs a breath. "I kept waiting for her to return to the sea after the captain sunk with his ship, but she never did." For a species that believes in protecting its own, Marina's mother seems to be the outlier.

"That's awful," I say more to myself than to her.

She leans her head back, face turned up to the stars as she says, "Yeah, well. You know what they say about our kind. Merciless, soulless creatures." She harrumphs a laugh, brushing off the insult.

"Why do you choose to spend your time in that ship, when it carries so much hurt?" I probe, my words coming out too blunt.

She looks me dead in the eye. "That's too much to unpack on such a beautiful night," and leans back on her elbows, swaying her amethyst tail in the water.

"Have you ever shifted? Spent any time on dry land?" I ask, hoping to lighten the mood.

"Just once to search for my mother. Calypso told me not to go, but I didn't listen, hoping she might have been wrong about my mother. I didn't have any luck finding her, but I did quite enjoy the music and delicacies of the people. But it was dangerous being what I am and walking on land. I was scared I would be discovered . . . and I craved the sea. Needed to wet my skin with sea salt once more."

"What's it like? To shift. Having only experienced it once, I'm not sure exactly what was real and what was in my head. That night is kind of a blur to me now."

She looks at me quizzically, like she can't quite figure me out but continues, "I'm guessing everything you remember is truth. If you remember excruciating pain, your memory serves correctly. Some say it compares to childbirth. Some say it feels like death by suffocation while your limbs are burned off. Which is why most of our kind prefer not to do it at all. There's nothing we need on land anyways. We belong in the sea. It's our home."

Her words hit me right in the chest and my eyes well, swelling with emotion. *It's our home.*

Where is my home? Clearly going through a transformation that compares to childbirth is not something I want to experience once a month for the rest of my life. Nor is it feasible. I can't have a home on land and at sea. Worry settles in my gut.

Even if all goes well and I do manage to break this curse, lifting a veil of infertility from an entire species, where do I go from there? Where will my life lead?

Land or sea.

I look out at the vast horizon, the line barely visible in the night. The ocean is now just a hair darker than the sky, and I know deep down that I could never leave it. Having a taste of this life, in this body. There is no other life for me. But to never see my family again or walk the halls of the palace . . . to never taste another almond crescent again. I just can't see that either.

The only constant I can count on no matter my fate is my beloved willow. She will always be in my life, whatever I choose.

"So, is Calypso always so—"

"Yes," Marina answers my question before it even leaves my lips completely. I laugh at her quick response. "She's always been a force of nature. Rough around the edges, and fierce enough to scare the scales off of you, but her loyalty has never faltered. She takes care of her pod as if we were her offspring, made from her own skin and blood."

I nod in understanding, feeling a small bit of tightness in my chest release.

Marina must register the uneasy look that lingers on my face, because she asks, "Are you sure you want to come with us to the Island of Bones?" I instantly correct my expression, but she continues, "Brea and I really don't mind if you stay behind. It's a dangerous trip and no one would think any less of you for staying with the pod. You are already doing so much for us by agreeing to risk your life to break this curse for us."

Her use of the term "risk your life" is quite telling. My stomach folds in on itself at the comment. So there is a risk involved in breaking this curse. A risk that could end my life if gone awry. I want to ask her what she means by that but her bright eyes swirl with so many emotions, I can't decipher one from another. Pain, gratitude, hope, and sorrow all bundled into one.

So instead I say, "No. I want to go. Really. It doesn't feel right to sit back and wait." I square my shoulders, feeling the softness of my dried curls brush my dorsal spike. "If this is my destiny, then I want to own it. I'm not afraid to get my hands dirty."

Her eyes narrow to slits as a smirk tugs at her mouth. "I knew I liked you, Princess."

I smile in response. But what I don't mention is that I know what it does to a person when the right to bear children is taken away. Aside from my aunt, my mother also struggled to have a baby for years. I was essentially a miracle for the King and Queen of Aqualasia Islands. My mother wanted a castle full of children, running down the many halls, but was only blessed with one. Despite her gratitude for birthing one healthy baby, I see how it haunts her to not have been able to gift my father with more. If I can change that for an entire species, that has to count for something.

"Has Calypso told you how exactly I am to break this curse? Once you procure the witch's ring, what am I to do with it?" The question flows out of my mouth with such urgency that I can't even feign any sort of neutrality. I need to know. Brave or not, my life is on the line here with or without Calypso.

"I only know what Calypso has told me, plus the legends that have been whispered through pods all across the seas for years."

We both dip further into the water, feeling the itch on our skin settle from the cool dry breeze of the night. I can feel my pores open up and drink in the water as I submerge up to my neck. Marina does the same, feeling the same need.

"But hearsay can often be unreliable. Muddled after years of reiteration. Some say the sacrifice to break the curse is your tail, which would ultimately be a death sentence. Others have said that to break the curse, you must burn the Dark Witch's bones to dust. Some say there is no breaking the curse." Her webbed hands glide through the water, creating small rippling waves as she speaks. "I believe it's not the breaking of the curse, but the reversal of it. I only take my information from Calypso, who had only the best and the brightest decode the riddle that the Dark Witch left our kind with on that fateful night." Her eyes stare at me with a palpable intensity.

"You must wear the ruby ring upon your right ring finger while reciting an ancient incantation." The intensity settles as she continues. "When the curse was first cast, merpeople were frantic for a solution. But once the prophecy was revealed and we knew there was nothing we could do until you came along, we stopped searching, knowing it could be years until you were born. Years where research could be forgotten or skewed. They are still learning the details but that is all I know."

I only nod in response, trying desperately to ignore the bumps crawling up my flesh at her words. I resist the urge to ask her if she is serious, but I know she is. She leans her head back, dipping her hair into the water.

"Witch riddles are such fickle things to decrypt."

Eleven

T hunder rolls across the earth as the storm comes in. Tonight we head to the Island of Bones to procure the ring of the Dark Witch, a vital part of breaking this curse. The gloomy day dragged on for ages as my nerves tripled with every minute that crept by. I passed the time as best I could by helping out around the pod.

Apparently, the quake that hit the cave a few months ago destroyed a section that the merfolk used as a spiritual temple, where one could go to connect with the Mother and recharge their energies. I spent the day helping remove debris and carving out a new structure. I got a lot of practice manipulating water as we moved the fallen rocks from the statue of the water goddess at the center of their sanctuary, her stone hair forever floating around her pointed crown. Luckily the damage to her was minimal, and she is still very much a symbol of everything the merfolk hold dear. The stone pillars that were carved from the rock below the caves reminded me of Marina's art in the ship with their intricate decorative patterns. What a beautiful place the temple must have been before it was ruined by the quake.

I met Kai today while working to clear the rock that crumbled in the entrance. He and a few others have been tasked with rebuilding the temple. From what I gathered, this lot of both male and female seems to be the brawn of the pod, with their rippling muscles and unnatural strength. Each one of them carries three times the amount of rock I ever could. But it was as good of a task as any to pass the time today while anticipating the journey ahead. Kai is strikingly handsome with his chiseled silhouette and his kind hazel eyes. The obvious kind of handsome that can be noticed from afar. That might have you making assumptions of a person before meeting them. Part of me wonders if Marina knows what waits right in front of her. They would make beautiful merbabies, once the curse is broken if that's something they both desire.

While hauling debris from the entryway, I noticed he had a few aquamarine gems along the tip of his ear, marking him with badges of honor. Being deep below the sea I can't properly ask him about them, which is all for the better. If you don't ask questions of others, you won't get any in return.

Now I swim alongside Marina and Brea as we venture towards the Island of Bones. Kai gave me a large hooked harpoon for safety, and I swim with it strapped to my back. It is beautifully adorned with mother-of-pearl and gold chains on its shaft. The spear is made of solid steel. He explained that every warrior names his or her most trusted weapon, honoring it as if it is a part of their person. So I named my beautiful weapon after the legendary goddess of fertility, Atargatis, who was said to have protected her people for millennia, residing in a pool of deep blue. Both Kai and Okiro approved, knowing the story of the goddess well.

He and Okiro were kind enough to teach me how to wield the weapon while Calypso was away. The muscles in my arm still ache from the practice of hauling that thing through the water as I tried to hit the various targets they set up for me in the cove. Okiro said it will take time for my muscles to develop enough to really get a handle on it and that it will eventually become second nature to use. But at least for the time being, I can use it easily enough without worrying that I will stab myself instead of my opponent. But I shouldn't need it today. I have been given strict orders not to enter the island and to stay out of trouble.

We've been traveling for hours now, only stopping once for rest and to hunt. Even with our heightened speed, this journey is far. But we planned accordingly, so we'll arrive just before the storm when the water will swell over the island enough for Marina and Brea to access the graves at its heart.

The sky has begun to mist, blurring the ocean's surface. But the thunder is so loud that I can feel it in my chest, booming with anger. The sound penetrates the water. Brea and Marina have already donned their armor in anticipation for when the hail begins to strike. Luckily, I will be far enough below the surface to avoid the icy pelts. My specific orders to not go into the Island of Bones still don't sit well with me, but I have been trying to make peace with it, reminding myself that my task will come soon enough. And if Calypso's discoveries are correct, it will be monumental enough to make up for not assisting in this one. Breaking this curse will be the most significant thing I've ever done in my eighteen years on this earth. But I hope it isn't the last. My father has always told me I am destined for great things. I've always assumed he was referring to bringing Aqualasia to greatness, but what if . . . what if he meant something else entirely?

I push the pure nonsense of that thought away.

The dark abyss gives way to land as we approach the island. Strange plant life creep up the rising ocean floor as we near, and I strain my vision through the dark night to see it more clearly. Wild, thick plum-colored fronds sway underwater, surrounded by a patchy carpet of neon moss. I look to the two mermaids with wide eyes and they both nod, marking our arrival. We break the surface before we get any closer to the shore and the sharp clinking sound of rain hitting the sea pierces my ears. A stark contrast to the muffled drops from below. The rain has picked up dramatically along with the wind. Massive waves from the ocean swell and dip, reminding us that it is as alive as we are. We rise and fall with the waves as the ocean's surface surges and dips. The white waves up ahead crash into the rocky edges of the island as an avalanche of water spills over its sides, causing small waterfalls to drain back into the sea. The sight is calm and chaotic all at once.

"Like nothing you've ever seen before, huh Princess?" Brea's beads twinkle in her hair like ornaments as she bobs beside me, water pelting our backs harder now. She's right. With Pearle Castle residing right on the water, I've seen my fair share of sea storms, but never like this. Watching them from a stone tower window is nothing compared to being in the belly of the beast. It's incredibly humbling.

"The Mother is angry today," Marina counters, eyes wide as she sizes up the island.

"A great reminder that we are never really in control," I realize aloud. "Watching it from a safe distance is nothing like being in it." Brea tilts her head back and barks a laugh, rainwater sprinkling her tanned face. She turns and eyes Marina as they both nod to each other, not wanting to waste any more time.

"You ready?" Brea eyes Marina as we rise and fall with the waves. Three small creatures just along for the ride.

"I was born ready." Marina's lips peel back, revealing the smile of a huntress.

The vicious waves carry us up, down, and sideways with their movements. The feeling is disorienting coupled with the pouring rain, and I can barely keep my bearings. As we swim farther inland, past the rocky edges, I see them, covering almost the entire shoreline. *Viper vines.* Thick, silver rope-like vines twist and tangle through itself, scattered around the island's edges, like thousands of slithering snakes. My body tingles with unease at the sight of them. The hooked thorns glisten in the night as they cut through waves.

Deadly.

Everything about this plant looks deadly. A trap set by the Mother herself. I look at Brea and Marina with worry when I think of how they are going to maneuver around this protective barrier. Not an ounce of fear shows on their flawless faces. Pure tenacity shines through their eyes like the brave warriors they are.

Not a word is spoken as we approach the island, waiting for the tide to rise. I can almost feel the chaos of wild magic swirling around the island, leaving an uneasy feeling in my gut. I look to the others to see if they feel it too, but their gazes are fixed, eyes on the prize.

The roaring of the thunder and the crashing of the waves with rain pouring into the sea are the only sounds amongst us. When the tide rises to the desired level, the females must time their entrance right to when a large wave can pull them over the viper vines without a scratch. They must follow the flow of the wave to avoid entanglement. Just as I think the armor might not have been needed, the hail begins. Pain sears my back with each blow and we duck below the surface completely. I watch as the ice pellets pierce through the water like arrows, a trail of white behind them. The mermaids adjust their positions beneath the surface so the armor protects their backs as I dive down deeper, safe from impalement. Marina looks back at me before giving Brea a nod and I watch as their tails propel them forward into the Island of Bones.

Twelve

My heart is in my throat as I watch the two females I now hold dear anticipate the perfect wave to ride onto the island on. I am deep enough below the surface that the waves aren't affecting my movements, but up ahead, Brea and Marina are rising and dipping with each wave that banks the shore. Hail pelts down on them. My blood rushes in my ears with nervous energy as I idle in the deep blue and wait, my tail swishing on occasion to keep me still, my arms swaying through the water, just waiting for them to make their move.

The song of a whale echoes behind me somewhere in the distance. The arc and bellow of her voice soothe my frayed nerves. Somehow, I know the whale is female just by the sound of her, the feel of her. Just like I knew the manatee was a female. When I encountered the sea cow, I thought I assumed her sex by the calf she was calling for, but maybe . . . maybe in this body, I can sense the very being of marine life. Not just their presence in the water and the space they take, but their very essence. Somehow, in this form, I have more of a connection to others that dwell below the surface. I hadn't noticed it until now. Until this whale's alluring melody hit me right in the chest, and an overwhelming feeling rises up my throat. But I am too focused on Brea and Marina to turn around, to see the mammoth creature creating the song. It would probably shock me into unconsciousness to encounter such a creature anyway. Better if I stay alert and focused on the mission.

Thunder cracks above the surface as a huge swell carries over my head towards the island and I know this is it. This is the wave that will take them over the vines and into the heart of the island. I swim closer in, closer to the surface to see, allowing the hail to hit my back in tiny blows, knowing bruises will soon form, but not caring. I hold my breath, squeezing my webbed hands into fists as I watch them ride the wave closer and closer to the thorny edges. Arms stretched out in front of them, tails whizzing behind, I cringe as they arc over the silver ropes so quick I almost miss it. I fear for their delicate fins that flutter behind them, but they graze right above the vines like butter, nearly missing a snag. My shoulders settle once they disappear over the vines.

As the wave settles back into the ocean, I pray they both have something to anchor them, holding them back from the pull of the wave. I smile to myself when they don't return to the ocean with the settlement of the wave, knowing they made it unscathed. I sink back into the deep, letting the song of the whale lull me while I wait.

Seconds.

Minutes.

Hours go by as I wait and wait for their return. My mind has been busy coming up with unlikely scenarios of what could be happening on that haunted island above. Most prominent that Brea and Marina are trapped up there, injured . . . or worse. I push the thought away, knowing it won't do anyone any good to continue down that never-ending path. The hail has subsided back to a heavy rain and the thunder has decreased to distant rumbles. Every so often, I break the surface and swim as close to the island as I dare, looking for any signs of them, any movement at all. But nothing has changed, aside from the palms whipping in all directions with the wind.

An ice-cold shiver runs down my spine when I catch a glimpse of the vines, through the frothy white waves crashing onto the shore. Relentless. The silver coils, wet from the waves, glistening under the sliver of moonlight, and more than once, I could have sworn the vines were moving. Coiling in on itself like hundreds of snakes protecting the border of this dark, sacred island of the dead. Magic lingers within, like lost souls, lagging behind.

I huff a sigh and sink, my gaze following the curve of the base of the island, growing wider and wider as I descend before the sea floor drops dramatically. The island base is too wide for me to see the ends. Sand and rock litter the roots, slowly turning to dense vegetation. I wonder how far in they had to travel to reach the graves. If there were any more obstacles to defeat.

Movement catches my attention from above, far ahead of me where land meets sea. My mind registers the telltale movements as uniquely mermaid. The body rolls snaking down to the fluttering fins, marking the dark creature as one of our kind. But only one. One set of fins. One tail. One body. Not two.

My heart sinks like an anchor as the realization hits me in full. Someone is still on the island. As the mermaid nears, I barely make out the dark braided hair that belongs to Brea. She swims towards me at lightning speed, one arm outstretched, one tucked close to her middle. Her tail undulates through the dark sea, sending her closer to me with every tail pump. I follow her lead as she turns skyward.

Brea breaches the surface, and I with her.

"Cealene, here." She tosses the ancient treasure into my shaky webbed hand. "Take the ring. I need to go back. It's Marina. She's trapped. When the wave tried to pull us out, she got caught in the snarls of the tree roots." My chest constricts with fear. I look down below the surface at Brea's shredded fins. "I tried to grab her, but the water was too strong, pulling me from her grasp." As she says it, I see the bloodied trails on her arm from where Marina's grip must have dragged. She tries to close my hand around the ring but I pause, calculating the scene laid out before me. She looks bone-tired.

"No. You are in no shape to go back in. Let me." I rest my hand on her cold shoulder, handing the ring back to her, and closing her fingers around it. "You need to rest for the journey back. I can handle this. I promise." I say the words but I don't believe them. I will my face to show a fierce confidence, enough for her to trust me with this, even though I'm not sure I believe it myself. I can see in her face that fatigue is settling in her bones. Fatigue and grappling fear. She isn't thinking clearly. Her eyes are frantic. I don't know what they encountered in there, but it is clear that Marina needs rescue from someone with a level head—and that leaves me.

"But Calypso said—"

"Calypso isn't here right now," I cut her off. "It's just you and me." Even as I say the words, unease roils in my gut. Calypso gave me specific orders not to enter that island. Nothing sounds more terrifying than defying Calypso in any way, except entering that island of death and darkness. I cannot let my fear show. I cannot let Brea get even a whiff of my uncertainty.

"Something tells me that Calypso will forgive us if it means keeping her third from turning to sea foam on that island." I point my clawed finger towards the vined beach ahead.

I watch as the wheels turn in her mind, making sense of my words, and my offer. Giving her an alternative solution. I watch the hesitation cross her face, but ultimately settle as she nods in agreement.

"Yes. Okay." Her breath is shaky as she gulps down the air. The swell of the waves bobbing us up and down in the wild sea. "Wait for a big one. Mark the height of the waves on the rock outcropping at the edges. When a wave comes that clears almost all of the rock, ride it in. As close to the crest as you can. Watch your fins as you go. Don't allow the natural sway of your tail to bring you in. Just ride the wave until you pass the vines." Her fierce eyes bore into mine, and I bury my fear deep down, where even I cannot find it. For Marina.

"From there, veer left and you will spot her. Just as the forest starts."

I nod, too frantic to speak. Too pressed for time. Without a second glance, I turn towards the island and swim.

It takes me only moments to reach my destination, and I watch as the waves heave up and over the rocks, pounding into the sides. White tips like snow inching higher and higher on the largest of the rocks as I wait for the perfect one. The one that will take me over the barricade and into the island. To Marina. My chest seizes as I think of her lying there on the sandy earth, alone and hurt. I look around me as if I will find anyone else to take on this task, but there is no one else. There is only me.

My heart thunders in my chest with adrenaline and anticipation as the next wave nearly covers the outcropping. I duck under the water as I wait to feel the push of this final wave behind me. The one that will carry me in.

I close my eyes for a moment, just a moment to gather myself, to remind myself one of my own is trapped on land. The one who has welcomed me into her circle with open arms, the one that seems to understand me completely, after only knowing me for such a short time. She needs me. And I am her only hope now.

My eyes open as I feel the water pick up around me and begin to carry me in. I keep my arms to my sides, allowing the wave to do its job as I near the shore. Closer and closer as I stay near the surface, my dorsal fin cutting through the water as I move. The sandy floor is below me, and I am weightless as the vines come into crystal clear view. Hooked thorns as sharp as shark teeth glisten through the water, hungry for a bit of flesh. Panic rises in surge when I know my body is too close to the thorns.

I'm not going to make it.

I can almost feel the bite of the thorns before they've even pierced my skin. Like anticipation has manifested pain all on its own. The vines rise higher towards my body as if they're calling for me. There is not enough water to pull me through. Not enough space between my body and the vines.

Too soon, I feel the scrape and tug of the thorns sinking into my flesh, pushing through my scales. Agony fills my every nerve as I feel the tug of the vines holding me back. I resist as my body tenses when suddenly the wave swells at an unnatural rate, and I know Brea has summoned up enough strength from the ocean to push me through. Somehow she knew it wasn't enough, and the Mother allowed her to intervene with her storm almost like she wants us to complete this task. The wave pulls me over the threshold, lifting me higher and I feel the hooked thorns break from my skin, leaving jagged puncture wounds in its place. By sheer luck and help from a sea sister, I've somehow passed the wrath of the viper vines alive.

As soon as my fins are in the clear, I grab for purchase at the nearest thing, because the threat isn't over. I can't allow the pull of the wave to carry me back into the vines. My hands find a stump of a fallen tree just past the wall of vines. I dig my nails into the soft grooves of the bark as the wave recedes back into the ocean, leaving my body curled around the tree stump. My soaked hair clings to the side of my face and down my neck. My body feels like a wet mop, limp and lifeless without the water floating around me, bringing my hair and fins to life. I look down at the damage from the thorns and feel like a sea sponge as blood leaks from the various holes littering my front side.

Before I have a moment to contemplate it further, a hollow sound howls around me on the island. I'm not convinced that it is from the storm winds passing through the trees. Like a distant screech. Like a song of the dead. Even through the rain, a heavy fog settles over the island, gray and eerie, making my skin crawl. Now that my body has switched over to breathing air, the stench of the island warps my senses. It smells like death. Dark decay, slick, and wrong.

When the last of the water trickles through the vines, I quickly push up onto the stump, arms straight as stilts, searching for Marina. My tail raises me up only so high, like a snake ready to strike, but I strain my neck to see more of the island. If only I could stand. If only I could run. My eyes adjust to the dark dense air around me, but the effort is futile because I can already hear her screams.

My stomach turns to liquid, and I drag myself towards her through the sandy earth. Moss and sea grass litter the ground beneath me. I never realized how heavy my tail was without the buoyancy of the ocean to carry me. But still, I trudge forward, digging my nails into the ground as I haul myself farther, toward the sound of her voice.

I squint my eyes, trying to see her more clearly through the darkness. Only a pale sliver of moonlight brightens my path. The slate clouds block out every star in the sky. Stray bolts of lightning illuminate the island for mere seconds. I half expect a wispy figure of a ghost to emerge from the thicket of the trees during one of these flashes of lightning.

My senses heighten when I see her. When I make out the shape of her thin body trapped within the snarled tree roots, broken and jagged from the storm.

Impaled.

She is impaled, just as Ezera's father was. But this time there are no tools to free her. This time it is only her and me. This time it's Marina staring death in the face. The mermaid who saved my life without hesitation and shared a piece of herself with me. For that reason, it makes the scene in front of me hurt just that much more.

"Marina!" I call to her, letting her know that I am here. That I'm coming. That she is not alone.

When I approach, I assess the scene laid out before me. Rain and blood mix together as they trail down the sand, creating tiny streams of crimson. A blood bath. Her side is impaled on jagged wood where her tail meets flesh. Damaged skin and scale flap open from the wound created by her attempts to free herself. The sight is enough to make me gag. Her whimpers strike true to my heart, squeezing tight and shaking the queasy feeling.

Immediately my hands are on her, assessing the damage, vision blurred through the never-ending rain. Open cuts litter her arms from attempting to pull herself free.

"I'm going to pull you from the tree. Just be still and trust me." I nod to her, my face an open book with wide eyes, needing her to trust me—needing her to not thrash with pain when I begin. She nods at me, her bloodshot eyes lined with fear. I watch as the muscled cords in her neck strain with agony. "On three," I warn as I wrap my arms around her middle and anchor my tail to the base of the tree.

"One." I pray to the Mother that the tree hasn't hit anything major.

"Two." I hold tight to her middle, careful not to puncture my nails into her.

"Three." I hold my breath as I pull her with all of my might, my arms and tail straining in different directions. Pressure builds behind my eyes, and my muscles begin to shake. Tail pushing against the base, arms pulling my dear friend, she begins to move. Her screams pierce my soul as I pull, steady as ever. She moves towards me inch by inch off of the tree jutting from the earth, ever so slowly. Warm blood runs through my hands.

As soon as her body is freed, I feel the absence of the tree holding her body back and lay her flat, moving to her side. I place my hands on her open middle, blood spilling out in rivers. The flesh sinks into the wound, but in the dark, I can barely see the damage. She moans in pain as I apply pressure, and I grind my teeth as I try to ignore it, knowing this is the only way. "I know. I'm sorry." I look her in the eyes. "You are going to be okay."

I nearly crumble when her pleading eyes look back at me as she says, "Please don't let me die here. Not here. Not yet." Her voice is weak and too airy. "Not before I can become a mother." At her proclamation, I know this mission was so much more to her than just a piece of a puzzle we are trying to solve. So much more than just retrieving a ring. This mission put her one step closer to her dream, to the future she wants for herself. For all of our kind.

I look around for something to pack the wound, so I can move her towards the shore. Before we lose the tidal wave that will bring us out to sea, to our home. Frantic, my eyes dart from left to right, scanning the area covered in night and fog, knowing I can't go too far and leave her to bleed out. But then I see it, right beneath us.

Salt moss. Growing at the base of the fallen tree, creeping up like a spine. Perfect for packing a wound, and the salt will draw out infection. I frown when I realize that it will hurt like a bitch. But I know Marina can handle it. She's tough as nails.

I splay one hand over the wound as I remove the other, gathering as much salt moss from the trunk as possible, and begin packing the wound. Her moans quickly turn to shrieks as I pack the wound with the moss, disrupting her insides and creating more pressure.

"I'm sorry," I whisper as I continue to work. It takes everything in me to continue, knowing I am causing her more pain. Her shrieks turn to deep groans through ground teeth as I pack the wound.

I wrap her middle with the fronds I spotted earlier, my hand making quick work of tying it off and hoping it holds. I clasp her hands in mine when I finish, both sticky with blood.

"Can you move?" I ask her gently, not quite sure how I will haul her towards the shore, near the viper vines, so we can wait for a wave to pull us back out.

She grabs onto my hands as she pulls herself up to a seated position, eyes tight, teeth still ground together. Every muscle in her face is strained with exertion. But she doesn't stop until she's upright. Eyes prying open, she looks to me and says, "Let's get the hell out of here."

I nearly split my side with a delirious laugh that barks from my lips, but slide my arm around her and haul us closer to the vines. Luck must be on our side tonight because the waves from the ocean are barreling through the vines by the minute. The tide is so high, it is covering most of them. We make haste picking one, not wanting to waste another minute on this haunted island, and dive into rolling waters as it reaches us, pushing off with our tails against the sand.

With my arm tightly around Marina, we arc our bodies as we sail over the vines with a speed I wasn't prepared for, and nature be damned, I summon as much power as I can to manipulate the wave surrounding us, not knowing how much control Marina has over her body right now. As we glide over the barricade of the island, my heart races with glee to leave in one piece.

My fin snags as we rush into the open ocean and yank with the pull of the tide, knowing the tear will be far better than being beached in the strangled vines. I feel the white-hot burn as the delicate tissues tear away from my tail. Trying not to cringe, I squeeze Marina closer as we spill out into the open ocean.

As we right ourselves from the wave, I spot Brea already swimming towards us, grabbing Marina on the other side, "Oh, thank the Mother, you're alright. Another minute and I was going back in." Brea's words are a distant sound as adrenaline still roars through my ears. Marina turns to me with a knowing look on her face. Like some kind of understanding has settled between us. Like a connection of trust has been established.

"Thank you," she breathes, her eyes red-rimmed, the sound barely audible over the wind and the rain.

"We protect our own," I reply with a smile as Brea and I hold Marina between us and dive into the water for the journey home.

THIRTEEN

I hold the ancient ring out in front of me to inspect it. I begin to try it on but Brea clutches my hand, her skin hot against my cold fingers. "No. Do not put that thing anywhere near your finger. This magic is old—really old. And unstable. That ring holds power that cannot be trusted."

Her golden-speckled eyes bore into mine, and I realize how little I know of magic and all its facilities. Humans of course know that a certain level of magic exists in the world. That it is a natural occurrence in nature, just as fog is. But humans never understood how it could be wielded or controlled. It just exists of its own accord. Over the years, humans have attempted to somehow capture it for themselves, but it's always been viewed as a futile effort. Magic cannot be taken or controlled, at least not by humans.

"Countless things could happen if anyone tries to put it on without the proper knowledge of how to wield it." As if the ring suddenly burns in my palm, I'm quick to hand it to her, not wanting to test its instability by accident.

Our arrival back to the caves starts a flurry of activity, all for Marina's injury and our return. She's hauled from our grasp by Kai and Okiro, her limbs limp with exhaustion, and brought to the stone platform near the main waterfall. Kai's face is a pinched mess of worry. Concern claws at him, and my mind snaps back to her comment on the island. *Don't let me die. Not before I can become a mother.* I wonder if Kai and Marina have had that conversation with the curse about to be broken.

As mermaids begin to work on Marina, Brea and I recount our story to Calypso and Lorelei, who has taken over working on Marina's wound. Her hands are quick and precise as she works to remove the salt moss and inspect the injury. "Did you pack this?" Her cerulean eyes glare at me with an edge that could cut through glass.

"I . . . yes." I stumble through my words, hoping I didn't cause more damage.

"Nice work," she smirks, turning her attention back to Marina. I release the breath I was holding.

Lyla presents us with two opened shells filled with white fish and greens. Brea and I take them to the sandbar within the caves, so we can still keep an eye on Marina. We both dig in with vigorous hunger. After I've gotten half my meal down I stop and look over at Marina, asleep in an old weathered canoe lined with soft green seaweed. How they got it in here is a mystery to me.

"What was it like?" I ask Brea between bites, as we scarf down our first meal in eighteen hours.

"The island? You saw it. Like Death's paradise." Her response is muffled by the white fish in her mouth.

"No, I mean . . . the gravesite. Where the bodies reside." I pick at my bowl, wondering if I really want to know at all. She stops eating and glances at me with haunted eyes, and I wonder if I asked her too soon to recount the memory of that place.

"As soon as we entered the catacomb at the heart of the island, I could feel it. The lingering magic in the air. Like a heavy mist that clings to your skin. The air sang with it, like an electric current." I think back to the dense fog that covered most of the island's ground and shiver.

"Taper candles were our only source of light. They lined the interior walls." Brea's eyes suddenly seem distant. "The endless flames were kept burning by some ancient spell. They lit the room well enough, but the flickering created shadows that didn't help with the tension in my muscles. The witch's sarcophagus sat on an altar at the very center. Larger than all the rest, it made her seem like the most powerful being to reside there—infamous for her curse set upon us all those years ago." She pauses to take a sip of freshwater tea that Lyla brought to us. "It was beautiful though, molded from pure gold and onyx. There were symbols etched around it from an old language long forgotten. Even I couldn't read the symbols and I've studied the ancient tongue. But the lid . . . it was heavy. So heavy to open. Nearly impossible with just the two of us. But we managed. Even if our claws suffered for it, we got the job done." Suddenly, her eyes glaze over, lost in the haunted memory.

"The scent in that catacomb was enough to burn all your senses, even with years of not receiving any new residents. The magic lingering within the dead created a scent that probably won't leave me for days. Ash and sulfur and something . . . wrong. Decay." My meal threatens to reemerge.

"Marina took the liberty of fetching the ring off of that knobby finger. The witch's hands were crossed over her chest and bound in iron manacles in the event that anyone ever came searching for her wild magic and attempted to use her body as a conduit. As if the iron would do anything against it. Once Marina had the ring, we bolted as quickly as we could, not wanting to spend another minute surrounded by lost souls and unclaimed magic."

I like to think I would have had it in me to endure the inside of the catacomb with courage for the greater good, but something tells me that the haunting feeling wouldn't have left me for weeks. Even just being on the island was enough to haunt my thoughts, which is why I didn't put much effort into trying to get any sleep for the night.

When Lorelei mentioned running low on taeopaen root, the yellow sea plant known for staving off infection, I jumped at the opportunity to go out and fetch some, knowing it grows abundantly near the mangrove forest. Most of the pod is still asleep, exhausted from the night's events, but my body won't wind down. My mind refuses to shut off. So I figure I might as well do something useful. Something helpful.

It's still early. The sun barely peeks over the horizon, causing the sky to glow in various shades of lavender. Dense fog is still settling over the water from last night's storm. The ocean is less than pleasant to swim through this morning, which is probably why Lorelei was thrilled at my offer to head out for supplies. She didn't want to venture through the murky, disrupted waters, and I would prefer she stay close to Marina. The storm's wrath really churned the ocean up last night, leaving it roiled for my morning swim. I pull another piece of stray seaweed from my hair when I finally enter the mangrove forest and emerge from the water. I bet the palace staff is already clearing debris from what the storm left behind. I imagine the groundskeepers in a tizzy over the state of the gardens.

Everything is so quiet here. Only the sound of the water lapping up the roots of the trees. Not even the birds have made an appearance yet.

I dive below the surface and skim the sea floor, feeling much too large for this community of sea life that resides here, until I find the stark white plant with the yellowed root, teeming with tiny blue fish swimming about. As I near, the fish scatter in a thousand directions and I begin to gently dig around the base of the plant, not wanting the roots to tear. When the sand gives way to the mustard color of the root, I gently tug, but my hands freeze when I hear the sound.

I release the plant and tuck myself deep into the forest brush when I see it coming.

The *Juliette*

Ezera's sailboat.

Of course he would be out here this early in the morning. It seems this man has just as much energy as he had as a child. Never tiring. Which is probably what makes him such a good fisherman with a crew of two. He never stops.

Slowly I rise to the surface and peer through the domed roots of the tree that arch from the water, protecting me from sight. With the sun barely peeking above the horizon, the shadows around me are plenty.

One glance at his sails and I can see he's replaced the worn rope. I wonder how long it took him to return to the water if it pains him to be away like it pains me to be away from the sea or my willow. I always thought that my love for the tree was due to the solitude I found there, but maybe it was because she drank from the ocean. That small piece of the sea streaming into the center of the island and fueling her with its endless wonder.

I watch as he navigates through the nearly impossible path through the forest, waiting until I can continue my task. For reasons I don't care to explore, I don't want him to go. I want his presence to linger here, trailing through the fog beneath the trees.

Something about him is more wondrous to me than even my own newly-discovered species. Even more alluring than encountering someone from a different world. This isn't the same story of a mermaid being drawn to a human. No, it has nothing to do with our difference in species because I know what it's like to be human. I know how it feels to live on land. I've done it my entire life.

This pull towards him is something different. And there is no denying it when he turns in my direction and those enchanting blue-green eyes stare right into my soul—at me. *Shit.*

He is looking at me, not at the forest. Not at the tangled spider web of tree roots, but at me. At my eyes peering above the water.

The look on his face is pure shock as if I've startled him from his very skin, like my very presence has just pulled him from the only world he's ever known.

My body freezes as I watch his face go from surprise to panic, to . . . *wonder.* Not fear, not rage, but wonder.

Without tearing his gaze from mine, he moves ever so slowly to lower his sail, his hands unhurried as he pulls the rope down. And then I know he's not going anywhere. I'm not getting out of this one. Part of me realizes that I could absolutely dive below the surface and swim away before he could get his sails back up, but the louder part of me, the more stubborn part of me, doesn't want to—and what would be the point? He's already seen me.

Matching his slow pace, I emerge from the safety of the trees. From beneath the tangled roots. I mark the awe on his face as he watches me swim towards him with inhuman grace. He knows I possess no legs. But to my surprise, he's unafraid. He doesn't back away like I might have if our roles were reversed. Instead, he leans closer over the edge of the boat, to get a clearer look at me. To make sure I'm real.

Hesitantly, I emerge from the shadows of the forest, my shredded fin nearly dragging on the shallow sea floor at this depth, and into the light. My skin pricks, and not from the brisk morning after a storm. My tail is on full display beneath the clear blue water at this depth. He can see me for who I am, almost as if I am naked before him. I try my hardest to remember the beauty of a mermaid, and not feel the self-conscious parts of me emerge. I try to remember that I have never felt more *me* than I do in this form. I peer up at him from below and watch as the breeze blows his sun-bleached waves from his face. He drops down to a knee, the boat bobbing from the motion.

"Cealene."

My name on his lips sounds like a song. One I've never heard before. He recognizes me, and I recall the night of the Full Celestia when I helped free his father at the docks. His calloused hands grab the side of his boat as he leans over, white linen shirt hanging open, revealing the taut muscles of his chest. Muscles built from endless amounts of hard labor on the water and at the docks. Hard labor that I've seen firsthand when I ran into him hurrying home for the party. Running to my fate. That day seems like years ago now—like a lifetime ago.

I settle a few feet from him, not daring to go any closer, not allowing the invisible thread between us tug to pull me nearer.

"Ezera," I say, my voice barely a whisper on the wind. A voice I barely recognize as it leaves my lips. He visibly shudders, like I've sent a cool chill down his spine. His deep eyes widen, but narrow to meet mine, a hint of a smile on his lips, weathered by the sun and the sea.

"You're . . ."

"Different. I know," I say, swaying my glimmering tail beneath the surface, still trying not to feel like an oddity.

"How did you—"

"That night, with your father. I never made it back to the palace." I explain without delving into the entire events of that night again. The transformation, when I plunged into the black sea, that memory is mine and mine alone.

"You've been here, in the sea, since that night?"

"I have."

"Your parents must be worried sick." His comment is laced with sarcasm, not really concerned with how my parents might be faring, but with it, anger boils up in me, threatening to spill over.

"Oh, they know where I am. I'm sure of it." Before he can ask, I continue, "They knew this was a part of me but chose to keep it from me. Until I figured it out on my own." Unintended anger lines my words as he absorbs this information for a moment. Mulls it over. Digests it.

"Well this form . . ." he finally says, looking me over, " . . . suits you." His smirk undoes something within me, and his eyes dazzle with mischief as he says this, not trying to hide the compliment one bit. I blush like a young maiden, instead of the predatory sea creature I am. Before I know it, I'm close enough to smell him on the breeze. Cedar and sunshine, and something more . . . something I can't quite identify. He leans over the boat a bit more.

"It seems you have an affinity for sea creatures," I muse, swaying closer to him, noting the irony of the fisherman meeting a half-fish, half-human. We are now mere inches away. If I reached out my hand, I could touch the muscle that flutters at his jaw.

"It seems I do." The inches between us shrink as he leans in, and suddenly the world falls around us. There is only him and me and we are trapped in this vortex of make-believe where boundaries don't exist and enchantments do. I can feel his breath on my neck, sending electric heat down my spine. My hands tingle with the need to grab him by the shirt and pull him into the sea with me. He reaches a hand up towards my face, slowly, and my breath catches in my throat. Frozen in place. My heart rams in its cage with anticipation and—

I hear it before I have time to turn around but know from the creek and groan of splintering wood that it's coming, sending the hairs on the back of my arms to rise. A giant mangrove damaged by the storm is losing a battle with gravity. Without even a thought I gather my strength from within, holding the water surrounding the boat with my mind. Before I have time to speak, I shove the boat out of the way by manipulating the water it sits in, sending Ezera tumbling forward from the jerk of the wave, almost into the water. We both turn in time to watch the tree crash into the sea. Its leaves flutter as they sail through the air and hit the water with a smack, spraying seawater into the air. The tree bobs for a moment before slowly settling into the water. I look back to Ezera and he's already staring at me, face speckled with drops of seawater from the splash. Our enchanted moment is long gone.

"That was—"

"Incredible," he finishes. I was going to say *close*, but incredible works too. His face is bright with amazement, causing my mouth to quirk up in a smile. "You saved *Juliette.*" He brushes a hand down one of the sails. "It seems my debt to you has now doubled." It takes me a moment before I know he is referring to his father, that night at the docks.

"How is your father?"

"If you asked him, he would tell you he's back and ready for action, but I know it will still be a few more weeks before he is fully recovered—if that."

I nod, remembering the day I saw him sitting at the front of their fishing boat. "I'm glad he's okay."

"As am I." His eyes gloss, shining in the morning light. "Truly, if there is ever any way that I could repay you . . ." He trails off.

"Actually . . . there is something you could do for me. If you're up for it." I wait to hear if he trusts me enough to oblige.

"What did you have in mind?"

"Have you noticed the missing posters lining the docks lately?"

Recognition fills his eyes. "I have. They seem to be more frequent as of late." It's refreshing to finally speak to someone about this that doesn't immediately dismiss me or roll their eyes in exasperation.

"Those are my thoughts too. Something about them seems. . .different than the others. More frequent, but also—they seem to be females around similar ages?" I watch as he mulls it over.

"You know, now that you say it, the posters do seem to be of young women more than men lately. Which is odd, considering men typically sail the seas."

"Exactly! If you see any more flyers, would you bring them to me?" I hesitate, worried I'll get the same reaction from him as everyone else. "I've been keeping an eye on them trying to figure out a pattern or something that could help find them."

I watch him as the sea breeze blows through his hair and he looks at me like I've captivated him.

"You are going to make one hell of a queen someday." His words catch me off guard as I was anticipating scrutiny. That may just be the kindest thing anyone's ever said to me, and I'm not even sure if it's well deserved. Ezera sees what I'm trying to do here, and he doesn't think it's a waste of time. He thinks it makes me a better leader. He sees me.

"Thank you." Emotion swells in my throat so unexpectedly I nearly choke on it. But I push it down, not wanting him to see me break down over a simple comment. But to me, it was so much more than simple. More than he could ever know.

"And one more thing," I continue, not wanting to forget an important part.

I ask Ezera if he would be my eyes and ears in the castle while I'm out here. At least until the curse is broken and I can make my decision before the upcoming full moon. I tell him about how he can enter the castle undetected and get to the third floor, where the living quarters are as well as where he will find the most gossip. The kitchens. They've always been a kind of hang-out for the staff to gather and converse.

Without hesitation, he agrees to my request, no questions asked. I ask him to keep close to the kitchens and staff areas to listen for any gossip of the upcoming Full Celestia celebration, any talk of mermaids, or where the heir to the throne has been. I ask him to listen for talk of my parents' well-being as well as the rest of the royal family.

As I explain a bit about the castle's layout and what to keep an eye out for, he silently listens and nods with understanding, his feathered locks falling into his eyes. We agree to meet in the mornings, right here in the mangrove forest, before he has to be at the docks with his father.

Understandably, he asks a few questions about our kind and what it's like to live in the sea. I tell him about my ancestor and the pod, about the world that exists below the surface, and of the Sea Wars, which he has never heard of. He asks how I feel about what happened, and I truly don't have a straight answer for him because I simply don't know.

Talking to Ezera comes so naturally to me. I'm not sure if it's because I've known him for so long or because he's the only human I've spoken to in weeks, but it's comforting to tell him what's been on my mind these past few days. I wonder if he feels the same.

"Ezera . . . about that night. Your father was badly injured, and it didn't appear to be accidental." I watch again as the wheels turn in his head, trying to find a way to explain. Trying to think of a good lie to spew.

"Please don't insult me by telling me I've mistaken the situation. I know an assault when I see one. I've been to the palace dungeons too many times to count. Your father was attacked. Why?"

It's possible I've overstepped. It's possible he doesn't feel as comfortable delving into his secrets with me. It's possible he will lie to me regardless. But I need to know the truth. I need to know what is happening in my own land. But as my words strike him, I see his shoulders deflate, his head bow. He will not lie to me.

"Hollow Bones."

I shudder at the name of the southern pirate clan notorious for their lethal dealings. The group my father has been trying to end for years. It has been said that if you cross them, they'll suck the marrow from your bones, leaving nothing left for the crows. They're a ruthless group to tangle with, and if Ezera and his father are somehow caught up with them, I'm surprised they left his father alive that night.

Fear grips my throat as I think of all the ways the Hollow Bones could be torturing this man and his father. Whatever the case, there is no doubt in my mind that Ezera and his father didn't come to this predicament lightly.

"I'm paying off a debt that was long ago paid." His eyes are hollow with grief. They must have something on him or his father. Something that is forcing his hand in a game he has no business playing. I can see it written all over his sun-kissed face. He's ashamed to tell me this secret. But I also see the fury simmering beneath the surface. He despises these pirates and with good reason. They are nothing but parasites, feeding off others with no regard for anything or anyone. They take advantage of people who are pressed between a rock and a hard place, seeing no way out. That's how they thrive—off of other's misfortunes.

I wouldn't be surprised if they had a hand in most of these missing person disappearances.

And then I remember the marked symbol on his calf, the one I saw when he saved the manatee pup. "Your calf . . . they did that to you." He nods in submission, as he rubs the scarred skin and I realize now what the symbol is. It's the symbol of the pirate clan that rules the southern seas. How despicable must you be to maim another's body? To mark them as your property?

On more than one occasion, I've seen the guards haul a member of their clan into the dungeons for one reason or another. Their inked faces are slicked with sweat, their mouths spewing profanities as they're tossed behind an iron gate. But my father has never been able to squash their existence completely. Whenever we cut off a piece of the clan, another limb grows in its place, continuing the vicious cycle.

"You don't seem like the type to cross paths with such heathens." I search his face for answers, but I can see him struggle again to put his shortcomings into words.

"I'm not." His words sound defensive like he doesn't want me to change my view of him. And I understand the fear that someone might think differently of you for something that is out of your control. But I was raised with compassion for my people, and I know the world is never black and white. The gray areas always hide between a question and an answer—a problem and a solution. It hides in places that people cannot always see, but it's there. It's always there painting our world with depth and uncertainty.

"It started a few years after my mother passed, when my father spent all of our money on tonics to heal her. Nothing worked, of course. But we couldn't just sit back and do nothing while she withered away. So we paid for any and every treatment we heard of to try and save her. But nothing ever did.

"When she was gone, we were left with a hole in our hearts and a debt we couldn't manage. One night my father comes home battered and bloody. Says we got a side job now. Something that will keep us afloat for a while. Just a while he assured me." He shakes his head in disbelief. "Turns out *just a while* can mean anything when you're at the mercy of the Hollow Bones." He looks out over the horizon, not meeting my eyes as he recalls the story of what brought him here. I hold my breath as I wait for him to continue. To reveal what has him so unnerved.

"They have us smuggling blue somnia into the city for them. Once a week, I dive for the plant and bring it back in our crates with the day's catch to be dispersed amongst the city. So the Hollow Bones can fill their pockets with coin while leaving the people hungry for more." My heart sinks at his admission. Pilfering blue somnia is illegal. The plant is dangerous and highly addictive. It can be ingested fresh or dried and ground into a powder. What Ezera and his father are doing could ruin an entire ecosystem, not to mention feeding a monster we have a hard enough time stopping. The plant can be unpredictable when ingested, sometimes resulting in paralysis, heart attack, or even death. It all depends on the potency and the person. It affects every individual differently. With all the variables of such a plant, I doubt it could ever be deemed safe for anyone. Even the way and location of how it develops in the sea can alter its effects.

"Every time we think we might have our heads above water, the clan finds a way to keep us down for another month. And then another. And another. The night you helped us, was the night they sent a message for my stupidity." A breeze catches his golden hair, pulling it across his forehead.

"You see, I was sick and tired of working ourselves to the bone for those heathens. Sick of being controlled by them. So I did something about it. I realize that it wasn't the smartest plan, but it was more of a reaction than anything. That day instead of delivering the marked crates to the drop-off, I delivered my fists instead. And my father paid the price. I should have known it would come to that. But I just couldn't do it anymore. I couldn't be responsible for poisoning our people anymore. For lining the pockets of the Hollow Bones and making them stronger." The shame that covers his face is enough to make me want to tear out the throats of the Hollow Bones. Not only for what they've done to Ezera and his father, but what they've done to countless others on Aqualasia.

"Ezera . . ." I know if I tell him that what happened to his father was not his fault, it will fall on deaf ears.

"I've tried to find other ways. I lie awake at night thinking of a way to free ourselves of them, to keep my father safe, to stop polluting our lands with drugs. But every time, I come up short." He drags his hand through his hair and down his neck. "So I fought back the only way I could. In a language they're fluent in." Something tells me that if I offer my help, he won't take it. But I don't plan to let this arrangement continue. How can I when it is my duty to protect our people?

They know where to find Ezera and his father, and any members we capture will only result in another taking their place. So there's only one way to end this.

"Here's what you're gonna do." I straighten my shoulders, showing him that I mean business and that he will take my help, whether it wounds his ego or not. "We are going to get your boat marked with the

Royal Insignia so your daily catch will be inspected by the guards before being delivered to the palace. That way, the pirates will see they can no longer use you to smuggle, knowing your boat has been compromised, now that your catch is specifically sent to the palace instead of sold in the town markets." I know this isn't a fix to the bigger problem, but it is the best I can do from here.

I tell him who to speak to at the docks, and how to get his boat marked for palace deliveries. He will tell the head of *Catch and Deliveries* that Cealene sent him.

I write a curt letter on some spare parchment stowed away on Ezera's boat, the webbing of my hand making it difficult to grip the pen. But I sign the bottom with my signature hoping it will be enough. I tell him that his payment per crate will increase and he will make close friends with the cooks that work in the kitchens of Pearle Castle, knowing Chef has a very specific list when it comes to his raw ingredients. Once the pirates see Ezera's boat marked with our Royal Crest, they will steer clear of them, not wanting to risk their operation further. The rest can be dealt with when I set foot on land . . . *if I set foot on land.*

Before he goes, Ezera guides his boat to the edge of the fallen tree and frees it from its tangled roots, cutting away the attached section with an axe. Not because the fallen tree was blocking his path back home, but because it might block someone else's.

I try not to gawk at his muscled body at work under the sun. Once he hauls the tree into the forest, we say our goodbyes with a promise to meet here tomorrow morning. When I turn to go, before diving beneath the surface for the taeopaen root I promised Lorelei, he stops me.

"Cealene," again, the sound of my name on his lips like a melody, "thank you . . . for coming into the light." I smile as I look away from the intensity of his gaze, knowing exactly what he means. I look back to him and nod, before diving beneath the surface, tail fluking on full display.

FOURTEEN

When I get back to the caves, the pod is alive with activity, like a beehive in spring. I make my way to Marina, who is still resting in the worn canoe, Lorelei at her side. I'm pleased to see Marina awake and moving her arms as she sips something steaming from a small shell. Since living among the merfolk, I've learned that not only do we have the ability to manipulate water, but some—although rare—have the ability to heat and cool water as well, creating steam and ice with enough concentration to a small amount at a time. I've heard it takes years of practice to perfect, but Lyla, the chef of the pod, has it mastered flawlessly.

As I approach, I hand Lorelei the bundle of roots she requested.

"She's doing well, thanks to you." Lorelei nods to me when I near.

"And to you," I counter, knowing without her expertise, Marina might not have made such a quick recovery.

"Finish that tea and stay put!" Lorelei gives her orders and leaves us with some privacy, slipping off the edge of the platform and disappearing into the water below. Her delicate fin tips are the last things I see before turning my attention back to Marina.

"How are you feeling?" I ask, curling my tail around myself beside the old canoe.

"Oh, this isn't the first time I've cheated death. Just the latest. It's going to take a lot more for me to turn to sea foam." She winks as she sips the hot tea from the salmon-striped shell. It smells of lavender and something more, but I can't quite pinpoint the other notes.

"You lot never cease to amaze me. How on earth do you have access to lavender?" I inhale the blissful scent wafting from her.

"Oh, we are more clever than the average human. We find ways to enjoy all things humans do, if not more." She sips her tea before continuing and I admire her braided locks flowing down her shoulder tied off with thin rope.

"The dried herbs we use come from a small garden a few of us tend to in a secluded part of a nearby beach. It's tough to grow it through mostly sand, but over the years the plants have adapted. Once we harvest them, we dry them here in the caves with the help of Lyla's heat magic."

I nod in astonishment. Truly these merfolk are more intelligent than most humans. But they've been living undetected for thousands of years. Of course they've had time to perfect and ease their living to accommodate whatever they desire.

"Well, I'm glad you're healing. The world is a better place with you swimming its waters." With that, her cat eyes look into mine as if I've stunned her, but she recovers quickly and says, "You're not turning into a guppy on me now, are you?"

I giggle at the accusation but don't have it in me to protest. Not when Marina is the closest thing to a friend I have under the sea. Calypso has welcomed me into her pod with grace and taught me almost everything I know thus far, but I don't know if that truly falls under the category of friend. Something about her demeanor won't let anyone get close enough to create that bond even though she is my family. Calypso just doesn't quite fit the same way as Marina does.

"How's the wound?" I gesture towards the now healing skin on her side.

"Missed my gills, thank the Mother. But still tender."

"When will you be back in the waters?"

"Lorelei says a couple of days, but *I say* that's too long." She grunts as she sinks down deeper into the water that fills the canoe. "You know how our tails sing with need to glide through the current after too long in one place." I nod, understanding the need she describes because I really do know the feeling, as if it were a real, tangible thing. Something drives us to travel through flowing waters, never staying put for too long.

Calypso finds us after a moment, stealing the conversation.

"Cealene, my dear. Just the one I was looking for. When you've both finished up, come join me in my cove. We have many things to discuss. Marina, I'll have Kai fetch you so you don't have to strain your healing muscles." We both nod as she heads in the direction of her cove, but my tongue is heavy with questions.

"I guess she's deemed it time to reveal the next step in breaking this curse." Marina's voice is laced with irritation, and I wonder if this might be the first time she's felt this way towards the leader of the pod. "I won't lie and say that the suspense hasn't been weighing on me. All the secrecy and withholding information gives me pause." We both turn towards the water breaking behind us. Kai emerges from the depths, slick with the sea. "I wouldn't worry, Cealene. Calypso is one for dramatics, but she wouldn't put us in a compromising situation without a well thought out plan." Her voice doesn't waver as she says it, but a small part of me still hesitates to fully believe her statement. Even if she does.

"The survivors of the Island of Bones. Alive to tell the tale," Kai jokes as he leans onto the edge of the platform, his brute muscle nearly covering the entire slope. The scarred body of a warrior from ages ago—a warrior who fought in battle and also survived to tell the tale. The comment was meant for the both of us, but his eyes haven't left Marina's since he emerged from the water.

"How's the pain?" He is nothing but concern and adoration.

"It's the strangest thing. It just subsided when you arrived." Her face brightens with amusement at his concern, but a blush creeps up her neck and into her cheeks. Try as she might, Marina can't hide her feelings for this male.

"I do have that effect on most creatures." His grin is wicked when his brow raises at me.

The laugh that escapes my lips echoes through the cave and sends Marina into a fit of giggles as well.

"Come on, charming. Before Calypso has our fins nailed to the sea floor." With Marina's command, Kai guides the canoe down the slope and into the water, steering her to Calypso's cove, and I follow in their wake.

When we enter the cove, Brea, Okiro, and Calypso are already huddled around the space examining the ring, and I swear it emits a low hum of energy that echoes off the walls. The many facets of the center stone shine in the dim glow of the cove, red and glorious surrounded by gold symbols. Kai guides Marina towards the group and I take a space near Brea, peering over at the ancient ring. Calypso lounges on her shell throne like a queen. Although it is lined with sharks' teeth and skeletal bone of some poor creature, the sea salt that sparkles the edges really makes it look quite exquisite.

My mother and father's thrones are made of the highest quality materials. I thought they were beautiful pieces, but they just do not compare to what Calypso sits upon.

"Now that we're all here, I'll begin." Calypso nods to Brea who gently drops the ring into Calypso's open palm. She places the ring in an opal-faced oyster shell in the center of the group and begins.

"With this key piece, we can move forward with the plan. Brea and Lyla have been working diligently with a neighboring pod to the north on witch curses and incantations. Years ago, before their clan broke apart, the northern legion of witches resided in the Ice Mountains, and pieces of the Book of Spells have been found and confirmed as legitimate.

"As I suspected, we must travel to Ember Island, which has an infamous volcano to break the curse. It will take a few days of travel if we take minimal breaks and hit the Melodian current on our way. Once there, Cealene will offer up a personal effect of her choosing and will don the ring and spill her prophesied blood into the mouth of the volcano while reciting the incantation from the book. It must be done when the moon is at its fullest, high in the sky."

Calypso's words are like a sworn vow. Now that she's said it out loud, it has been set in stone, like something has been put in motion that cannot be stopped. My mouth goes dry and I look around the cove at the others as they take in this information.

"Why must this be done at Ember Island? Over that specific volcano?" I barely recognize my voice as I ask the question. Anticipation and fear warp my senses.

"This island holds a very unique kind of magic within its soil. It is rare and potent, heightening any incantation. Some believe it is due to its unique coordinates, some believe it's because it is the first piece of land the Mother created. The truth is, no one honestly knows why this island holds strange potent magic. But what we do know, is that breaking the curse there is necessary. It was where the curse was born, and it is where the curse will die."

Silence once again fills the room. This group will join me on a journey that will change the course of our lives forever. But only I will spill my blood under a full moon. Only I will don the dangerous ring that holds raw and wild power. I look to Marina, but her eyes are glued to Calypso, as are everyone's. The cove is silent, save for the babbling water rushing through.

Okiro's voice breaks the silence. "How much blood must be shed?" At his question, I can feel that very blood pump harder and faster through my veins, not even thinking of the question myself.

"As much as it takes." Her tone is clipped, not giving any more than that. My heart drops to my stomach.

"Will it kill her?" Marina's voice is nearly a shriek.

"Of course not." Calypso's syrupy voice holds too much confidence to be true. The crescendo of her words works its magic to lull us into submission, but they come too quickly, without any hesitation, and I know better than to fall into her spell. Something deep within my chest coils tight, my fate wavering in the near future.

"You mentioned a personal effect. What kind of personal effect? All of my most valued things are in Pearle Castle." I think of the aquamarine stone in my ear and wonder if that would work well enough as an offering.

"Yes, well, that is another issue that needs resolving." Calypso's look is one of irritation. I don't have time to think of anything because Calypso throws another bit of information our way.

"But because of the nature of this curse, Cealene will need an anchor during the incantation, to keep her grounded in this world, this reality. So she is not swept up into the vast black hole of realms. The power held within that ring coupled with the other elements of the curse breaking is immensely strong, stronger than most can handle. It can be enough to rip the mind to shreds, to warp it from its original form, and send scraps through different realities, lost to its owner forever." She looks around the group with a haunted stare. I don't want to know what that must feel like, to lose grip on reality, with your mind. My insides quiver with the possibility of losing what makes me *me*.

"And because I have no intentions of letting that happen to you, my dear granddaughter, you will need an anchor. Someone who you can trust to hold you to this earth. We will not let you get lost in the power of the spell. This anchor must be someone who is grounded in this world, with a strong mind of their own. Someone strong enough for two." As Calypso speaks, my eyes slide to Marina, remembering how she battled the sharks with ease, thinking of no one else who could fit this role for me. I know she is the only person I would want by my side, keeping me grounded and anchored to this world. But immediately I feel guilty, knowing she has barely recovered from the last trip she took to help break this curse.

Before I can turn back to Calypso, Marina meets my stare and smiles. Just small enough for me to notice. And then I know: no matter how many times we save each other from near death, there is no tally. No debt to be paid. And there never will be because that's what friendship is, that's what love is. It's endless support for one another. Love is limitless.

In such a short amount of time, I have found a friendship with Marina that most don't find in a lifetime. I think of Angelina and my heart aches with the memory of her. We've only been separated for a few weeks and I miss her fiercely. Our relationship was always one of fun and laughter. A connection you share with someone who's known you for your entire life and shares a childhood with you. Angelina and I have had deeper conversations on occasion, but for the most part, our friendship tends to stay on the lighter side. I wonder when I will see her again after the curse is broken. Will it be soon or in a few more moon cycles? Or will I disappear from the world on land entirely, getting lost to the sea?

But this friendship with Marina, though new, is deeper and richer than anything I've ever experienced with anyone before. We understand each other on a deeper level than most. With thoughts of connections, my mind drifts to Ezera, the only being on this earth who knows me on land and sea, who has a connection to me in both forms. Both worlds. He is the only other person who has both shared a childhood with me and has been connecting with me on a deeper level. But something about our relationship is incomparable to what Marina and I have. Something about my relationship with Ezera holds a spark of some kind. An electric current that connects us.

"There is no doubt in my mind that you are strong enough to break this wicked curse. You were born to do so. But precautions must be taken. I will not have our hero in mortal jeopardy." Although intended to bring me comfort her words sound as cold as the deepest sea trench. Barren.

"So let me get this straight," Kai's low voice fills the cove. "Cealene dons the ring, and recites the incantation while spilling her blood directly into the volcano . . . under the full moon."

"That is correct, Kai." Calypso's stare pierces Kai, challenging him.

But instead of rising to the challenge, his eyes shift to mine. "I am forever indebted to you, Princess."

"As am I." Okiro chimes in, holding the necklace that he always seems to wear. The thin gold chain features some type of fanged tooth. Whale maybe? Shark? When I look up to his silver eyes, it's suddenly hard to swallow. Gratitude fills the room and my chest, melting the icy cold feeling. I've never had so many people address me in this way, and I never thought I would until I became queen, hopefully earning the gratitude of my people by taking care of them.

The word he used to address me strikes a chord. *Princess.* How has that title followed me down here beneath the waters? I know the merfolk have ways of getting information from above. They aren't isolated from the world on Aqualasia, but they certainly don't follow its laws or traditions. Does my title even hold any weight here? If I decide to live the rest of my days on land, as soon as my feet hit the sand, will the shadow of the crown still be as heavy as it once was?

"Is there anyone you can think of who you would like to name as your anchor?" Calypso asks, her emerald eyes gleaming.

Again, I look towards Marina, but before I can even ask she's already nodding, puffing her chest with pride. "I would be honored to anchor you, Cealene." A smile creeps onto my face and it matches her own. Pride and loyalty connect us to one another. *We protect our own.*

"Then it's settled," Calypso leans back into her throne. "Marina, you will accompany Cealene during the incantation. You will anchor her to this realm with your mind and your hand in hers." Her onyx tail curls around the base of the throne, fins sweeping the water below.

Kai shifts in his seat, sloshing the water around him. "Is there a danger for the anchor? Is it possible they can both be swept into the void?"

Something deep within me melts. Marina has someone who genuinely cares for her well-being with no benefit to himself. A selfless love that is unapologetic, and I worry he resents me for choosing to put Marina in danger once again. Even if Marina has expressed time and time again that she can handle herself and doesn't need anyone taking care of her, it's in his nature to look out for her, like my father has always looked out for my mother. They may not always see eye to eye, but when it counts, they show up. Every time. And asking Marina to be my anchor may have threatened that. I wait for Calypso's response, praying there is no danger for her. She looks at Kai, her eyes softening.

"The truth?"

"Please," he insists.

"I don't know." Calypso's voice is a mere whisper. In the weeks I've known her, not once has Calypso's voice ever sounded anything other than commanding and sure. But this response comes out watery, like admitting to not knowing all the answers is a sort of weakness. I guess to her, it is.

Kai looks between Marina and I. Guilt and shame wash over me when I see the worry on his face. He doesn't like the uncertainty of that answer, and neither do I.

"I'm sorry. I—" But Okiro's voice breaks my fumbling words as I think of an alternative anchor.

"Oh, come on Kai. Marina is the closest thing to a warrior I know without actually ever being in a war."

"He's right, Kai. Plus, if me being an anchor for Cealene helps break this curse, then I can be that if it means we get our freedoms back." Marina's voice does not waver. The uncertainty will not deter her. Not that I needed the reminder, but Marina does not back down from a challenge. And Kai knows better than to shelter her with his worry. Hesitation lines his face, creasing his brows and corners of his mouth, but eventually, he releases a slow breath. He hates this.

"I will be with you every step of the way." His face visibly softens when he looks to her, and I swear her soft smile could burn the sun.

"Let's not forget Cealene holds the trophy for the most dangerous part of all this." Brea breaks the bubble of romance with a truth I was trying to forget.

"Thanks for the reminder," I retort, a low chuckle escaping.

"If that sums up the questions for now, you are all dismissed," Calypso calls the meeting with a flick of her wrist and heads to the waterfall trickling to the right of her throne. "And if you do come up with any inquiries, you know where I can be found." Her webbed hands glide down her silver locks as her claws brush away any tangles.

With that, we all leave the cove, Kai pushing the canoe that holds Marina into the pool of water. I trail behind them, the last one to leave. But before I do, Calypso stops me.

"Cealene, dear." I turn back towards her at the cove's edge.

"I would be careful at the company you keep, girl. Humans are precarious creatures." Calypso's voice is sharp as a knife, and I can't be sure if her comment is more of a threat or a warning. My insides turn molten as my cheeks heat. How could she possibly smell human on me after I've traveled through the sea after meeting with Ezera? It's preposterous to think someone's sense of smell could be so keen. But then I think of all of the scents that linger within the ocean water as I pass through it and know. We are predators with heightened senses.

And she is Calypso. Of course she knows all.

FIFTEEN

When I was a young girl, my mother gifted me with a diadem on my tenth birthday. It had been passed down the royal line for generations. As soon as I saw it perched in its crystal box, I knew what it was, recognizing it from the paintings in the great hall of all of the queens that came before.

Framed in their heavily carved wood, each portrait portrays a regal queen with the diadem across her brow. It's bold and beautiful with the purest of gold delicately twining like vines and coming to a point at the base of the forehead. At its center, a large iridescent pearl represents the moon surrounded by the deepest of blue sapphires, dark as night. Aquamarine and diamond adorn the points of the corona to symbolize the waves of the sea that surround and protect our island.

The diadem is something that demands attention. Its sparkling brilliance claims your eyes, but it is also more than that. It is like the power of each queen infused the diadem with bravery and perseverance, with strength and grace, each ruler who wore it expected to live up to its predecessor. At ten years of age, I didn't understand much beyond the beauty of it. It was simply a sparkly thing that would one day be mine to wear, marking me as a queen like my mother.

I wouldn't understand the weight of the crown until years later when I learned the real cost of ruling a kingdom. When my father and mother started allowing me into their council meetings and accompanying them on trips to neighboring lands, I began to understand how heavy the crown could be and what that diadem truly represented. That's how I knew it was the personal effect I needed to offer up in order to break the curse.

The heirloom became more of a symbol to me than an object to be worn. I would stare at it every night before I fell asleep, thinking of what kind of future I hoped for—what kind of leader I wished to be. I looked up to my parents as rulers, accepting their guidance and knowledge. But I also had my doubts about how things were done in the name of tradition. There could be better ways if one only took the time to look. A thriving kingdom is one where all its people are valued and protected—not just the ones who are close enough or loud enough to make noise.

But regardless of the baggage it carries, the diadem has become a sort of comfort to me. It is a reminder of where I belong and what is expected of me, like a compass always pointing me north, steering me in the right direction. I know my parents will be devastated to lose such an heirloom, but if they trust me enough to one day rule, they need to trust me to make my own decisions as I see fit. And if this is the cost to free the merfolk from extinction, then so be it. We have many more heirlooms in our vaults, as well as crowns. So although the diadem is precious, it is also replaceable. These creatures aren't.

So when I asked Ezera if he would bring the diadem to me, I knew it would be no small ask. Although it will ultimately be lost to the volcano's wrath, I am hoping that it brings me clarity and maybe a little bit of guidance while in my possession. It's always given me direction in the past when I was faced with difficulty, and I hope it can lend some now too.

I haven't yet figured out how I will tell Calypso about the personal effect or how I received it, but it's not as if she has much room to disapprove. She needs this, for her people and for herself. I know the curse weighs on her more heavily than others, as she believes she is to blame. Her love began this chain of events, whether she wanted it to or not.

Who knows, maybe this diadem was around when the mermaids lived freely among the people. Maybe a queen with merblood had once donned it years ago. Maybe my mother isn't the first.

Last night, I decided that Calypso's opinion on who I spend my time with doesn't hold any weight for me. I am the heir to my parents' throne and have yet to decide if I want to give that up. I still have a responsibility to the people of Aqualasia, regardless of what Calypso thinks of them. Remembering the aquamarine stone that she gifted me that first night, my fingers graze my pointed ear and I know I have a small bit of leverage where Calypso is concerned. I am her curse breaker. If she wants to challenge my choices of interacting with a human, she will have to decide if it is more important to her than breaking the curse of infertility.

When I reach the mangroves the next morning, I can see from below that Ezera is already here. The belly of the boat creates a shadow in the water. The small anchor is nestled in the sand below, rope pulled taut against the waves. Suddenly, when his watery silhouette from above comes into view, flowers bloom within my chest, stretching and filling. I realize I am more nervous to hear about life on land than I anticipated, or maybe I'm more worried that he will have another missing poster for me. With everything going on down here, I haven't really had the time to think about what must be happening on the island regarding my absence.

I surface the water and approach the boat, noting the rising sun peeking through the morning clouds. It creates the softest glow around him. He stands with a foot on the ledge of the boat and an arm outstretched from the rigging. His back is to me, facing the rising sun. His messy hair is pulled back at the nape of his neck today and tethered with a thin strip of rope. The breeze blows through his shirt, causing it to flutter around his stone-still body, and it carries his scent to me. Cedar and sunshine. When it hits my senses, it's a welcome familiarity now. One I've come to cherish. It is the one connection that I have to both worlds. Both parts of me.

"Hey, sailor." My tone echoes over the surface of the water. It's sound alluring even to me. Never has my voice had an undertone of . . . allure. Without effort, it laces my words like it's riding the coattails of my voice. Slowly, he turns towards me.

"Cealene." His lagoon-colored eyes bore into me with just a hint of a smile wrinkling his nose.

"You failed to mention your home was more labyrinth than castle." His voice is deep enough to bury secrets. He strides towards me, and amusement fills my soul thinking about Ezera sneaking through the castle, following the map I created for him. I try to hold in the chuckle, but a smile curves on my lips despite my attempt.

"Trouble navigating your way?" I remove Atargatis from around my shoulder and place it along the boat.

"Oh, I found my way . . . eventually." His voice is playful as he sits at the edge of the boat, rolling up his pants to dip his legs in the water and submerging his scar.

"Well as long as you weren't compromised." I kick my tail out in front of me, gliding in figure-eights around the back of the boat.

"Not in the slightest." Although we are only playing, my chest releases at the news of nothing going awry at the palace. I know what he did for me was a huge risk and would likely end badly if he were discovered. I could never forgive myself if his kindness destroyed his life. I idle in front of him, arms swaying in the water.

"So, tell me what you discovered while spying in the palace." He huffs a laugh as his legs make small circles in the water.

"Well, the king and queen aren't happy. Which came as no surprise." Despite my anger towards them, my heart sinks at his words. No matter the reason for lying to me, I still love and respect them. Not just as my parents, but as the King and Queen of Aqualasia. To know they're hurting . . . it doesn't sit well. I remind myself that they probably know what happened to me and know exactly where I am. They are likely leaving me alone to avoid drawing attention to what I am and what lives beneath the sea.

Pulling me from my thoughts, Ezera continues, "But it seems the story is that you have been staying with a distant relative, learning the trade routes of the Saona Sea, and meeting with royal merchants."

"A clever story that my father, no doubt, conjured up."

"I thought so." He leans forward, resting his elbows on his knees, and continues. "There's talk amongst the staff of canceling this month's Full Celestia celebration. I heard rumors of the queen not wanting to celebrate without your presence, and people are . . . skeptical."

"Sure. The importance of celebrating another moon cycle has lost its luster when the true reason behind those silly soirees has been discovered." My tone is clipped and full of anger, despite the many days I've had to process my parents' motives. I swim up to the boat and rest my elbows on the platform next to where Ezera sits. His body heat radiates towards my cool skin.

"Our boat is marked with your crest." His eyes swirl with hope and gratitude, and I notice the lightness in his shoulders as he rests with ease. I can see how the lines in his brow have smoothed out with relief. A brightness is there that was missing the last time I saw him. How could I not have noticed it immediately upon arrival? Regardless, it makes me smile.

"I'm glad. Now you won't need to pummel any more pirates in your free time," I muse.

"Cealene, I can't even begin to explain what you did for us. For my father and I." His words catch in his throat as he looks to me through thick lashes. If only I could do more. If I could grant such a favor to everyone in need.

"It wouldn't be very responsible of me to allow such things to continue in my lands," I joke, trying to make light of a heavy situation and ease the weight of his gratitude. I watch his eyes soften as he allows it.

We sit in silence, listening to the breeze and crinkle of the leaves, and the moment that passes between us is one of tranquility. Moments this sweet barely exist in the palace where there's no time to admire the vibrant colors of the mangroves and the rich, clear blue of the water surrounding us. Birds chirp, the breeze carrying their song along the waves. The moment passes and I ask a question I've been curious about since the moment I spotted Ezera sailing these waters.

"Who's Juliette?" The words tumble out and, as soon as the question leaves my lips, I wish I could take it back. Suddenly the question seems too intimate and personal, and I don't want the answer for fear it might burst this bubble we're in. Without speaking, Ezera leans back on his palms as he takes a deep, heavy breath, tilting his head back to the sky. I swallow thickly as his body language speaks to me. The loose blond hair has escaped the rope and falls back from his face. His throat bobs right before his lips part.

"Juliette was my mother." My mind snags on the small word. *Was.* Reminding me she's gone, and my heart breaks for him again. No matter the age, a mother is a comfort like no other that cannot be replaced.

"This boat belonged to my father before it was mine. Sailing became his passion over time. He built it for my mother as a gift, so she would always feel the wind in her hair. They spent many years on this boat, sailing the seas. She was the love of his life, and when she died . . . a part of him died too."

The ache in my chest throbs as he speaks. He looks out to the horizon, where the sea meets the sky, as he speaks. As if looking into another's eyes while telling this story might unlock some deeply buried emotion, bringing it to the surface. Making it palpable and exposed.

"His passion for sailing died with her but he couldn't bear to get rid of the boat, so he gifted it to me. I've found comfort in sailing the *Juliette*, feeling the wind rip through my hair as it once ripped through hers. I feel like it somehow brings me closer to her. My father won't sail this boat anymore because there are too many memories of her lingering in its sails, but that's exactly why I love it. As if the memories might seep into my mind, so I might see her again." I look up at him from the water, eyes brimming with unshed tears as he speaks. His head tilts as he looks at me, pupils shining in the light.

"That must sound crazy to you . . ."

"No," I place my hand on his knee, "it sounds like you miss her. Very much."

He nods in response as he stares at my hand resting upon his knee, webbed and scaled. Once I realize what I've done, I pull my hand away worried I've done something wrong, and fold it into my crossed arms on the platform of the boat.

"I've been lucky enough in my lifetime to not have experienced such a loss and I do not envy you for it." I dare to look up at him again. "I'm sorry you lost your mother."

"Me too." He whispers, the wound still feeling fresh. A manatee passes beneath the boat and as if Ezera was expecting it, he pulls fresh greens from a bin nearby and tosses it towards the slowly floating creature. A moment passes and then her gray whiskers poke through the surface as she snatches up the greens. I giggle when she passes by my tail, grazing slightly. I watch her glide into the forest channel and when I turn back to Ezera, I see the light has returned to his eyes.

"You know . . . life at the castle," he says, "it's loud and busy. For all its lavish beauty, I truly don't know how your mind can think in such a place. It's so—"

"Noisy?" I offer. His laugh shakes his shoulders and exposes his bright canines.

"Yeah, noisy. Such a stark contrast to living on the water."

I imagine his days hold a calm that I could only ever find at my willow before that night. Every day on the water with a small crew, the work speaking for itself.

"You're right. Court life is often too much for me. When I was a young girl, I found a place to escape to. To get away and just . . . be."

"Yeah?" His brow raises with intrigue.

"Deep in the forest behind the castle, there is a big beautiful willow. It's where I go to think. I call it my sanctuary." As I expose another part of myself to him, I wait for his response, tentative to see if he'll find me silly or strange.

"It sounds dreamy."

"It is." I smile, missing the willow's limbs caressing me as I stare up through the swaying leaves.

"Take me there sometime?" His kaleidoscope eyes glow like burning blue flames.

"Okay."

The seagulls call above us, and Ezera pulls one leg up from the water and plants his foot on the edge of the platform, resting his arm on his knee. Casual and free. So comfortable in his own skin.

"I've spent most of my days on the water for as long as I can remember, and I still cannot imagine what it must be like to live below the surface. Or to even imagine that you live below." I watch the muscles in his jaw flutter as he speaks. "As many days as I spend on the water, it will never compare to what you experience. I will never know it the way you do. What you are, it's a gift." Although there are many negatives that come with this life, I know exactly what he speaks of, and I know he is right.

"Do you want to find out?"

"Find out . . . what it's like to live the way you do?"

"Mm-hmm." I nod with a smirk tugging at my lips. His eyes turn to saucers at my confirmation.

"How?" His boyish grin lights up his entire face.

"I may not have the ability to transform you, but I can manipulate water. And that might be all I need to show you a bit of my world." *My world.* Even as I say it, I feel guilty for calling the sea my world when my entire life up until recently has been spent on land. Like I'm some sort of traitor to my people.

"Show me," he says, and a moment later I am controlling a swirling sphere of water around his head, holding an air pocket around his mouth and nose to breathe in. Allowing oxygen to transfer through. It takes more concentration than anything I've done with water thus far, but I hold on to the power, willing the water to do as I ask. Calypso taught me that the magic we possess is about give and take. It requires a balance. If we take from the earth, we must also give to it. Replenish what we use. To manipulate the water around us, we must respect its boundaries and show humility. So I am gentle as I hold the water in the air, defying gravity. I try to pull it away from Ezera, to complete my task, but I pulled too soon, too quickly, before I had a true hold on the entire sphere.

The bubble bursts and the water splashes down, soaking his hair and shoulders. I hesitate, worried he will be mad for soaking him, but once the water trickles down his body he shakes his head to the side, spraying me like a dog, but his smile couldn't be brighter. His wet locks glisten around his face, and his playful eyes swirl with delight as he pushes off the edge of the boat and plunges into the sea.

Concern must still remain in my eyes because when he breaks the surface he says, "Don't worry, Princess. Water's never bothered me in the slightest." With that boyish grin on full display, I splash him with my hands, a small curling wave drenching him once again.

"Alright," I say, letting the worry subside, "let's do this." I extend my hand to his under the water and I suddenly feel the vulnerability creep up my spine as I wait for him to take it. It's not the delicate feminine hand I had as a human, but the hand of a sea creature long forgotten. A hand with scales and claws and webbing. My heart pounds in my throat as I look from my extended arm to his face and am met with a look of wonder and awe. Like I am offering him the keys to a world unknown. Not a hint of fear or disgust in his eyes.

As his feet kick below the surface, he places his hand into mine, warmth spreading throughout my palm and up my arm. As soon as our hands touch, electric heat swims up my arm and down my spine, causing a tingling sensation to spread throughout my body. Our gaze meets and his kaleidoscope eyes of blues and greens swirl like the depths of a lagoon. His soft smile reveals a small dimple in his cheek and the heat in my belly sinks low.

"Lead the way, mermaid."

Sixteen

I bring Ezera to the kelp forest nearby and we swivel in and out of the tall stalks together like two sea lions, all the while his air bubble stays intact. My confidence soars with every turn we make and the air pocket holds. Water manipulation is no small task, but once you hone the energy it holds, the power just moves with the water as one. It's like holding the shape in your mind, bending it to your will, and keeping it there. Allowing instinct to take over instead of resisting the impulse to overcorrect.

My intention to swim slowly was more of an effort than maintaining the air pocket, once we were fully submerged. At every turn, I forgot how much quicker a creature of the sea is in water than one built for land. Even Ezera's strong legs are no match for the large muscled tail of a mermaid.

We swim through the reefs near the mangroves and through the cave outcroppings that Marina showed me. I would have shown him the shipwreck, but I feel like that is Marina's place and not something for me to share.

Every time I look back at Ezera, his eyes are wide with wonder, taking in the secret world below, something that once had limits to him, holding him back from everything the sea has to offer. If his experience is anything like mine when I was first able to discover the ocean on a different level, he must believe he is dreaming, because the world down here . . . is nothing like the one humans are accustomed to. It's almost like quiet becomes a feeling more than a sound. The pressure of the water against your body is soothing and freeing all in one. The textures are the signature of the sea for their unique properties.

The sounds below the sea are so different and foreign to our ears that we hear each and every one of them—the muffled echoes of whales and the tinny clinking of shells. Even the slight swish of a tail creates a noise you cannot find on land. Colors seem to come alive in salt water. They almost take on their own shape, their own feeling. There's something cleansing about swimming through this underwater ecosystem. It's almost intimate.

I don't have to be an expert to know how much the sea means to Ezera. His entire being looks like it was made for the water with his tanned body and bleach-blond hair. To be able to give this experience to him brings me more joy than I could imagine.

As we swim back toward the mangrove forest, I stop him, grabbing his hand again. He idles in the open ocean, floating weightlessly in the abyss as his eyes hold me in my place. Intense and depthless. Simply, I point with my other hand to the sky above, beyond the surface and his eyes scrunch with question. A laugh escapes me as my grin turns wicked. I muster up a bit more energy in the water surrounding us as we idle together in the water and sink down lower. I watch as his face turns curious, but not scared. He trusts me.

When I've decided we are low enough I begin to pump my tail, propelling us up, up, up. Manipulating the water around Ezera to move him with me. When we break the surface of the water, the sun assaults my eyes hanging high in the sky now. I squeeze his hand tight as we arc through the air as one, water spraying around us. My tail curves as we pass our peak and begin to descend back into the sea. The cool water rushes past my ears as we plunge in. The last thing to disappear below the surface: two fins, two feet.

I swirl around him as we right our positions and resurface. His eyes are bright and wild, smile dazzling in the sun—his lips wet with saltwater.

"That was incredible." Heat rushes to my cheeks as I smile back, feeling exhilarated from the jump.

"It always is."

"I mean, of course it was. But never in my wildest dreams did I think . . ." His words trail off as he pulls his hair back from his face with his fingers.

"I know what you mean." This morning I woke up to the song of a whale echoing through the cave of waterfalls I now sleep in. An actual whale woke me up this morning. *Wildest dreams* would be putting it lightly.

"Thank you, truly." His lashes drip with sea water and I can't help but stare. To feel a pull towards him that I cannot explain. I want nothing from him, but I want everything from him. He floats so close to me, that our breaths mingle in the space between. Heat rises in my cheeks as he looks into my eyes. But my nerves threaten to spill over and I kick my tail in front of me, swimming backward towards the sailboat.

A moment later, he follows suit swimming alongside me, and I feel like a coward. Not letting myself open to someone who, depending on my choice in a week, I could never have a relationship with. Two people in two different worlds.

When we get back to the boat, he pushes himself up onto the platform, the muscles in his arms contracting as his shirt sticks to his body like a second skin. He pivots and sits on the ledge, breathing deep from the swim back. Guilt and cowardice fueling my belly, I decide to mimic his motions and sit up on the ledge beside him, tail dangling off the back of the boat and disappearing into the water below.

"Thank you, Cealene. I will never forget this day."

"Neither will I." I smile as I lean my head back, allowing the sun to hit my freckled face. I feel the boat sway as Ezera jumps up and closes a worn silver pocket watch, hooking it back around a pole extending from the hull.

"Shit. I'm late." He begins unraveling rope, preparing the sails. I sink back into the water as he rushes around the boat. "I'm sorry, Princess. It's like time doesn't exist when I'm here with you."

I blush at the implication but nod in understanding. "It's alright. I need to be heading back too." He waves his goodbye as the wind picks up. I wave back and turn to depart.

"Cealene," he calls my name from the boat, and I turn around just in time to catch the red, waterproof pouch he tosses my way. As soon as I catch it, I know what it is from the feel of the hard metal within. My mother's diadem. *My* diadem. A gift passed down to me, like Ezera's boat.

"Thank you," I call back, holding the pouch to my chest. He nods in response, a crooked smile revealing that dimple once again.

Seventeen

When I get back to the caves, I'm thankful for the distraction of others. The entire trip back, my mind would not stop churning with thoughts from the morning spent with Ezera and of my parents. Happiness bubbles up in me when I see an all too familiar amethyst tail swaying above me just below the surface. Blue tipped fins ripple with each sway. It seems Marina has been given approval to swim again.

I surface next to her and sit on the rock just below the waterline.

"Back to flipping fins I see." I nod towards the empty canoe at the far end of the cave.

"Finally," she says flatly, like the small amount of time she was on rest was an eternity. "Ugh, I thought I would wither into sea foam if I had to stay in that sorry canoe any longer." She shows off a bit by twirling around the water, tail spinning. But I can see the hesitation in her torso as she turns, the injury still tender.

"Kai took me on my first hunt today. I needed to get back in the water, and feel the tides beneath my fins. I told him if he tried to help me catch my prey, I would be having him for lunch."

"We wouldn't want that. Who would do all the heavy lifting around here?" I muse. Finally, letting my eyes roam from her, I look closer at what she's working on at the ledge of the cave. Strands of deep green sea vines are wound with tiny pink berries attached. "What are you working on?"

She looks down at her project and holds it up for me to see. Like garland, with tendrils of laced vines cascading down.

"It's for tonight. Just some decorations. You excited for the ceremony?" I swim closer to get a better look. Marina has really outdone herself. The garland is delicate and simple, yet full of detail.

"It's beautiful," I remark. "And, actually, I really am. I feel like I've missed so much of this culture that I need to make up for. Plus, on the island, the violet moon was never celebrated like the traditional moon. Just a night or two spent under the stars to view its visit. Which is odd because you would think its rare appearance should be more celebrated than the Full Celestia." Of course, my parents had no need for an occasion to fill my time during a violet moon like they did for a full moon. No worries of me accidentally slipping into the ocean to discover my legs have turned to fins.

Marina nods at my explanation, but her eyes tell me that our lack of attention to the rare viewing of the violet moon's appearance is strange, to say the least, and can't help but agree. Although the violet moon visits our sky twice a year, Marina explained that this night won't be like the others. When the violet moon passes over tonight, it will travel directly in front of the endless ring constellation, causing the large purple sphere to have a corona of stars surrounding it. Because they are so rare, I've never actually seen one myself, the last one occurring when I was just an infant. But the merpeople, having an extended lifetime, are bound to see its glory at least a few times while on this earth.

"You're going to love it. Honestly. And not only because of the stellar afterparty that I've planned."

I giggle as her smirk reveals nothing but wonder. Without prompting, I help her string the vines together and wind them up when we're finished as she tells me more about this violet moon and its importance to creatures of the sea.

We work together in silence for a few moments before she pulls something from her netted bag and slides it over to me. My hands falter for a moment when I realize what it is sitting in the small round disk. *Aquamarine.* A petite perfect stone, glimmering in the light filtering in through the rocks. I cup the disk in my hand as the stone rolls around, sparkling at every turn.

"For me?" I ask as I look at her, shocked to be gifted such a thing. Something that is traditionally so honorable and rare. I've seen plenty of mercreatures that have no stones to their name and I somehow have two. Marina smiles back at my uncertainty.

"Of course, for you. You saved my life and risked your own in doing so. I can never truly tell you how much that means to me." She grabs the tiny disk. "Here, let me."

I turn my head and she lines up the stone directly below the other that sits right beneath the point of my ear, and anchors it in. A sharp sting burns my ear for a second, but quickly subsides to a dull ache. I reach up to feel the stones, a small collection beginning to form. "Thank you," I whisper.

"My gratitude is yours, Cealene." She grabs my shoulders and pulls me into an embrace, squeezing my frame into hers. And for a moment, I still, not expecting the physical connection. But I wrap my arms around her small frame and hold her tight.

Night has fallen, and everyone is here for the ceremony. Pods from neighboring seas have come to partake in the ceremony as well, which I've learned is common for a violet moon celebration.

Calypso will be leading the ceremony tonight, but other pod leaders have led them in the past. I'm excited to see her in action and to experience this tradition. An array of merfolk mingle through the water, talking in low voices. To see this many of our kind in one place is dizzying. It still boggles me that not only do these creatures exist, but the number of us, even with the fertility curse, is almost unbelievable.

All of this time, the people of my island have no idea what lives beyond its shores, and what beauty thrives despite their defiled past. Some pods have donned elaborate headdresses for the occasion, and some carry spears and armor. It's a wonder how they traveled here in one piece. Seeing the variety of cultures is fascinating. I almost can't get enough. Despite our differences, the blood that runs through our veins is the same and that knowledge is humbling.

My thoughts come to a halt, along with the low chatter, when Brea blows the shell horn, creating a winded boom over the water. We turn our attention to Calypso, who has donned a spiked crown of shark teeth herself, as she begins.

"This day marks the beginnings of many things . . . as well as the end. It is the push and pull of time. Of balance. A time to rejoice and a time to reflect." She pauses, glancing around the cave as if to search every one of our faces.

"It is no coincidence that the great whales of the sea begin migration on this night. The same night when our violet moon visits our sky and the tides are highest. This night, we are reminded of who we are, of why we are here. We are the keepers of the sea. Protectors of the waters, and of everything in it. Including each other." Calypso's tail curls around the rock she is perched on like a snake strangling its prey. Her scales catch the dim light, giving shape to her form and the pattern of her tail. She looks every bit a sovereign as her voice bellows across the water. Her silver hair blows freely behind her.

"Let us witness the beauty that the Mother has created for us tonight. Let us show her our gratitude."

With that, we follow as Calypso dives deep from her rock and swims out of the caves.

We trail Calypso out into the open ocean, only peaks of black waves for miles, like inky lava molten in the heat. The dark line where sky meets sea is usually barely visible in the night, but tonight, doubling the size of our regular moon, the violet moon lights up the sky to an almost unnatural level. The cold wind tries desperately to blow the wet hair from my face as I float on the surface of the water, moving as one. Up and down. Like we are one entity, we move together with the waves, forever grateful that we are allowed to live in the ocean's glory. As we idle in the water, the violet moon illuminates our skin with a purple glow.

I was born under a violet moon, just like this one. I imagine my mother cradling me in the ocean as we basked in the purple glow. I picture us together in the elements, both our bodies craving the sea as our blood comes to life. I wonder if that is why we never made a big celebration of the violet moon. Because, to my mother, it means so much more to her than to anyone else. Maybe she prefers to honor it in her own way. How mediocre our Full Celestias must seem in comparison to this glorious glowing orb. The large purple moon seems to shine from within, and the sky is unusually bright like during a lightning storm where your skin crawls with anticipation of the next strike. When Calypso turns to us, flanked by Marina and Brea, we stop and form a line across the water as she begins to speak.

"White lilies grow where blood was once shed, where lives had been lost. They hold the memory in their veins. They hold the sorrow and the souls. Join me in remembering the many fallen soldiers we lost long ago." Calypso's voice carries over the open ocean, through the never-ending wind, echoing in my ears. A tiny wooden boat glides along in front of us, filled with white lilies. I watch as everyone takes one as it passes. When it nears the end of the line, I see that it is a thick log carved hollow from a spruce. The lines are smooth and sleek. The aroma from the lilies fills the crisp night air, giving it a floral sweetness that's foreign to the middle of the sea. I take the delicate flower from the arrangement and hold it above the water, admiring the specks of pollen dusting the inner petals.

Calypso raises her arms high up to the violet sky, the petals of the lily like a fallen star. She says what sounds like a small prayer, but her voice is too low for me to hear. Her prayer is not for us but for the dead. A moment later, dozens of arms are being raised in the same fashion, and I follow suit, feeling the cool water run down my arm like a stream, small bumps rising in the process from the cold delicate sensation.

As we bring the flowers down together, letting them float on the surface of the water, one by one they set forth in a row of white against the black sea. I watch as Calypso raises her palms up to the glowing sky and brings them together. She brings her palms to the water and the lilies trail one another out into the distance. A faint green glow follows each flower as it travels farther away. Each lily represents a fallen soldier from the sea wars and their souls moving on, sending them peace wherever they may be.

I try not to feel like an intruder in this world. Not to feel like I don't belong, but I'm still learning something that has been innate to merfolk for centuries. I glance at my sides, peering down the line, and see that some are weeping, Okiro being one. For such a brutish male, I would have never thought anything could bring him to tears. But it occurs to me that I really don't know what they endured during those days, fighting for their lives, or what memories Okiro, Kai, Calypso, and Brea had to battle to be here today to mourn their comrades in arms. The deep maroon of bloodied water, the metallic replacing the salt. I've seen the scars that cover their skin, which haunt their eyes. But I have no inkling of how they were created or what story lies beneath each mark. The only stories they ever share are ones of small happy moments between the blood and gore. Moments that bonded Okiro and Kai forever.

Marina told me that she was never on the front lines of battle, but by Calypso's side or tending to the injured. She used her mind, and working strategy, more than her body.

As I watch the endless ring constellation circle around the moon, I thank my lucky stars that I am a stranger to war and what it entails. Thankful that the Sea Wars were years before my time. I watch as Kai places a hand on Okiro's broad shoulder, which only makes him weep harder, bowing his head low. His shoulders hunch forward like a wilting flower. If these many years that have passed haven't dampened the sting of loss, then I fear no amount of time ever will. I ache for Okiro and everyone who had to fight to live those many years ago.

With another speech of remembrance from Calypso, we slowly change positions to float on our backs, staring up at the night sky as the moon compliments the ring of stars. I'm taking in the beauty above when the low ethereal hum begins to vibrate the water around me. The merpeople have begun to release their song in a melody that could never be matched on land. It sends chills down my spine as more voices harmonize with one another in layer upon layer of alluring echo. *A siren song*. The sound is so moving, I feel it deep in my chest. In my bones. As if my body is responding to the energy it holds. It sounds like stars, like diamonds, like bubbles. It's equal parts eerie and inviting. Light and dark. I find that I never want it to stop.

The song rises to a crescendo so powerful that my eyes prick with tears. As if this is the moon's coronation, and she's just been crowned queen of the sky. The stars' light coupled with the moon's glow causes hazy rays that shoot out in every direction like the icy sister to the sun.

Too soon the siren song ceases, calming the waters around us.

Slowly, we descend under the sea to complete the ceremony near the caves. Glowing jellies disperse from the area as we move through the water, lighting our paths like neon lanterns, pulsing to their own beat. The scene is more wondrous than any Full Celestia I've been to. If Ezera could see this, he wouldn't believe his own eyes.

The next part of the ceremony is all about balance, according to the quick lesson Marina gave while assembling the decorations earlier. Each time the violet moon soars over the endless ring constellation, our kind must give back for all that it takes—an offering to the Mother as a sign of good faith and gratitude, on the night when the violet moon is at one with the earth. Where the skies are perfectly aligned, it balances the scales of magic. We must sacrifice a part of ourselves so our wells of magic will be replenished. As the tide swells to its highest points, so do our wells.

Blood is the sacrifice we offer to the sea, to the Mother herself. Calypso begins the ritual by slicing her palm with a serrated shark's tooth. When she drags the tooth along the smooth skin, tendrils of dark blood emerge from her hand like twisted snakes. Her blood swirls and mixes with the sea, until she drags her hand through the water, dispersing the red until it disappears in a cloud of salt and blood. The tooth is passed down from one mercreature to the next. Blood fills the water around us in silence. Although my mouth is closed, I swear I can taste the metal of blood. As if the gills at my sides are filtering the liquid of life through my system.

When the shark fang makes its way to me, I take it from Kai with a hand I force not to shake. All eyes are on me as I make my sacrifice, slicing my palm in one fluid motion. The sting of pain sharpens my senses as I watch the prophetic blood leave my body and wonder how much will be required of me to break the curse. How much of my blood will be needed to free these wild creatures from their hold?

When everyone has completed the blood sacrifice, a strange thing happens. All of the small creatures below scatter, leaving the sea floor bare of any movement like they feel a shift of energy around them and know to scatter for what comes next. I was told many things would occur tonight, and to be ready for anything, but this is not what I expected in the least.

In the darkness, the sea floor appears gray, along with the rocks and coral. After a moment, the ground begins to shake, and the water around me pushes against my body like a vice. My eyes dart around at the others, but their faces are clear of fear. They only seem eager, engaged, and maybe a bit uncomfortable, which tells me that this is normal. That the pressure will stop before I implode. I hold on to that knowledge as I squash the panic that begins to rise with the growing pressure. All eyes are focused on the sea floor below us, so I look down in the darkness at what they are trying to see. And that's when I see it at last. The blood from each of us has gathered together above the sea floor in a spiraling circle, spinning like a sun with rays hovering around its center. The ground opens up beneath us, taking in the blood like a vault, drinking in our sacrifice until the last bit disappears into the sandy floor below.

My eyes nearly bug out of my head, watching this all unfold. I'm seeing it, but I still don't believe it. It's a literal sacrifice to the Mother, giving back to the earth for what it has given us. There's nothing metaphorical about it. The earth literally took in our blood in exchange for magic. I try to consider that these creatures have seen this time and time again but for me . . . I can't seem to believe my eyes, but I'm incredibly grateful to have been a part of it.

Humans have always known that magic lingers between the trees in the night or can be manipulated by the hands of a witch. But they do not have the means to use it themselves. Nor do they know that it can be used, for that matter. Humans have no idea what it can really do. What it can be. Like a living, breathing thing that surrounds us. That holds such power within it.

Calypso raises her arms for us to join her as she turns and swims to the caves to celebrate with food and drink. We swim together in a swarm of reflective scales and shadows in the darkness, an army of predators in the night.

Eighteen

As we enter the caves one by one, we break the surface to see the interior aglow with the neon algae and the pink glowworms hiding in the crevices of the rock. The garland Marina and I worked on earlier lines the walls of the cave, giving it a botanical feel. Everyone mingles around the rock outcroppings which hold shellfish and seaweed salads. Glasses of dark wine travel around the room, pilfered from an unlucky ship earlier this week.

I wasn't surprised when I heard Brea was put to the task, remembering what she said about close observations of the human world. Her ability to sneak in and out of a place undetected is uncanny, like a shadow in the dark. Just the other day she was telling me about these gold bangles she snatched off a Hollow Bones ship in the middle of the night. While the men were three sheets to the wind, she boarded the ship, completely unnoticed, and grabbed whatever she fancied. If it weren't the Hollow Bones she stole from, I might have felt a pang of pity for the poor ship, but the Hollow Bones deserve every foul bit of luck thrown their way.

From the way Brea speaks of the Aqualasians, you would think she walks among them. Lives in the villages with them. She must be incredibly stealthy to get so close to the lives of humans without being spotted, slipping into our waterways, and observing us from close quarters.

Music plays from somewhere within the caves, loud enough to be heard over the rushing of the waterfalls. I scan the area for the source and finally find it at the far corner of the caves. A small group of mermaids creates music with only their voices and a few instruments created from the sea.

Marina quickly finds me and hands me a glass as we make our way towards Calypso, who is conversing with merfolk from other pods. Whereas our pod typically forgoes finery, these creatures speaking with Calypso are bejeweled in glittering gold chains and bejeweled armor. They look beautiful and fierce, but it must challenge their movements as they travel through the sea.

As we near, Calypso spots our presence and extends her arm out to me as she says, "Thanks to my brave descendant, Cealene, change is upon us all." My cheeks heat at the attention as the strangers take me in. The weight of my fate to break this curse is starting to feel heavier than the weight of the crown. I should be used to this by now, the stares and expectations of strangers, but I'm not. The weight of their stares cracks my shell of confidence, exposing the soft interior within. "By the next violet moon ceremony, may we be free." The others nod and cheer, clinking their glasses to one another before taking in a heavy swig. Marina and I clink our glasses and drink deeply, knowing the end is near.

After Marina and I mingle for a bit, Kai and Okiro direct us to the party. Okiro looks much better than he did at the start of the night, his smile brighter than ever in the glow of the cave.

"Your favorite," Kai offers a fresh scallop still in its shell to Marina. She takes it into her clawed hand, her wicked smirk revealing the small dimple on her cheek.

"You remembered," she sings. "Are you trying to flatter me?" Marina tears the scallop from its shell and pops it into her mouth.

"Maybe," Kai teases. "Is it working?" He looks at her with glittering eyes, like he's just discovered light for the first time. She moans in pleasure as she chews the shellfish.

"Get me another one, and we'll see." With a wide grin, Kai saunters off in the water to the huge display of food Lyla prepared for the night, and I watch as the tattoo on his back bends with his movements—two massive harpoons crossing one another in an X on his back with a blazing sun behind it. Kai is a male that Angelina would refer to as *stupidly handsome.* The obvious kind that you could spot in a crowded room. I look to Marina who is outwardly ogling at his muscled backside while he fetches more snacks. She's shameless.

"Oh, you are so love-struck," I tease. My face breaks out into the biggest grin at her facial expression. Her eyebrows shoot to her forehead and the whites of her eyes are clearly visible with her mouth agape like a fish, betrayed by my comment.

"Am not!" she protests. But even Okiro can't help but laugh at her denial. Marina eyes him with a look that could kill. "Who needs another drink?"

Okiro raises a webbed finger, and I drain my glass in response. With that, she turns to grab more drinks, flicking her tail up to splash us on the way over. Which only makes us burst into more laughter. Splashing a mermaid with water is like tossing sugar on a cake. You can never have too much.

"So, your first violet moon ceremony. What did you think?" Okiro drains his glass. His side reveals the red ink that patterns his back and extends onto his shoulder. From what I can see, it's a tattoo of a trident trapped in a wave, coupled with the different phases of the moon. The dark red ink matches the maroon scales of his tail as if he had his true colors in mind when getting the art inked into his skin.

"It was incredible," I answer. "It's hard to believe I've lived my whole life on land, not knowing any of this existed. Every day I learn something new about life in the sea and every day I'm spellbound by it. Not even my wildest dreams could have conjured this up."

"I'd imagine I would feel the same had our roles been reversed. To me, it seems ignorant for humans to not remember our existence. To not have the faintest of idea that we may still be here."

His words send a small stab of pain to my chest, but he's right. How naïve we are to believe we are the only intelligent beings to exist. I nod, thinking of all he must have been through in his many years in the sea. I'm not sure of his age, but he's old enough to have lived through the Sea Wars, and that is plenty more years than I've had. What it must be like to have so many years of life behind you. To have so many more ahead. My eyes drift down to the ivory tooth that hangs from around his neck. Always adorning his person, like it is a part of him.

"Who's missing a canine?" I nod to his necklace, a beautiful contrast to his perfectly dark skin. He follows my gaze and looks down to the bone pendant, grabbing it in his palm.

"Believe it or not, it's actually from a crocodile that wandered into our territory looking for food." He leans an elbow on the stone before us, looking out at the crowded cave. "When I was just an adolescent, my brother and I were in the wrong place at the wrong time when we encountered it. Echo, my baby brother, took on the croc all on his own, thrashing in the shallow open waters. He saved my life and kept the fang as a souvenir." My brows raise in disbelief. How rare for a crocodile to wander into open waters to hunt. How unfortunate for Okiro and his brother.

"How lucky you are to have him as your brother."

"I was." He nods, and I catch the implication immediately. Suddenly my insides don't have enough room as my emotions grow. Okiro didn't need to tell me the story of how he got the necklace. He didn't need to share that part of himself with me. But he did. And that means something to me.

"Something tells me he was lucky to call you his brother as well." I smile at him, admiring the ivory tooth hanging from the chain.

"Maybe . . ." he counters. "It should have been me." Silver lines his eyes as they begin to well. "I was the eldest. I should have been protecting him. Not the other way around." Even without his words, his body language speaks volumes about how much this weighs on him. The guilt is like a shadow that never leaves.

Before I can tell him how it wasn't his fault, Marina returns with an entire fully corked bottle of rum in each hand just as Kai arrives with a whole tray of scallops.

"Who wants to take this party elsewhere?" Kai asks, brow raised in question.

"You don't even need to ask." Okiro's comment is barely heard as he puts down his glass on the rocky surface and is already diving below, his massive tail rippling a wave around us all. I look to Marina for more context, but she only smirks at me and says, "Oh, come on. That would ruin the surprise," and dives in after Okiro, bottles in hand. Kai dumps the tray of scallops into a netted bag and tells me to follow his lead. We dive below the surface and I follow his dark shadowed figure through the sea.

As we pass through the cave tunnels and out near the mountains of coral and seaweed, I notice the glowing jellies still lingering around the area, lighting the way through the darkness. Not that we need it.

Our night vision allows us to see figures and depth, but the slight glow certainly helps.

When Kai begins to slow, I know exactly where we are. The Grotto. The rock outcropping that arches above the water, creating bridge-like structures that seem to defy gravity. As we break the surface, I see that the violet moon has found space in the sky with the traditional moon, lighting up the night. I watch as Kai pulls himself up the arched rock, perching himself on a ledge high above the water. Others are already there, tails swaying from the rocks, or curling around its structure. Laughter bounces off the water like sprinkles of rain hitting a tile floor.

I hoist myself up and clamber to a small alcove near Brea and Marina. No wonder these sea creatures have toned, built upper bodies. Hoisting myself up with just my arms is nearly impossible. My tail weighs a ton and without the water giving me that weightless feeling, my muscles quiver under the pressure.

Bottles are passed around as we admire the millions of stars above and watch as the violet moon fills the sky for only a few more hours, leaving the traditional moon to take over in its absence. It's only a few days before the next full moon appears. The one that will change the course of our lives if I get it right.

As the bottles get lighter and lighter with each pass, I listen as everyone swaps stories of past ceremonies and pod gossip. In this moment, I look around and know that there is nowhere else in the world I would rather be. Nowhere else in the world that I feel more like myself. I belong to the sea. Her music of waves lulls me. Her sea salt washes me with clarity. My body is most alive when I am here. It pains me to think that I couldn't imagine going back to life as a human right now. Legs would be foreign to me. The lack of fluidity, the etiquette of acting a certain way. *The promise of a crown and a kingdom.*

Commotion stirs my thoughts as I watch Kai push off the rock with his hands and dive head-first into the dark sea. Midway he tucks his tail around his body into a ball and spins midair. Before he hits the water, he uncurls his body, straight as an arrow, and drops in. Okiro follows after, diving off the top of the rock arch, arms out wide in a T before spearing into the water at rapid speed, disappearing into the black abyss with barely a sound.

"Here we go," Brea says as others begin freefalling into the black mass below, giving me the notion that this isn't the first time this lot has done this. Pushing fear aside, I look down at my friends swimming about, as my hair curls around me in the wind, reminding me how high above sea level I am. As my hands grip the rocky edge of the alcove in anticipation, sandy pebbles stick to the fresh wound on my palm. I push off the feeling of gravity taking its hold and dive in. Living life as it should be. *Wild and free.*

Nineteen

That night I sleep a dreamless sleep, deep and undisturbed. And I can't quite remember the last time that occurred. My nights are typically filled with many dreams. One rolling into the next. Endless scenes play in my head the entire slumber. Sometimes when I wake, I have to take a moment to let the lingering thoughts from the dreams settle, to remind myself that they weren't real. Most of them leave me feeling confused and out of place. My mind feels more exhausted from the pseudo-memories playing in my mind the whole night than before I fell asleep in the first place.

But last night was different. Last night, my sleep was undisturbed and as black as the sea. It left me feeling a little more levelheaded this morning as I made my way out of the caves and into the deep blue. And with my newfound clarity, I realized something from last night. Living in the ocean, you can't grow roots in the water as you can on land. You can't anchor your life into the soil beneath and hang on tight to the comforts of home. In the ocean, you are fluid and free to move as you please, with nothing holding you in place, tugging you back. That is the lure to living wild and free. The freedom to just *be* and move where the waves take you.

Limitless.

The water seems crystal clear and smooth today. Like the violet moon from last night lulled all of the currents to sleep. With Ezera and I not meeting again until tonight, I decided to spend my morning at my willow. It might very well be the last time I can make this trip before we begin our journey to Ember Island to break the curse, and I need to visit Alana again before I do. I think she can answer some questions I've been having as of late. Whatever comes our way, and whatever happens on that island, I want to visit my willow one last time before I go.

I pass a school of yellow-striped fish, and they part down the middle, swimming around me before meeting again in a cloud of yellow and black. A part of me has been avoiding my favorite place because of my last encounter with the Lady of the Lake. After hearing her story and feeling the parallels between the two of us, I was ashamed to feel a connection with her. To have any similarity at all to someone like her, so sad and alone. But I felt her pain, nonetheless, and as forlorn as her story is, it isn't mine. She could use a friend, someone to talk to. What kind of leader would I be if I left her there abandoned and alone?

I still get chills every time I think about the years I spent here sitting in my willow without ever realizing I wasn't alone. It just goes to show that perspective is everything.

I swim through the dark tunnel, my eyes adjusting to the absence of light, and quickly emerge into the vast opening of the pool, light spilling out from above. Looking around the edges of the water for the Lady of the Lake, I stop short at an all too familiar noise from above. *A voice.*

Someone is here.

And not the ethereal creature that lives here, but a human. A woman.

Adrenaline courses through me as I duck behind the shadows cast over the pool where the dense forest is thickest. Willing my nerves to calm from fear of the unknown, I take a moment to compose myself and break the surface. Emerging only enough for my eyes to see over the water. I grab onto a tree root that has grown into the side of the pool for stability when I see a woman kneeling at the base of my willow. Her head bows forward enough that I can only see her back and shoulders covered with a maroon cape. As her voice carries over the water, it hits me like a blow to the chest.

I know that voice. I know it better than I know my own. It was the first sound I heard coming into this world. It was the voice that lulled me to sleep every night as a child. It's the voice I hear in my head when I'm in need of direction.

That's my mother's voice.

What could she be doing here? And how does she know about this place? I've never once seen her here at the willow, let alone anywhere near the forest behind the palace grounds. What reason would a queen have for traipsing around in the forest?

I lean forward as if that will give me an advantage of hearing her more clearly, but her voice is quiet and sounds a bit shaky. She tilts her head back, looking up at the big, beautiful tree, and I dare to move closer.

"I know your life in the palace hasn't been an easy one. I know your father and I have put a tremendous amount of pressure on you, and I know how much you loathe the court. But I also know this is your favorite place besides at sea."

Her voice strikes a chord in me, breaking down any and all barriers surrounding my heart and soul. My eyes well and my throat constricts at her words, at her presence so near. The anger I've felt for my parents these past few weeks dissipates into nothing the instant I hear her voice. As my mother speaks to this tree as if it were me, it seems like she is grieving, and then I realize that she doesn't think she will ever see me again. She doesn't believe that I will come home. And her main concern isn't for the crown, or for what the future of the kingdom will hold, but is for me. She's terrified she'll never see her child again.

Sorrow and shame heat my face as I watch my mother kneel beneath the willow, its green vines swaying around her. Her figure looks so small at the trunk of the tree.

"Everything I have ever done since you came into my life has been for you. Always for you. I know you might not believe it or might not fully understand why we kept this from you, but you must know it was a decision not made lightly. It was a choice that hurt but a choice that needed to be made. I never wanted you to be someone others might use to get what they needed. I never wanted you in a situation that blurred your future. If I could take your place, I would. I would lay my life down for you over and over again if it meant securing your safety."

Tears roll down my face in rivulets disappearing into the pool as the sorrow spills over. Her voice is gravelly as she speaks through thick emotion, and I can barely stand the sight of my mother in turmoil. She was the one who protected me as a child, who made sure I was safe. If she crumbles, so does the world around me. So does that feeling of security mothers provide for their children. I wish I could emerge from the shadows. But I can't. If I do, I fear that I won't go through with the curse breaking. That I will use my mother as a crutch. I will fall into her arms and let her take me to safety. I will leave all of those beautiful creatures of the sea stuck, with no future. I will abandon them. Abandon Marina.

I can't do that.

I won't.

I don't trust that I can make myself known to my mother. I don't trust that I can see her and not run to the safety of her arms. I also cannot trust that she won't make the decision for me and haul me away from my fate.

I have to do this. I have to break the damn curse that has plagued an entire species for years and years. I am part human, and for that, I feel partially responsible. It would be cruel to abandon my fate now after feeding them hope. It would be cruel to them and to myself. I am not a coward. I am better than that.

"Cealene, my baby. If you can somehow hear me out there, I love you. More than anything in this world. More than you will ever truly know. Please come home." My mother barely gets out the last of her words before crumbling into a mess of sobs that rack her body as she bows her head beneath the willow. I squeeze my eyes shut, willing the pain in my chest to go away. To subside.

"Merla, dear. Come on. Let me take you home." My father's deep voice fills the air and my eyes spring open. He kneels beside her in the soft, mossy grass and places his hands over her shoulders. I watch as he brushes a strand of hair away from her brow. Two guards stand at a distance as their mares drink from the flowing stream.

"Did we do the right thing? Keeping it from her?" My mother pleads as she looks up into his soft tawny eyes, as if they hold all of the answers in the world.

"We did our best. We are to protect her, always. And that is what we did." He pulls her into his embrace, his cape enveloping them both. "Do you remember the night she was born? Out in the sea under the violet sky . . . thousands of stars winking to life? I told you not to go out that night, but you were so adamant that the sea was where you needed to be." My mother nods, resting her head on his shoulder as they huddle at the base of the willow. I duck further into the shadows as they talk.

"The baby was so restless all morning. Kicking and squirming. The muscles surrounding her contract the entire day. I knew she would settle in the sea. I knew she needed it, as I did. I could feel it in my veins, like a pull from within me." As my mother talks, my father nods as if remembering the story for himself.

"Once you made up your mind, I knew there was no stopping you."

"I should have come back to shore when the tides shifted. I knew better. Knew something was wrong . . . but the pain. It was crippling. I couldn't fight the sea. All I could do was hold on to that crescent rock. It was like the tide was trying to take her from me. Like the sea lured me there to claim her as its own."

"But you would never let that happen."

"Never." She says the words with fervor. "Even when that wicked silver-haired creature came to reveal the prophecy. Claiming she must take my baby. Humph." My mother chuckles to herself. "Over my cold dead body."

My jaw nearly drops to the pool floor when I hear my mother mention Calypso. Salt water pours into my mouth agape with shock. Calypso tried to take me as a newborn. I was probably still connected to my mother. Wicked, indeed. That is how my parents knew about the prophecy. About my fate. That is why they kept the secret from me my entire life, why they created the Full Celestia celebrations. I should have known my mother had encountered Calypso at some point. How else would she have heard of my fated future?

I watch as my father helps his queen to her feet, and they walk hand in hand towards the guards and their mares saddled for the journey back home to Pearle Castle.

As they disappear into the distance, I realize that I forgive them for the lies. For the secrecy. I forgive them for doing the only thing they have ever tried to do—protect me. To shelter me from harm. I will not fault them for loving me too much. For trying to keep the weight of this curse from crushing down on my shoulders. But there is no going back now. And I don't *want* to. I want to help these magnificent creatures. I want to help my friends. I will see my parents again, soon. But first I must meet my fate.

Twenty

Once my mother and father left the forest, I removed Atargatis from my back and emerged from the water, hoisting myself into my trusted crook in the willow. Lying along the thick branch, I watch my tail sway with the vines while I contemplate where I go from here. I know I cannot abandon my parents or my duty to the crown. I also refuse to lose this part of myself. The merblood in me has always been there. It cannot be denied, and now that I know what this life entails, now that I know what I truly am inside and out, there is no going back. There is no forgetting the last few weeks. And what about Ezera? Can I have a relationship with him in this form? No.

So, the question I really should be asking myself is what do I want more? What can I not live without?

My thoughts are halted by the slush of water, and I pick my head up from the branch, curls dragging through the coarse bark. My claws grip the tree tightly as I lean over, less steady with a tail than with legs.

"You're lucky to have a mother who loves you so fiercely." The Lady of the Lake—Alana—emerges from the pool, that ethereal voice sending shivers down my spine. Again, her features strike me as she approaches, gliding through the water. I try not to stare at her double tail from above, but the effort is lost. Each half moves in tandem with each other. Not quite like legs but not quite like a mermaid's either. Her pale skin glows in the sun as she turns her flawless face up to me.

"I am." I sit up straighter, glad that she's come to visit. I knew she would be here. She's always been here. But, still, her presence startles me.

"I've always wondered what that feeling must be like. To experience a bond that's stronger than anything in the world. To have a visceral connection that is stronger than a lover."

"What bond?" I ask. Her words sound disjointed as if she's speaking in riddles.

"Motherhood, of course." She says it so matter-of-factly. I almost feel embarrassed for not immediately understanding. "I think I would have enjoyed being a mother." Her long lashes blink with a pained expression, and I remember the first time we met. The story she told me of the king and his sword. Of how she felt for him and was cast out because of it. I look down at her from the willow, admiring her intricate crown of braids atop her head, in place of the crown she will never have.

"Did the king ever come to visit you? After you were . . . sent here?"

"Ha." Her laugh is humorless, hard with years of resentment. "Once my people decided my fate, I was as good as dead to him. His love was conditional and I didn't meet the standards." She was once a different person before she was isolated for so long. It must do something irreversible to the mind, to be alone for so long. As much as I love my solitude, I wouldn't want it forever.

"I'm sorry," I offer, not knowing what else to say to make her sorrow ease. She turns away from me, looking out towards the stream that feeds into the pool.

"I should have known. Falling for humans must run in our blood. Seeing what my sister's actions did to the world should have been enough to teach me."

I look at her curiously, never thinking of the possibility that this creature could have close family, ones that abandoned her here for the rest of her days. Or maybe they're gone. Maybe they have long since turned to sea foam. But before I can ask, she offers up more.

"You know the Sea Wars was a direct result of Calypso's stupidity." With that, I look at her dumbfounded. She is saying that Calypso is her . . . sister? Her elder sister, if timing plays a factor in their stories. How could Calypso allow such a thing to be done to her sister when she, herself, knows that you cannot choose who you fall for? I knew Calypso was a sharp edge of a female, but this is just plain cruel. The Sea Wars must have hardened Calypso's heart to unimaginable levels. Levels that made her forget her own weakness, if you can even call it that.

A thought suddenly appears in my mind as I remember what Alana said. She said falling for a human must run in our blood. The same blood that runs through her veins runs through Calypso's . . . runs through mine. This creature is my ancestor too. Immediately I think of Ezera and reject the notion that this tragic flaw could be inherited altogether.

Alana must see the contemplation on my face because after a moment she asks, "Someone on land gripping your heartstrings?"

Heat floods my face, but I push it down, not wanting to be so easily read. "No. I—"

She stops me with a raised hand. "No need to explain. You owe me nothing." As strange as this creature is, I can't help but like her. Maybe. . . we could be friends.

I shake my head to the side, wondering if I've been up here too long.

"See you around, Princess."

"Wait!" I sit up from the branch and dive into the bright pool below, barely making a splash. As I submerge into the water, my body becomes more alive. I break the surface before she has a chance to disappear around the bend. Her eyes are already on me, curious as to what I want from her.

"I was thinking, maybe we could talk."

"What would we talk about?" She swims towards me, her interest piqued.

"The Sea Wars, what it was like to live through such a thing. What it was like growing up with Calypso for a sister. What fills your time these days? Anything, really."

"So you want to get to know me." It isn't a question.

"I do."

"Well, the first thing you must understand is that I've been here a very long time, which means I have had a very long time to think about the world and my place in it. To think about what I'd do differently if I had the chance."

"Like what?"

"Well, for starters, I would have never asked my pod for their blessing to live on land." She leans back, floating on the surface of the water. "That was my first mistake." She closes her eyes, lashes fluttering. "Or maybe my first mistake was falling for the king in the first place."

"I don't think one can control that sort of thing." That's what makes love so irrevocable.

"Unfortunately for us all, you are right about that." As she floats around the cerulean pool, I relax a bit, swimming in lazy circles.

"I would have left my life in the sea without a word. Silently, never mentioning where I was going or who I was going with. Then they might have thought that I died or swam away to a new ocean. Nevertheless, once I was the king's bride, they would have no hold over me. I would have been free to live happily."

"Would you have missed your sister, if you lived a life on land instead?" I don't realize I've asked the question more for myself until I hear it out loud. Her laugh comes immediately and I cringe knowing what comes next.

"My sister is a foul creature. Always was. When we were just young merlings, she would find pleasure in slicing the tails off of sharks. Said she was saving the sea turtles from a gruesome death. But I saw the look in her eyes. The way they glistened when the shark would flail as it dropped to the sea floor. The way she would watch as other sea creatures feasted on it before it took its last breath. Gills fluttering to a close for the last time."

A sick feeling fills my bones as bile rises to my throat.

"I think it was her only way to mask her tendencies. To disguise it as merciful instead of calling it what it was."

"And what was that?"

She stops to turn to me before speaking. "Wrong."

The feeling in the pit of my stomach sits uneasily at the thought. To purposefully maim a creature like that and then to watch it suffer. That is not the Calypso I know. That is not the fearless leader who taught me how to hunt, how to breach the water like I was flying.

"You don't believe me." Again, it is not a question.

"No, I do. It's just . . . the person you described doesn't exactly match the person I've met."

"Well, my sister has always been exceptionally good at trickery of all kinds. She's always been skilled at hiding her darkest parts, distracting the world with her fierce beauty and perseverance." Alana's eyes bore into mine with a strength that makes me want to look away, the intensity almost too much for me to take. It is then that I notice the resemblance between the two sisters. Their eyes are strikingly similar, not the color so much as the shape. The big bold pupil with the perfectly curved slant of their eyelid lifting to a point at the edges.

"Stop at the trenches just beyond the mangrove forest before you head back. There's something I think you should see."

The look on Alana's face makes me hesitant, like I may not want to see what she would like me to. I try to push the possibilities that swirl in my head away and instead nod, taking the information in.

I try to work Alana's opinion into my thoughts of Calypso and all that she's been through. The war, the loss of her child, and her lover. In a way, she lost her freedom too. Freedom to swim along ships and interact with humans as she once did. But then how could she possibly turn around and do the same thing to her own sister if she knows the feeling so intimately? How could she want to spread that loss?

None of it makes sense. But I do believe Alana. What purpose would she have to lie? This new information about Calypso doesn't change my decision to break the curse. It isn't about Calypso. It's about Marina and Kai and me and Alana. And all of the merfolk who are left.

I ask Alana about the Sea Wars and what Aqualasia was like then, about what she fills her days with now. I ask her if there's any part of her that fancies the willow as I do, which she informs me she does. She tells me about how the Sea Wars tore everyone and everything apart, how no mercreature nor human was ever the same after.

She speaks of her time here like it's chipped away at her sanity one day at a time. With each word, my heart reaches out to her more and more. I have to figure out how to free her from this prison. There must be something Calypso can do.

I don't tell Alana about my mission to ask Calypso about freeing her sister. I don't want to give her false hope if nothing can be done. But I refuse to believe that. I will find a way to free Alana from this unfair captivity.

We say our goodbyes and I watch as the Lady of the Lake turns from me as she sinks lower into the cerulean pool and I watch the small ripples expand from where she dipped below the surface. The circles grow larger and larger until they reach the edges of the pool and disappear into the land.

I waste no time grabbing my harpoon and darting through the tunnel that leads me back out into the ocean, having a new curse to break.

When I spill out into the open waters, I slow down, taking my time. I decide to hunt on my way to the trenches before I head back to the caves, but as soon as I begin tracking a school of yellowfins, a shadow appears from above, blocking the sun rays that beam down through the water. Without looking up, I know I've been caught below a ship, ruining my meal. Abandoning the fish, I dart to the right, careful to avoid any potential nets trawling behind. I pump my tail, sending me out of harm's way and back into the rays piercing the waves. I descend further to be sure I'm not spotted from the ship and watch as the dark belly of the boat passes by, pushing through the water, and creating a wake that ripples out from its path.

Once it passes, I take a different path, entering the underwater forest that spreads south of the mangroves. The plant life here is incredible. Trees like large mushrooms pock the sea floor, shadowing the sandy bottom like huge umbrellas. Other trees shoot out from the sea floor extending skyward for days, olive-colored algae hanging from their branches like wet clothes on a line. Sea turtles filter through the plant life at a leisurely pace, floating through the copse. The further in I get, the darker the forest seems to be.

Gliding through the sea grass and kelp, I notice where the sea floor begins to crack, creating a sort of opening—the trench. I peer into the crack but see only blackness. What is it that Alana wanted me to see?

I swim farther along the trench line as it opens up, a bit of light filtering in from above. This part of the trench seems to be filled with something, the void no longer there, and a shuttering chill wracks through my body. I mark the quiet stillness that surrounds me and realize this place of the ocean seems...*disturbed* in some way, like it's been tampered with, or altered by an outside force.

Pushing past the feeling, I swim closer, getting a better look as I grab Atargatis from my back, holding it at the ready and nearly combust when the figures come into view. Small bubbles escape my lips as my lungs constrict to near pain. I dart away from the opening, pushing away with my hands and kicking my tail, sending me backward. Sending me farther away until I am in a tangle of seaweed.

Bodies.

Human bodies.

Dozens upon dozens of corpses.

This trench is a mass grave . . . of pregnant women. Hundreds of pregnant women. Swollen bellies protrude from the bloated figures layering one another. Farther beneath, I see the stark ivory of bone. Some mouths are agape in a silent scream, eyes wide in a forever panic. Soulless, decaying bodies piled on top of one another, haphazard and forgotten. Pale skin flutters with the waves of the water, shredded and atrophied, like wet tissue. I vomit up seaweed and fish into a cloud in front of me. My mind spins for an explanation, for how this could be, and land on Alana. She wanted me to see this, she knew something was here despite being trapped in the pool on the island for years.

Why?

How did these bodies get here? Why are they all with child? To think of the little body decaying inside each of these corpses makes me want to tear my own skin off. My muscles seize and spasm at the sight. My hands tremble and I want to cry, but no tears ever come, for I am a mermaid, and our tears are nothing but seawater, making the pain all the more unbearable. Carnivorous fish feast on the fresher bodies at the top of the trench and my stomach threatens to spill again. My instincts kick in as my eyes dart around the forest for any other signs of life. Besides the animals that surround me, no human or mermaid seems to be around but me. How could this happen? Who would do such an unforgivable, heinous thing? And why?

Why?

Why?

Why?

Bile rises in my throat and the gills at my sides constrict. I look around at the dozens of bodies and see that they are all at different stages of decay. Some are mere bones, ivory skeletons a stark contrast to the darkness of the shadowed trench. Some are fresh with bloat. Clothing still intact, hair swaying around a frozen face.

Without a second thought, I dart from the forest trench as fast as my fins will take me, into the open ocean and beyond. I pump my tail as fast as I can, water pulling through my hair, and I head straight for the caves. Straight to Calypso.

Clouds of fish scatter as I swim through the reef and rock surrounding the cave tunnels. I see a few mermaids lingering about the coral, hunting. I pass them in a blur as I swim through the largest opening of the cave, bile still burning my throat at the thought of what I saw. Those poor women, holding the gift of life inside of them. Holding so much hope in their hearts. The most precious, innocent thing there is. To think of the families that never saw their wives, mothers, sisters, or daughters again. They just never came home—

Oh my stars, the flyers of the missing women. They were all with child. That was the connection. I wouldn't have known it from just a portrait of their faces, but if I had only investigated harder. If I had gone to visit each family member of those women, I would have discovered it. The drawn portraits of those women must have cost the families a couple of months' wages to be made, but it wasn't just the women they were searching for. It was the unborn child as well.

I know Alana is not responsible for this. Not only did she want me to find this trench, but she has been stuck on the island for years. These murders haven't been occurring that long, so how did she know they were there? What made her send me there? Did she know about my mission to solve the mystery? Did she see me pouring over the flyers?

This heinous act was deliberately carried out by someone. A serial murderer. Essentially mass genocide. To take a life is bad enough, but to take two? To take dozens? I can't begin to comprehend this fully. My mind spins and spins.

My heart cracks in two. Those were my people down there, and I failed them. *We* failed them. My father and I. I should have pushed harder—demanded more attention to the flyers. If my father knew this was where the mystery led, he would double the guards in the towns. He would send ships out to monitor passing travelers. Investigate this nightmare.

When I breach the surface inside the cave, it almost shocks me to see everyone going about their business as usual when something so horrific is lying miles away in a trench in our ocean. I have to remind myself I am the only one who saw the nightmare. None of them even know it exists, except Alana. Or do they?

"Cealene! I've been looking for you!" Marina calls me over to the waterfall, so cheery and bright, compared to what swirls inside my head. I hesitate before heading over to her, not wanting to waste another minute before telling Calypso about the trench. She and Brea lounge beneath the tumbling water. Before I can even open my mouth, Marina reads my face, detecting the worry that spreads across my eyes. She sits up, splashing the water around her waist. "What is it?" she demands and my eyes begin to well.

"I . . . there's . . ." I can't seem to get the words out. Or maybe I don't know how to put what I saw into words. Maybe something so monstrous shouldn't be put into words at all. Now Brea leans closer to me, my worry spreading to her too.

"What is it, Cealene? Are you okay? Are you hurt?" Marina's voice borders on hysteria, and I feel guilty for causing her panic. Brea rests a hand on my arm, peering into my eyes, "Take a breath. Tell us what happened." Her touch sends a jolt of calm through me and I gather my thoughts.

"I was swimming through a sea forest, south of the mangroves, and I came across a trench. It was filled with . . . bodies." I take a breath, willing my voice to stop shaking. "They were human. Females with child. It looked like dozens of them . . ." My voice trails off. Marina's slender fingers shoot to her mouth, covering her lips in disbelief.

Brea's eyes meet Marina's as she says, "Calypso. Now." Marina nods but doesn't seem to trust herself to speak.

Brea leads the way to Calypso's room in the caves, adorned with wicked things from the sea. A shark's skull. A trident made of steel and bone. A crown of eel teeth. And bone structures that look a little bit too much like human femurs for my liking. It's smart, I suppose, to use a discarded skeleton for building, but given the circumstances, it hits a little too close to home at the moment.

As we approach, I see her lounging in the small pool below the trickling waterfall. Her onyx tail spills over the edge, scales reflecting green in the dim light. When she sees us approaching with such urgency, she puts down her freshly sharpened dagger and rock.

"Something's happened," she predicts, her voice stern. Brea takes over, presumably knowing that Marina and I can barely contain ourselves long enough to explain the story once again. When Brea finishes, Calypso eyes us all in contemplation.

"Where were you *exactly*, Cealene?" Calypso's honey-coated voice calms me enough that I can recall my trip through the sea forest and exactly where I saw the trench. I told her about the ship from above and the bodies all piled on top of one another like layers of a fresh catch stacked in a wooden barrel. Calypso's glowing green eyes widen as she takes in my story. Her claws tighten around the hilt of the dagger as I finish answering her questions. Disgust curls her lips when she says to me, "Take me there."

I lead the way out of the caves and into the open sea as Calypso follows close behind, Brea and Marina flanking her on either side. Together we make our way past the mangroves and into the sea forest. We pass the mushroom-domed trees and filter through the tall ropes of kelp and seaweed shooting up towards the surface. Nausea roils my belly as we near the trench once again. If I never saw this place ever again, it would be too soon. But twice in one day . . . I cannot.

As soon as we get close enough to where the sea floor begins to open up and crack, I pause, not wanting to go any farther. I feel Marina halt beside me as the water whooshes past my shoulder, billowing my hair around me. I point ahead to where the dark trench opens up near the cracked coral patch and the sea grasses swaying around its edges.

Calypso swims ahead, dagger in hand, and Brea trails close behind her. Marina places her hands on my shoulders, giving me a reassuring squeeze before passing me and following. I stay behind, idling in place as they search the dark opening of the sea floor. I watch as they near the wide berth of the trench and peer in, getting a closer look. As soon as Marina makes out the figures she jolts back, just as I did, and turns her body away, her dark hair swirling behind her from the movement. Brea's claws come out feeling a threat, but no one is here to attack. Whoever did this is long gone now. The only things left behind are the hundreds of bodies in this underwater necropolis.

Calypso swims the perimeter, inspecting their faces and bodies. She looks around the trench opening, inspecting the sea grass and the brush as if to look for clues of who might be behind this. Trail marks, netting, anchors, tracks. But from her body language, it doesn't seem that she's come up with anything of use. After a few more moments of looking around the area, she nods for us to head out, and she leads us back home.

When we surface just outside the caves, we beach ourselves on the small sandy shore. Waves rush in, causing white frothy bubbles to line the shore with every crest. The sun peeks through the big puffy clouds, creating moments of direct sunlight on the beach. Crabs hurry along the sand in their sideways dance, avoiding the tide rushing in as they gather food. Brea looks like she's just seen a ghost, the warmth of her skin leeched away, and Marina hasn't stopped crying since we surfaced. Silent tears roll down her iridescent cheeks in succession. My hands still shake uncontrollably, so I fiddle with the straps of my harpoon in hopes of masking it.

"I'm going to put the word out to our neighboring pods to see if anyone has come across this trench before. Maybe someone has information. Though I doubt it is an act of the past. Some of those bodies near the top seem to be much too fresh for my liking." Anger floods Calypso's face as she speaks, but she doesn't look us in the eye. She just glances out at the sea, as if it might offer some answers.

I know how hard this must be for Calypso. She has been trying for years and years to bring fertility back to her kind, for her people, and herself, and someone out there is just throwing it away as if life has no value at all. I don't tell her that Alana urged me to visit the trench. It would only deepen the bad blood between them if I brought it up to her now. I would have to explain visiting my willow and how I came to meet Alana. My loyalty to my new friend tells me to let it lie. It's not like the information as to how I came across the trench is important anyway. It doesn't help us find the culprit.

"We will figure this out." I can't help but feel like her words don't hold much hope. She doesn't think we can find who is doing this and I'm not sure I disagree. I nod to her, not wanting to push any further. Maybe I can ask Ezera to help. Maybe he can ask around the docks to see if anyone's ever heard of anything strange going on near the trench. But if this has been going on for years and no one has detected it yet . . . I don't have much hope.

"I don't understand," Brea says. "It has to be by the hands of a human right? They must be capturing women on land and bringing them to the same coordinates of the sea to drop them there. Or diving down from a boat with the bodies? I've heard some humans can deep dive up to several meters. Hold their breath for up to twenty minutes." Her voice trails off as she contemplates her thoughts. "But why? Why would anyone want to harm these females? What purpose would it serve to anyone?"

"I don't know . . ." Marina's voice sounds distant. Almost a whisper, as she too looks out at the water for answers. Of all the things to bring to these three females, this is by far the worst I could ever dream of. A group of females who have been cursed with infertility have been presented with the tragedy of dead mothers. Guilt coats my insides for making them endure it.

But I couldn't keep it to myself. Someone needed to know in hopes of stopping it from happening again. The more who know about it, the better chance we have of stopping it.

I keep my plan of going to Ezera with this to myself, knowing how Calypso feels about mingling with humans. She wouldn't trust any intel that came from him anyway.

When we hear a ship near, we dive into the frothy waves and descend deep into the sea. Calypso turns left towards the reefs to hunt, while the rest of us swim lower, into the caves. As we surface from the water, Brea heads over to Lyla and the others to ask if they've ever come across the trench, while Marina and I head to the males, wielding weapons in preparation for the trip to Ember Island.

As Marina tells the males about the trench, I look up at the jagged rock wall that serves as the armory for the pod. Tridents and harpoons line the inner wall, along with daggers and swords. Some are made from materials from the sea, and some are clearly stolen from land, pieces that can only have been made by a blacksmith. These must have been treated with water manipulation to keep them from rusting in this environment.

Whether they were pilfered from ships or lost to the sea unintentionally, the one clear thing is that the steel swords with a golden inlay, adorned with jewels were not made by the hands of any sea creature. Some of these pieces even look like they could have come straight from Pearle Castle, from the royal guard's armory in the eastern wing. I don't dare ask about it. I'd rather not know. But my father has been aware of the slick and sinister pirates that sail the seas, and he's aware of their schemes and tactics. Some of these weapons have made it into the hands of pirates before finding their way here in the merfolk armory.

Admiring the wall of shining armor is a much-needed distraction as Marina recounts the story of our visit to the sea forest and what lies within the dark trench. The males put down their tools and stare at us both, wide-eyed and concerned.

Kai reaches out, grabbing Marina's hand. "I'm so sorry you had to see that." The gesture is sincere and heartfelt, his hand engulfing hers. I don't know how much Marina and Kai have talked about their future and what it holds once this curse is broken, but I do remember her words on the Island of Bones. I do remember her desire to become a mother. And Kai must know at least that much because he sees what this must have done to her.

Where sorrow and worry fill Kai's face, only wrath and anger fill Okiro's. "What kind of sick individual would ever dream of doing such a thing? Repeatedly." He shakes his head in disbelief, eyes closed. "If what you say is true, about the amount of bodies, and the varying levels of decay, it has to be a group. There is no way one person could be doing this alone. There must be some sort of clan out for some kind of vengeance. I just don't see the motive." He picks up an iron hatchet with engraved symbols on the handle and continues sharpening it with more effort and strength than he had been before. Anger flutters the muscles in his jaw as he works in silence.

"Calypso said she will alert the other neighboring pods to keep an eye out, but I don't have much hope in that," I explain, looking over to Marina. "If it's gone undetected for this long, they must have a pretty good system for staying under the radar."

"Unless we set up a system to oversee the area. Between the surrounding pods and us. We could monitor in intervals." A light sparks in Okiro's deep-set eyes as he explains. Marina nods in agreement.

We leave the males to their work and Marina heads out to her sunken ship, needing to clear her head. I also think she wanted to leave her mark on the ship one last time before we head out for Ember Island tomorrow.

Because Calypso plans to leave at first light, Ezera and I are meeting tonight to talk one last time before I go. I'm itching to tell him about the trench to see if he can get any more information about it on land. Especially working at the docks, he has a much higher chance of hearing something, even if it's a myth told between sailors at the saloon in town.

I decided to help Lyla prepare an array of foods we can take on the trip with us. Although we will hunt along the way to keep us fed, the long treks through the open ocean will be gaps of time where traveling towards the coasts or reefs to find food will slow us down. We certainly aren't going to take down a whale in the open ocean while traveling the seas. So as a precaution, Lyla is making each of us a few things that we can pack with us. We're also bringing a few medicinal items in case of emergency, which gives me pause. I know this journey won't be easy and I know it won't even be the most dangerous part, but I'm hoping nothing unexpected occurs in the next few days. Breaking the curse without any surprises will be enough of a challenge as it is.

Working side by side with Lyla has calmed my nerves and put some much-needed distance from memories of the trench. Something about her emits a sense of peace. There is a serene aura about her and wherever she is, whatever she passes, it infects her surroundings with that same calming aura. It's intoxicating.

As night falls and the sea gets dark, I make my way to the mangroves on high alert. The trip has become second nature to me now, but traveling a distance like this at night is a bit of a risk for anyone, especially for someone like me who is still learning. Different creatures lurk through these waters at night. Dangerous creatures, including myself. It's strange to remind myself that I am a top predator of the ocean now, amongst the deadliest of creatures.

But still, I'm careful as I swim towards the mangrove passage. If I were meeting anyone else here at night, I might be worried for their safety, but not Ezera. I know he can navigate these waters as well as I can. He is no stranger to the sea, even at night.

When I near my destination, I swim along the surface, letting the moonlight bathe me with a neon glow. The pattern of the water tells me that no one is out here at this time of night to spot me. And even if there were, the light of the moon is faint enough for a human to mistake me for some other sea creature.

I enter the copse of trees where the sea floor rises to meet the strange roots, and I can see the faint orange light of a lantern bobbing further down the trail on what can only be the *Juliette*. As I swim up to the boat, Ezera's silhouette comes into view. His broad shoulders are black against the glowing light of the lantern. More features come into view as I approach the stern. His pale hair is pulled back into a knot at the base of his neck, revealing all of the angles of his face. His jaw.

"Hey, sailor." My voice barely sounds like my own every time I hear it. Something about being in this body has given my voice an airy chime that was never there before. Spending most of our days underwater, I don't hear it often. But in the quiet of the night, it rings through the trees, sounding foreign to me. Ezera stands from his place near the mast and strides towards me.

"Princess," he replies, "or should I call you Curse Breaker, now?" Amusement lights his eyes, making me want to roll mine.

"Please don't. My nerves are already frayed enough at the thought." When I told Ezera about the curse and the prophecy deeming me as the one to break it, I thought he would look at me like I was crazy, like I swallowed too much seawater. Of course, that's absolutely impossible, seeing as I'm part fish. But I really did worry that he wouldn't understand. I was wrong.

So very wrong.

He took in everything I said about Calypso and the Sea Wars as if it were a history lesson. He was fascinated with the prophecy and the steps it will take to break the curse.

"So, how was your day?" His question is innocent enough, but if he only knew. I nearly burst into tears when I think of the easiest way to answer. I decide the best way is to just dive right in with my visit to the willow. I tell him about spotting my mother and father and about how it made me feel. I tell him about Alana and the sea forest just beyond these mangroves and the trench with the bodies. Once my words begin to flow, they seem to just tumble out. Ezera is easy to talk to about anything—even the bodies of those poor women. I watch as his eyes widen at my words and his jaw hardens. Shock and anger line his features as I continue my account of taking Calypso and the others there. When I'm finished, I sigh, taking a much-needed break from talking.

Several moments pass as Ezera takes everything in.

"Regretting asking about my day, huh?" I attempt to lighten the mood. He draws his hand up to rub at his face, the lantern now glowing from below.

"Never," he reassures me. "But I also wouldn't want to relive this day ever again if I didn't have to. And I just made you do that by asking about it."

"I wanted to tell you. I needed to," I say as I lean my arms against the boat. "I want you to ask around about the trench or see if anyone knows anything." I don't hide my unapologetic urgency from him.

"Done." He doesn't hesitate to answer, determined to solve this tragic mystery. For me, for himself, for those women. I don't know. I'm just glad he is doing it.

Twenty-Two

"So you leave tomorrow, huh?"

"At first light. Calypso will lead us through the waters. She said we'd make it there just before the sun sets and the full moon rises." I think of the long journey ahead and hope I can keep up with these seasoned sea creatures. Their muscled tails are strong from swimming miles and miles of ocean, while I only have a month of practice with my fins. Not to mention some have soldiered through literal war.

"And once you break the curse? What then?" His question hits me right in my center, as bold as my request for him to look into the trench mystery. I sink lower into the sea, trying to come up with an answer. After seeing my mother and father today, I know I owe them more than just disappearing from their lives forever. I know I must go back. But how? Do I keep this part of me a secret from our people? Do I make private monthly visits to my parents? Or do I give up the crown and my legs altogether and make a clean break?

"Honestly . . . I don't know," I answer in truth. "I cannot abandon my parents or the crown. But I also cannot deny that this life is a part of me too. This life in the sea . . . is who I am. Just as much as life on the island is." I look out at the water, the moon's reflection a wavy strip of white on the ocean's surface. "I guess I am hoping that breaking this curse will give me some clarity. Will give me an answer to where I go from here."

"Maybe it will. I've learned that when you're pushed up against hardship, your raw self is revealed, showing what you're really made of. It lines up your priorities in a way that you might not have seen before." I can't help but stare as his lips move with his words, caressing every vowel.

"When my mother died, I had to make choices that I never thought I would. Choices that would change the course of my life forever." Ezera's eyes seem pained in the darkness. The yellow light of the flame flickering around him. If I peered deeper into those blue-flamed eyes, I might see a memory.

"I'm scared," I admit, my voice a mere whisper in the dark. The lack of light creates room for my most hidden feelings to slip through, things I won't even admit to myself in the daylight. They can slither through the shadows of night without being claimed or recognized as my own.

"Come on, Princess. You aren't one to back down from a fight. Even I know that. That night of the Full Celestia, you didn't hesitate to come to my father's aid. Afraid or not, you jumped into action. And when you came across those three sharks you told me about? They didn't stand a chance." As he recalls these moments of my life I realize he's right. When given the option to fight or flee, I almost always stand my ground. When Marina was stranded on the Island of Bones, I didn't wait around for some miracle. I took fate by the reigns and gained control.

"Do you believe in destiny?" The words leave my mouth without approval, but once they're said, I want the answer more than I knew. He pauses, thinking it over, water dripping from his loose strands of hair.

"I believe the universe gives you direction. That the wind will push you down a certain path. I believe that if you refuse that push, the universe opens up a new path for you, one that might help you get to where you are going. I don't think there's one path paved for a person but multiple." His words are wise as he speaks, lined in starlight like he's lived longer than his body shows.

I consider what he says and find comfort in it. In the fact that you might have a bit of control in your life. That the universe, or the Mother, or whatever is out there is gently guiding us instead of the notion that our fate is set in stone. No matter what choices we make, we will always end up in the same place.

"I believe the universe brings certain people into your life for a reason—that if someone keeps appearing on your path, they must need to be there." My breath hitches when I think he might be referring to me—as kids playing on the docks, the night of the Full Celestia, and here in the mangroves. It seems the universe keeps pulling us near one another. For what, I can't be sure. But the way he's looking at me gives me an indication.

"I believe that when a striking creature finds you in the sea, you thank your lucky stars for it." Heat floods my cheeks as he speaks, his voice low and husky. His eyes glow in the night, like twin blue flames. I have no choice but to lose myself in them.

He leans closer, and the boat tips from the balance shift. He brushes a stray strand of dark hair from my temple, those blue-green eyes swirling with desire. I reach my hand up out of the water, dripping from the sea, and caress his jaw, my fingers curling around the soft spot behind his ear. Blood rushes through my veins at rapid speed, tingling my senses. Passion grows within me as his eyes bore into mine in the dim light. The only sounds are the waves lapping the sides of the boat.

In this moment, nothing else exists but him. The world around us has fallen away completely. His warm breath touches my lips and I am intoxicated with the scent of him. Sea salt and cedar. Sunshine and freedom.

I shudder a breath as his lips brush mine, the boat tipping further into the water. He leans into me and I wrap my arms around his neck at the same moment he presses his soft lips to mine, the contact nearly enough to kill me. And before I can stop myself, I pull him under.

Bubbles erupt around us and we descend into the black sea head first. His arms tighten around me as we dip below the surface and he deepens the kiss, opening my mouth with his. I brush my hand along his jawline and into his silky hair, loose from the water. His skin is ablaze with heat. When my mouth opens more, water floods in with his tongue. If this were any other human, they might be sputtering for air, but Ezera has spent his life on the water. He's done countless deep dives over the years. He was made for this kind of kiss.

I feel the gills at my sides register the change in atmosphere and begin to filter water through. His arms are wrapped around my waist but travel up my back, a hot and fluid motion. It's hard to tell if his legs have tangled around my tail or if my tail has curled around his legs. Either way, we are wrapped up in each other.

Arms, legs, lips, hearts.

Maybe it's from being upside down, but for a moment I almost don't know where I end and he begins. As he pulls me closer, hand cupping the back of my neck, we move in the water, tilting on an invisible axis, our worlds spinning in tandem. I taste sea salt and crystal blue on my tongue. Lights and colors flash behind my eyes as the kiss intensifies as our mouths collide.

I pull away from him, a vague sense that he must need air, and stare deep into his eyes as they open. Bubbles leave his swollen lips as he exhales the last of his breath when he looks at me, and suddenly it is just me and him in the water, sharing this moment in the dark. A secret from the rest of the world. He breaks the connection first as he kicks his legs, propelling him up to the surface. I follow after him, my tail pushing me skyward with too much force. I shoot out from the water up to my chest before gravity pulls me back down, the sea now lapping my collarbones. Ezera's breaths are heavy, and it's hard to say if it's from the kiss or the lack of air. The smile on his face tells me it might actually be the former, knowing his lungs have a stronger capacity than most. His pearly teeth flash in the moonlight. That dimple makes an appearance.

He grabs my hand from the water and places a kiss atop it, obliterating any insecurities I had earlier when I placed it on his knee. Flowers bloom in my chest, filling me up.

"Goodnight, Cealene."

If I had any sense, I would be embarrassed at my reaction to the way my name sounds on his lips. In his mouth. I would scoff at the way my body reacts to a kiss from a sailor. What a cliche I've become. Like the paintings in the great hall depicting a similar story. Two beings who were once enemies long ago. In another lifetime, we might have been at each other's throats for an entirely different reason. But now . . . tonight, there is no denying the connection. The attraction. The syrupy tension that has filled the air.

"Goodnight, Ezera." My voice chimes in the night, and I watch as his smirk quirks up to the side. Our fingers slip apart beneath the water and as much as it pains me, I turn towards the caves, diving deep. My fins fluke out of the water as I go, leaving him and the *Juliette* behind.

Heading back to the caves, my body still singing with the fire from that kiss, I hear an echo of a call through the water, muffling the sound from above. A sound that brings me back to many nights at home in my bed in the royal residence of Pearle Palace. My window open, letting the midnight breeze from the ocean fill my room, billowing my ivory curtains. The sound of a siren songbird calling in the night. Its echo travels into my room from somewhere out on the sea. My heart sparks at the nearness of the sound. I've never seen one before, for they only sing at night. Most people have never seen them. They only emerge from the cliff trees to sing a midnight song, sailing over the ocean, near the shores. Some have said that they have wingspans as wide as porpoisette. But they are very rare and very hard to spot, blending in with the night.

My heart rabbits in my chest as I surface, anticipation fueling my nerves to finally spot this creature up close. I glide through the water, nearing the edge of the rock cluster jutting out from the sea. I hide behind a large boulder covered in barnacles and algae, my hands grasping onto the slick, wet surface. As I peer around through the rocks, the sound so close I can taste it, shock racks my body at what I see.

Long flowing tail, fins fluttering in the strong ocean wind. A mermaid sits atop the rock outcropping that domes our caves, one I've seen around the pod. The breeze carries her yellow hair behind her as she plays the long spiraling shell-horn, blowing her breath into the opening at its base. It takes me a moment for my mind to catch up with my eyes. With what I am seeing. The bird . . . the one widely known as the midnight singer, is no bird at all, but a mermaid. A sea creature no one even believes to exist.

All these years.

All of those stories of sailors spotting the siren songbird were all just fables. The echoed lullaby that sang me to sleep at night from my bedroom window wasn't some rare bird who only sang at night. It was a mermaid. One of my sisters from the sea.

I try to stifle my laugh, not wanting to disturb her. How silly humans must seem to the merpeople. Not that they know about the infamous bird. Or maybe they do if Brea's spy skills lent her that information. Immediately, I want to tell Angelina about my discovery, and my chest aches with a longing I didn't realize was even there. With everything that has happened these past weeks, even just today, I hadn't realized how long it has been since I'd thought of my cousin back at home while I've been out here. I miss her so much, my chest feels hollowed out with her absence.

No matter what choice I make come this Full Celestia, I will be sure she continues to be a part of my life. Somehow. I will find a way.

The lack of sleep I had last night has left me jittery with nerves as we depart from our home. Farewells were brief, leaving one of Calypso's oldest advisers in charge while we were gone. Not that the pod will need a leader in Calypso's absence. But if anything goes awry, the pod will at least have someone to go to for direction.

The ocean is cold today. My skin prickles with every shift we make as we swim past different landmarks along the ocean. We swim in formation, our positions forming a diamond with Calypso guiding the pod. My diadem is anchored firmly upon my head with intricate braids Brea weaved around its base. When packing up supplies, Marina pulled the diadem from its pouch and placed it atop my head, stating that I was a curse-breaking queen and should be seen as such. I laughed as Brea secured the metal to my head with ease, but I'd be lying to myself if I said I wasn't happy to wear the beautiful heirloom at least once before it becomes one with Ember Island's core. Calypso was pleasantly surprised when I told her of the personal effect. She clapped her webbed hands together in delight, but I could see the distrust simmering there when I explained how I procured it from the palace.

Sacks of supplies are strapped around us as well as weaponry. A bone-handled dagger is strapped to my triceps as well as Atargatis, strapped along my dorsal fin. As my tail undulates through the water, I still worry I'm going to impale myself with the pointed end even after days of training, but Kai has assured me I'll be fine. I swim staggered between Okiro and Marina, following in Marina's wake as Okiro follows in mine. My nerves are on edge with anticipation, but I find the silence of swimming through the sea with no conversation relaxing. Almost therapeutic. I leave my scattered thoughts behind me as we swim ahead, towards Ember Island—the island of rare and potent magic where the curse was born.

Every time we pass a whale or shark, I fight the urge to freeze in place. With only a month of familiarizing myself with this life, I don't know if I'll ever get used to passing a creature eight times my size or a spotted whale the length of Pearle Castle itself. The fact that these creatures merely exist is enough for me to believe in anything.

After hours and leagues pass by in a blur of various shades of blue, we stop to hunt along a coral reef filled with colorful life. Most of us graze on shellfish and easy catches, saving our energy for the journey. But not Calypso. She hunts down a squid with techniques that must have taken years to master. I watch in amazement as she outwits the sea creature, avoiding each tentacle that lashes out at her. The squid is quick, but Calypso is much quicker, and when she spears the animal with her barbed fin, blue blood fills the space around us, clouding the water.

When we've had our fill, Calypso leads us through the endless waters, towards Ember Island. Closer to ending this curse that has plagued these creatures for much too long.

Twenty-Three

All I see is blue. Above me, below me, and in every direction around. Blues of all shades and textures; the deepest blue of night, a dark thick sapphire; clear turquoise blue surrounding the sea turtles that float through the water under the powerful sun; the royal blue of the foggy open ocean that stretches on for miles and mile; and the flame blue eyes that pierce my memory every time I close my lids.

The only thing to occupy our time is our own thoughts and the smooth rhythm of our tails propelling us forward. No other agendas, no conversation or expectation. This far out from land, there are no ships that pass overhead, so we swim closer to the surface, letting the sunrays find us. When deemed safe, we surface to take tabs on the group. We plan to camp tonight for some much-needed rest once we find a spot that will shelter us from anything or anyone for the night.

My shoulder aches where the strap from the harpoon sits and the muscles in my back and tail begin to cramp with fatigue. Rest cannot come soon enough. The further we swim, the cooler the water gets, chilling my skin and bones. Swimming along the surface is a welcome reprieve from the chilled waters below. I try to soak in the heat from the sun as much as I can as if I can savor them for when I need them later. With nothing else to occupy my thoughts, my mind swirls from my parents, to the Lady of the Lake, to the duty of the crown waiting for me at home, to my impending curse breaking, and of course . . . to Ezera. To the kiss we shared before I left. To what it means for us. Just another reason for me to return to land.

How can a human have a relationship with a mermaid? History has taught us time and time again that it never works between two different species. Calypso's relationship was the straw that broke that camel's back and began the Sea Wars in the first place. Why would I think that I would be any different? I'm not on my way to break one curse just to jump into another one. If my life leads down a path with Ezera, I don't see it being in the sea. But if I truly decide to live the rest of my days on land, I won't be fulfilled. I will be missing a part of myself. And if I am not whole, can I truly rule the kingdom efficiently? Justly?

Am I kidding myself to think that I can still have both? That I can take entire months off from my duty to live in the sea? Who would rule in my absence? Where will my advisers believe me to be? Do I come up with an elaborate lie that I am taking trips to neighboring lands? Alone?

My brain hurts from the strain to find a solution. My only comfort in these thoughts is that the king and queen are young and healthy enough that my coronation will not be for years to come. A small comfort at best.

As the sun descends, turning the sky a vibrant periwinkle I tell myself to not borrow tomorrow's problems today. Right now I need only to worry about breaking this curse because that is something I can control now. Because that is the right thing to do. An easy decision to make, as it always has been; help the helpless, as my mother has always taught me. Where my father is the ruler, making the hard decisions, my mother has always been the one to rule with mercy and compassion for those who struggle on the island.

As well as our kingdom has done thus far, it is not without its worries. Pirates still raid the seas, and neighboring kingdoms still try to advance on trades that don't belong to them. People will always be power-hungry and try to cut corners. But my parents make quite a pair when it comes to ruling. Despite their differing views on things, they need one another to shed light on parts that the other doesn't see. When my time comes to rule, I hope to have that too, someone to shed light on the parts I don't see, to show me the gray areas.

Suddenly we halt, staunching my thoughts in the process. Calypso signals for us to follow through a sea forest and up into an outcropping of rocks extending out from the sea, like angled hash marks on an otherwise horizon of nothing, small, but enough for us to rest for the night. My eyes adjust to the clarity of life above water. After being below sea level for so long, I've forgotten how crystal clear the world seems above water. Sharp lines and angles differentiate my surroundings. The sparse palms that reside on the small bit of land are enough to give us some coverage if a ship were to pass in the night. That's if they have enough light to shine this way. As we approach, I am pleasantly surprised to find a small bed of sand between the rocks, feeding into the cracks and crevices. It seems Calypso has found us the perfect resting place for the night.

A few coconuts litter the uneven ground and we all begin to work at cracking them apart. Okiro is the first to pierce the hard shell of the fruit. "Sweet Mother, thank you," he calls as he tilts his head back, pouring the milk into his mouth, a trickle spilling over his lips and trailing down his dark skin. One by one we open our fruits and drink the liquid from within. As we feast on the white meat inside, a moan escapes my lips, enjoying something grown on land, something without the lingering taste of salt. The sweetness brings back memories of pastries at the palace; almond crescents, honey-sweetened tea, chocolate drizzle.

Until this moment, when my tongue recognizes the natural sweetness of the coconut, I hadn't realized how much I missed something as simple as sugar.

"In the morning, we'll hunt from the island before venturing out," Calypso commands as she scrapes the meat of the coconut with her clawed finger. No one argues, content with the plan to fuel ourselves before the long swim ahead. We have a view of this entire stretch of land that peeks out from the ocean in just a few movements, small enough to view the other side by perching on the highest rock. Nothing and no one resides on this rock tonight, especially with our presence known. Most animals know better than to come near our kind, particularly in groups.

Maybe it's the uncertain future that lies ahead, maybe it's the exhaustion that racks our bodies, or maybe it's the stillness of the night, but when Marina curls up against Kai, resting her head on his broad chest, I'm surprised she's stopped resisting her pull towards him, and I'm glad for it. It's exhausting fighting your feelings.

Brea and Marina fall into easy conversation as they recount the memory of visiting the Island of Bones and retrieving the ring from the sarcophagus.

"Can I see it?" Kai asks Brea, curiosity getting the best of him. She pulls the granite-colored clam shell from her pack and hands it over to Kai. Slowly he unties the vine wrapped around the shell, keeping it contained, and lifts the top shell. The ring shines in the darkness of the night, like the thousands of stars above. I swear a hum fills the air as if the ring and all the power it holds seeps out into the open. Careful not to touch it, Kai examines the jeweled piece within the shell. "It's . . ."

"Alive?" Okiro jokes.

"I was going to say opulent, but alive works." Kai turns the shell, watching the small reflection of the stone bounce off the light of the moon.

"How did you take it from the body?" Kai asks the two females.

"Marina was the lucky sucker who had the honor of actually retrieving it from the body," Brea explained.

"You're welcome," Marina jokes, her voice light.

"I am forever indebted to you," Brea claimed. "The strangeness of that place and the lingering magic had me all but bolting back to the sea. I wanted out of there."

"What she's trying to say is that if it weren't for my bravery, there would be no ring." Marina's sarcasm isn't lost on us as she explains further. "Grabbing that ring from the witch's cold, dead finger was enough to make me want to jump out of my own skin."

When Kai closes the two halves of the shell together, I hold my hand out for it. When he hands me the shell, I open it with as much care as he, not wanting to push my luck or disturb any magic within. The multiple facets of the stone reflect as I turn the shell at different angles. As creepy as it is, the ring truly is beautiful. Old and ancient, but beautiful. The gold band still shines after what I can only assume was years of wear. As I turn the shell to the back, I notice an inscription engraved on the inside of the band. Subtle but there, small black letters appear on the thin band.

Liquid life pays the price.

Before I can speak a word, the inscription vanishes from the gold band as if it were never there at all. Heat creeps up my throat as I look around at the group hoping I can see through their eyes if any of them saw something similar when they had the ring. But I already know without asking. Of course not. Of course there was no inscription on the gold band. It would have been mentioned. It would have been discussed amongst the group.

And the phrase that appeared. What could it mean? It's daunting enough that it leaves me feeling uneasy. I fight with myself on whether I should tell the group or not. I look over to Marina, who's now carving our silhouettes into the thick trunk of a palm tree with her dagger. Will they even believe me? A thought snags in my mind, demanding to be examined.

What if it's trying to tell me something? Only me.

If the power of the ring can relay messages to its holder, wouldn't it have appeared to the others if the ring wanted it to be known? But it only showed up for me and disappeared before I could show anyone else.

Slowly, I close the shell and hand the ring back to Brea as she tells us a story of how she spied on a few Full Celestia celebrations held at the palace. The longer I keep my mouth shut, the harder it becomes to mention what I saw.

I glance towards Calypso who's lounging in the sand, staring off into the open sea, and contemplate telling her. But something tells me not to. Something tells me to keep it to myself, and I can't be sure what that something is. But I know enough to never ignore my instinct. I've learned that lesson time and time again. So I school my face into one of contentment and try and lose myself in the conversation around me.

Brea describes how she enters Aqualasia through the water channels. She has found access to our lands without ever leaving the water, without ever changing forms. She's learned about our customs, politics, fashion, our cuisine, and even town gossip. The more she explains how she's slithered her way through the island, the more I believe she is something of a spymaster.

No wonder she is Calypso's second. She's the ears and eyes on land. Just a shadow in our waters, absorbing life. She's so good I don't even have the nerve to be upset about it. Normally if someone had that much access and information to our lands, our palace, it would be cause for concern. But I know these creatures now. I know their desires and motives. I know Brea and nothing about her says she would harm my people. She just thrives on knowledge.

As the sun sets, seemingly dropping into the ocean below, our tired bodies settle for the night. Exhaustion hits me hard as I rest my head on the palm fronds we gathered earlier. The water covers most of my body like a blanket as I stare up at the night sky, mesmerized by the stars above and the sound of the lapping waves. Sleep finds me quickly as I let my mind wander to thoughts of Ember Island and what the ring was trying to tell me.

TWENTY-FOUR

The farther out we swim, the colder the water becomes. So far, we've passed several mountainous icebergs floating atop the freezing ocean. Calypso warned us what to expect when hitting this strange stretch of sea. She assured us that once we hit the Melodian current, speeding up our trip, we'd quickly enter warmer waters. But thus far, my fingers have lost sensation and I can feel my blood struggling to pump through my body. With nothing but silence and ocean around us, the cold is the only thing to keep me company, ever-present with every push ahead. As our blood vessels constrict from the cold water, our movements become slower, decreasing our speed. It's like I'm swimming through sludge instead of the crystal blue salt water. The aqua current cannot come soon enough.

The only other thought that found its way to me through the cold is that of the ring, the inscription on the band, and what it means. Not knowing if the ring has spoken to the others gnaws at me as I push through the biting cold.

We decided to forgo hunting this morning and push through this part of the journey. The quicker we get out of here, the better. I personally cannot get through this water fast enough. If I never found myself near another iceberg again in my life, it would be too soon. Nothing about this patch of sea is desirable. It's cold and dark and unwelcoming. Not much movement and not much to eat, not that any of us have any sort of appetite. Food is secondary to our need for warm waters.

When Calypso changes course with a swift turn, I almost cry out with relief. The current zooms by in a flurry of rushing water. Clear but visible in the dark waters, the Melodian current is our salvation. Never using a current this swift as a type of transportation before, my frozen nerves get the best of me when I wonder how exactly one enters the invisible tunnel of rushing water. It can't be as easy as the small currents back home.

From their many years of living in these waters, I can only imagine that each one of these creatures has used the major underwater currents at least once before. I watch in fascination as Calypso picks up speed alongside it. She merges in with ease, the water carrying her further from us with each passing second.

One by one each member of our group follows Calypso's movements and merges into the fast-flowing current. Okiro waits behind me, always the gentleman, ensuring that I make it through smoothly. I pump my tail as much as my body will allow, the muscles contracting painfully in the cold, as I swim alongside the rushing waters. With arms out ahead, I merge into the current and immediately feel the speed of the water pull me along. The absence of that chill is a welcome replacement from our earlier predicament.

As we follow single file behind Calypso, the speed at which we move within the water is almost disorienting. It's as if the world passes by in slow motion as we speed along through a vessel. Slowly, sensation comes back to my fingers and a slight hunger grows in my belly. But I know we have leagues to go before we will stop to hunt. This current will take us almost to the end of our journey where we will veer off a few miles before we hit the island. As I watch Marina ahead of me pull her prepared food from her sack, I do the same understanding now why we needed such provisions along the way. In an ocean full of fish, hunting is not always ideal.

With the packed food satiating my hunger and heat creeping back into my body, my senses become clearer, telling me that our trip is almost coming to an end. That it is almost time to break this curse.

As we merge out of the current, we swim up near the surface, enjoying the pleasures of the sun beating down on us, chasing away the last of the chill. Glorious heat wraps my body in these warm waters, and I swear I can feel my hair flowing more freely. We follow Calypso in our designated positions, still swimming at a quick pace. Although exhaustion begins to settle in, I have no complaints now that the icebergs are well behind us.

Without warning, Calypso rights herself, coming to a halt, and peers up from the water. We each do the same but sink down lower into the sea. She's spotted something or someone, and my spirits dampen with every passing second we wait. Calypso's eyes dart down at us, emerald orbs aglow, as she nods for us to follow close, staying low within the waters. It is clear that something has gone awry as I peer along the surface and spot a dark, blurry figure sitting on the water. A ship is in our midst. And the sounds coming from it are anything but merry. Deep voices shout profanities and cruel-edged words. Orders.

When we reach the shadowed water directly below the belly of the ship, I realize it's not one, but two ships idling side by side. Calypso signals for us to have our weapons at the ready and points to where we will surround the boats upon emerging from the sea. I grab Atargatis and place my hands on the shaft, ready to strike.

My stomach drops when I realize we are going to take a closer look at what's going on and from the sound of it, it won't be pretty. It sounds like a hostile takeover. If I had to guess—pirates. It's clear from the glances exchanged around me that everyone wants to further investigate the hollowed cries from above. My own chest squeezes at what situation will reveal itself once we emerge. Maybe Calypso thinks they captured one of our own, or maybe she finds this an opportunity to seek some revenge on humans, but for whatever reason, she has made the situation on deck our problem.

Water drips down my scalp as we emerge from the ocean, hugging tightly to the first ship in silence. Waiting. Assessing. We don't need to wait long to understand the situation at hand. The low grunts and filthy slang of the passengers above are enough to tell us that pirates walk along the hull of this ship. One glance at the flag tells us they've taken over a Bakhtian ship from the west. We must be near a trade route.

Calypso's eyes glow with a fury I've never seen before. When I follow her line of vision, I see what has her so enraged. Nailed to the tall mast of the pirate ship is a copper mermaid's tail, bloodied and limp. Serrated at the waist, it seems that it was hacked off carelessly and displayed on the ship as some sort of sick trophy. My stomach clenches with disgust when I think of the poor mermaid who died a painful and derisive death. If we had come across this ship only a few hours later, that tail might have disintegrated into sea foam, hiding any evidence of their crime.

As we creep up the wooden sides, manipulating the water for leverage, we get a clear view of what's inside. Soiled bandannas holding back greased shaggy hair, filthy, liquored faces covered in scraggly beards, empty bottles of rum roll along the deck, and weapons strapped to worn leather boots. And blood. Lots of blood.

Definitely pirates.

Bakhtian sailors are tied up against a mast with thick coiled rope. They look badly beaten and scared. Helpless cries come from the forecastle of the ship.

A young girl cowers next to a wooden barrel, shielding her face from the lifeless body before her. Her auburn braids fall over her tear-streaked face and my stomach churns as bile burns the back of my throat. This girl must be only eight and her shaking hands are speckled with blood, like she was too near when someone took a blow. The overwhelming urge to steal her from this ship is crippling. No child should have to witness such a thing, let alone be smack in the middle of it.

Kai and I are the closest to her and the brute pirate who antagonizes his prisoners, slicing one's face with a bloodied dagger. I know Kai can smell the rancid stench of liquor just as well as I can. The others make their way to the bow, meeting Kai and me just below their line of sight. I grip my harpoon tighter. There is no question of what will happen next. Our group will enter the deck and obliterate these fools.

Again, Calypso signals instructions on when and how to strike. I only recognize a few but I follow her commands, Atargatis at the ready, as we wait for her to make the first move aboard. Anticipation eats at my nerves as the whale-boned hilt of the harpoon cuts into my palm. I'm holding it much too tight, but I can't seem to loosen my grip as my eyes meet Kai's and he nods at me to be ready.

Sounds from above continue along, as if this ship weren't in imminent danger, as if these pirates haven't seen the last of their days. Even on my best day, I would never want to find myself up against the merfolk. They're fearless, predatory creatures who have fought for their lives on more than one occasion, who have earned the title of survivor twice over.

Calypso's eyes gleam with bloodlust as she lets her dagger fly through the small opening on the side of the ship, just above the deck, striking the tendon on the leg of the assaulting pirate. When he drops down to a knee, his screams fill the air as we board the ship, spilling water onto the deck along with our wrath.

Shouts layer one another as the pirates scramble for cover or their weapons. But we don't give them a chance. We rise like serpents ready to strike, and I feel the wooden planks grate against my scales. Kai and Okiro spear their opponents like fish and their mammoth tails knock oncoming threats from their feet.

Calypso is vicious as she uses her teeth and talons to disable her target. Just like in the ocean, Calypso prefers to feel the life leave her prey with her own two hands, no weapon necessary for a female with vengeance in her soul. A wicked smile transforms her face into something else entirely as she pins another pirate to the deck with her speared tail. I do not doubt that she is enjoying every minute of this, and I'm not sure I even have a problem with it. These lowlifes don't deserve our mercy.

Marina and Brea take turns fighting the pirates brave enough to emerge from the hatch below, disarming each one before their feet even hit the deck. Brea's strength and speed are envious as I watch her disembowel the pirate who tortured the unarmed merchant. His blood coats her dark skin in a slick sheen.

After fending off three men trying to capture me in a net, I feel the rough scrape of the deck steal my scales as I slither over to the girl curled up at the furthest end of the ship, uncontrollably shaking from the trauma. Or maybe it's all of the blood or the sight of our attack. Her skirts are torn and I wonder if maybe she was trying to get away from a pirate's grasp during their raid. Her hair has fallen out of her braids. I approach her with care, sheathing Atargatis, not wanting to frighten her any further.

"It's okay. We just want to help you." As I near her, it occurs to me that she might be just as afraid of us as she was of the pirates on this ship, depending on what stories surrounded her upbringing, and what myths and legends were ingrained in her from a young age. If she found her way onto a ship, I'm assuming she was told only the worst of the stories that paint us as the devil's servants.

"Are you hurt?" I reach out a hand but stop before reaching for her, waiting for her to react. Her eyes widen as she looks up, and fear etches every part of her tiny face. I believe it's by the sight of me, of my pointed ears or the gills at my sides, or maybe my scaled, webbed hand, but too late I realize it's from what approaches behind me. And then I realize my mistake.

I turned my back on the enemy.

A net blurs my vision as I'm dragged away from the girl, kicking and clawing as I fight for freedom. My dagger lies idle on the floorboard near the girl, fallen from my grasp in the ambush. Splinters threaten to pierce my tail as I'm dragged towards the open hatch. Fear rises in my throat as I see the darkness below. Once I'm down there, I won't find my way back out. I cannot let him toss me below deck.

I struggle to grab Atargatis strapped to my back, cursing myself for sheathing it to begin with, but my efforts are futile as the net twists and turns, throwing me off balance. I can barely make any sense of direction and the movements are only becoming more erratic. The pirate is no idiot. He knows what he's doing. How, I'm not sure. But his strategy is one born of either experience or intelligence, and I try not to let my panic cease my running thoughts.

I take a deep breath, letting the air fill every corner of my lungs, and try again to grab for my harpoon along my dorsal fin. Every time my hands grasp the shaft of the weapon, I am again tossed around in the net, losing my balance and my grip. As we inch closer to the hatch, I begin to spiral in panic kicking and clawing for a way out. The rope is too thick—the movements too abrupt. I cringe at every grunt the pirate makes as he tugs me across the deck, towards the opened hatch.

In the blur of commotion, I see Okiro's dark, brawny figure break our path and a cry escapes my lips. His back is to us as he fights off two pirates coming at him with swords flying. Okiro's movements are one of sheer skill and strength, doubling the movements of his opponents. As my captor nears Okiro with their backs to each other, I wait for the inevitable clash when I will make my move. I only pray that Okiro doesn't move away before then.

I can feel the pirate's fatigue as he hauls me towards the hatch. Fighting against gravity, friction, and my resistance has begun to take its toll. Exactly what I need for when he inevitably stumbles into Okiro's hulking form. I stop fighting, letting the pirate think I've given up or run out of strength as he backs farther into the merman's shadow. With my hands on Atargatis, I wait for the moment to make my move.

Okiro has been disarmed, leaving him with nothing but his wits and strength to fight, but he deflects each blow from the slippery pirate until he's pushed over the edge of a wooden bench and lays flat on his back. Fighting on land has its downfalls, and this is one of them. Okiro struggles to get upright or move away as the pirate advances on him. Okiro's face turns ruthless as he rips the thin chain from around his neck and plunges the crocodile tooth into the pirate's left eye, leaving him staggering back as he wails.

When he turns to me, Okiro's tail whip sends my captor onto his ass as a sly smirk graces his face. But I see the tightness in his eyes. The pain he feels for losing the one thing that tethered him to his baby brother.

Before I can dwell on Okiro's lost necklace I see the pirate who ensnared me begin to sit up. Without wasting a second, I'm on him, net and all. My claws find their way into the slimy pirate's skin and tear the flesh away from his face. His screams send a thrill through me that's wildly out of character. I've never been a violent person but, in this skin, pleasantries and decorum do not exist. I feel no remorse as I free myself from the rope and plunge the harpoon into the man's chest, pinning him to the wooden floor of the ship.

As blood trickles from his chest, spilling onto the floor, I yank Atargatis from his lifeless body before heading back to the girl. Her arms hug her knees so tightly around that her form appears impossibly small—such a young innocent life defiled by people who don't care about the damage they leave in their wake. Her shaking has yet to subside, so I open a leather-banded chest near the main mast, hoping for a jacket of some sort to drape over her shoulders, in comfort and in warmth.

Instead, I find bottles of amber liquor, a worn pair of leather boots, and at the bottom a thick wool blanket complete with tattered edges. I pull the charcoal blanket from the chest, knocking the bottles around with an array of clinks, and I bring it over to the girl, wrapping her up tightly.

The shouts and chaos from the fight lessen as I gently place my hand on her back, hoping not to frighten her. The last thing this poor child needs is another stressor from a stranger invading her space. Only ragged breaths and a few final groans litter the air. Marina and Calypso scuttle closer, not wanting to startle the girl. Okiro, Kai, and Brea seem to be checking the rest of the ship for any stowaways. With blood painting their skin, Calypso and Marina are a sight of nightmares.

"How is she fairing?" Calypso wipes the blood from her hands with the rumpled shirt of a fallen pirate, his eyes staring directly into the sun but not seeing.

"Hasn't said a word," I reply, feeling strange to speak of her as if she wasn't sitting directly to my left.

Marina ducks her head lower, attempting to meet the girl's eyes, "The threat is gone, child. You don't need to be scared any longer."

Only then does it occur to me that we've just left this young girl stranded on a ship alone in the middle of the ocean with only rotting corpses as company. Calypso cannot think to just leave her here now. We have a responsibility to see this through. Before I have a chance to voice my concern, Brea calls out to us as Okiro and Kai haul a man up from the hatch. "Found another one."

Brea's beaded braids shine in the light as she saunters over. As the man is flanked by the finned males, he holds his arms out in surrender, hands shaking. He squints in the sunlight as if he's been below deck for quite some time. His bald head is beaded with sweat and a dirty white towel is tossed over a shoulder. I feel the girl straighten beside me at the sight of him, eyes wide.

"Krysha . . ." The man says her name softly. "I'm so sorry, dear girl. They locked me in the kitchen. I tried to get to you." I watch as Okiro and Kai wait for the child's response before releasing him. When her lower lip quivers and she holds her arms out for him, the blanket falling behind her, he runs towards her, crashing to his knees before her and pulling her into a soft embrace. With that, she cries only harder into his robust figure, arms shaking with grief. "Shh. There, there, child," he coos, cradling her head with his worn hand. After a moment, he turns to us in astonishment. His eyes scan us intently as if he isn't quite sure we are really there.

"The folklore that surrounds you . . . it is wrong." His words tell us enough that although he may not have believed we truly existed, he certainly heard that our hearts were blackened with evil. "Thank you."

"How do you plan to navigate this ship with no crew?" Calypso's voice holds no affection as she directs her question at what must have been the cook of this unfortunate crew.

"We'll take the lifeboat south to Arias. That's where they were headed before . . ." his sentence dies off with the wind.

"This ship has a lifeboat?" Marina's question is full of surprise.

"It does indeed. I will navigate us to civilization . . . thanks to you. Then we can make our way back home from there."

He bows his head with grace as Calypso peers down her nose at him. "Very well, then. We will leave you to it." She turns and begins to pull herself over the side of the ship. "Kai, Okiro. Sack the other ship for anything useful for our journey."

The males nod as our leader disappears, not waiting for a response. Brea follows in after Calypso and Marina nods at me to follow. My body has begun to itch with the need for water, being out of the sea for too long. As much as my body craves to drink in the liquid life below, I find it hard to leave the girl.

I look back at her once more as she clings to the only other human left on the ship like a lifeline. The shaking has subsided now and her shoulders have sunk lower, losing the tension that held them high. I take those as good signs that I can safely leave her in the care of this man. And hope that they make it back home in one piece. Wherever that may be.

TWENTY-FIVE

The last leg of the journey might have been worse than the freez-ing waters we endured, if only for the anticipation constantly gnawing at my insides. How I long to lounge at my willow or swim through our waters back home, anything that feels like a soft blanket of familiarity. Instead, we race against time to meet the next Full Celestia at the very top of the volcano, as close as I will ever be to the glowing orb in the sky.

It occurs to me then that this will be the very first Full Celestia that I've been away from home. I wonder what Angelina will do tonight, with the celebration canceled. I wonder if there's a void in her life where I used to be like the Angelina-shaped hole in mine.

The sea floor begins to rise as we near the sandy beach of the island, uninhabited due to the massive volcano that threatens to erupt at any time. We surface as we near and I am surprised to see a small jungle of trees and lush plant life around the base of the volcano. I'd assumed that the island would be mostly barren due to the high temperatures of the rocks and the billowing smoke.

But as it is, lush colors of green and yellow drape the island, giving it a dreamy feel, with the mist hovering between the trees. Mossy green creeps up and over the rocks and bark. The lacy vines string along the wild vegetation. Dew drops twinkle as our tails brush the sand where sea meets land.

"Damn," Kai comments as the waves push us further up the beach, and it seems I'm not the only one surprised by the flourishing bed of this island. The smoke atop the massive mountain mingles with the clouds. The sun bruises the sky as it slips toward the horizon.

I can already see the moon's full belly, appearing almost translucent as it competes with the setting sun, which means we only have a few hours to make it to the top of the volcano. But the volcano isn't so much tall as it is wide. Its mouth is a yawning berth opening up to the sky above.

We have a small window of time to complete the incantation before we risk transforming under the Full Celestia. It was by pure coincidence that I was out on that cliff the night I transformed nearly a month ago. *Or maybe it was no coincidence at all.*

Although the moon appears full to the naked eye for about two to three days, it is only truly full for a moment in time before the waning begins again and the moon is ever so slowly hidden in the shadows of the world.

The group has absolutely no desire to spend the next month with legs, not to mention stranded on this island without a way to swim home. As for me, I have the option to shift into the form I was born in. *Human.*

If I decide to continue my life on Aqualasia, the group will bring me back home once the shift is complete, just as I was able to bring Ezera through the sea. They will bring me along for the brutal journey home in my human form, heating the cold waters enough for me not to freeze to death as we go. Something that I am not looking forward to in the slightest. If I thought the swim across seas was difficult as a sea creature, I can only imagine what it will be like in the form of someone who belongs on land.

Each of us takes a moment to admire our new surroundings, even Calypso as she cranes her neck to see the wide expanse, eyes darting for any signs of danger. She's been distant this trip, not that she was ever one for conversation. But it seems lately that the stress of executing this plan has taken its toll on her. An entire species reliant on her plan is almost too much to bear. I should know. If I don't break this curse, the merfolk will look to me as the culprit. As the failure. Not Calypso. No one would dare fault her for her efforts. After all, she was told the prophecy to begin with. Without her, none of this would even be possible.

I watch as she surveys the land, marking its landmarks and no doubt finding the best route to take up the mountain. Its rocky body is patched with green in spots. The rest is an ashy rock with rivulets of black snaking down its sides. Part of me wonders how we will make it up to the top without legs. We couldn't possibly scale the entire side of the mountain with only our arms.

"We have time, despite our detour on the ship. It shouldn't take us long to make it to the mouth of the volcano." Calypso looks at none of us as speaks, her silver hair already beginning to dry in the warm air. "I'm going to scout the area. See which route is best to take." Her tail slithers along snakelike, head poised like a viper ready to strike, leaving a trail in the sand as she disappears into the rocky terrain.

With our leader gone scouting our surroundings, Okiro lies flat on the wet sand, letting the waves roll around him as he stares up at the milky blue sky above. I find a space beside him and splay my arms out to my sides like a cross, and sigh heavily as the water bathes us with each wave. Our gills are rendered useless as the water slips into the lifeless vents at our sides.

"I'm sorry about your necklace, " I begin, hoping I'm not rubbing salt in the wound. His exhale is audible, and I close my eyes wishing I could backtrack.

"I'm . . . not." His words strike me with surprise, and I turn my head in the sand to look at him, his dark profile. Before I can ask, he continues. "I think the necklace was weighing me down with guilt. And when it left me, I felt . . . free somehow." He turns to look back at me, the waves rushing along our cheeks.

"You held your guilt around your neck for so many years," I speak my thoughts aloud, more to myself in realization.

"I think I did, without really realizing it. And he saved me again, even in death."

"A part of him will always live within you."

When the space between us gets too heavy, he brushes his tail up, splashing me with saltwater, "Look at you, ever the wise one." I sit up on my elbows ready to retort when Brea swims over and lies beside Okiro, stomach first. Her arms curl around her head, framing her face.

I decide to swim over to Kai and Marina immersed in the small inlet of water farther into the island near the jungled trees. It's warm from the sun's rays and reminds me of my baths back at the palace in my claw-foot tub, complete with steamy bubbles and rich aromas from the lathers. Somewhere deep inside, the human part of me aches for my room back at the palace, the familiarity of my home, and the small comforts I took for granted.

Kai pulls out a trochus shell freckled with violet swirls for Marina, placing it in her palm. The color matches her fins perfectly. I don't know if I should swoon or gag from the tenderness of the gesture. But the ache in my chest and the vision of cyan eyes are not lost on me as I watch the couple interact.

"So, Cealene . . . am I going to lose *my* anchor after tonight?" It takes only a moment for me to understand Marina's question and all it implies. She wants to know if I will go back to my life on land after I do what needs to be done. My heart swells at the implication that I, too, would be her choice as an anchor if our roles were reversed.

"No matter what tomorrow brings, you will never lose me." Holding onto this relationship I've forged with Marina will be the easiest of tasks if I decide to resume my role as a human. We can meet at the cove, or grotto, or even above the caves. "I'm not that easy to shake."

The sound of Marina's laughter fills the air like bubbles popping. When I look over to the two basking in the wet sand, I see that Brea has risen onto her hands, her back arched as she looks into the jungle. Her dorsal fin stands on end, spikes ready to pierce flesh. Her braids brush the sand as she stills, on high alert.

Okiro must detect whatever she searches for too because he curls his tail beneath him, sitting upright. The muscles in his back are taut as he listens intently, not moving an inch—weapon at the ready.

"What is it?" Kai rushes closer, his thick tail causing a small wave to roll in his wake. Okiro doesn't answer, but instead motions with his free hand to listen. As if on cue, the leaves of the jungle begin to rustle unnaturally. We move closer toward the invisible line where the beach ends and the forest begins, barely making a sound as we move through the sand.

Movement rustles through the trees as I hear my name carried through the mist and we all still, five statues made of stone.

"Cealene!"

I know that voice. I would know it anywhere. I move forward, and pull myself up on a broken palm trunk, looking through the forest when he emerges. Dampened hair and a machete cutting down the brush. Eyes wild.

"Ezera?"

Twenty-Six

"Cealene, you're okay." Ezera's voice is haggard with worry as his eyes search mine.

"Of course I'm okay." Dismay settles in my gut as pieces merge together. He sailed here in his boat, the small sailboat named after his mother over miles and miles of ocean to find me here. He looks as though he hasn't slept in days. His beautiful teal eyes are sunken and wild. He walks towards me with a limp, and it appears there is a gash healing at his hairline. His sun-bleached tendrils hang loose around his face as if they too are haggard with fatigue. So many questions fill my mouth, but only one surfaces, "What in the stars are you doing here?"

Before he has a chance to respond, Marina appears behind me, apprehension and confusion shaping her face. "Cealene . . . who is this?"

Now that I look at her straight on, I may even detect a bit of hurt on her face for not knowing who this male is who has called my name and seemingly sailed across the ocean for me. Maybe I should have told her about him. She did show me her sunken ship after all. Maybe I should have trusted her with this part of me I've been hiding. But then I would have to put this thing between me and Ezera into words. Then I would have to say out loud how I feel. I would have to admit further that I have a problem on my hands: to choose life in the sea or life on land. And I guess I just wasn't ready to do that.

"This is Ezera. He lives in Aqualasia. He's been keeping me updated on my parents while I've been away. He's the one who procured the diadem for me." Ezera walks closer to us as I explain who he is without giving up anything more.

"Looks like that's not all he's been doing," Kai comments under his breath, picking up on the connection between us. My cheeks heat and if the situation weren't so dire, I might have even laughed.

Okiro elbows him in the arm. "Quiet, you fool."

Hysteria threatens to release a flurry of giggles, though nothing about this is remotely funny. No. Nothing about the look on Ezera's face is comical at all. Whatever brought him here is no laughing matter. Nor is it amusing that he was able to sail across seas in such a short amount of time in his sailboat.

"Where is she?" Ezera's eyes dart above my head and around the area we occupy. "Where is that soulless creature with the tail as black as her heart?"

I grab Ezera's hands that hold my shoulders as if to keep me together and in one piece.

"Calypso?" My question is not so much to confirm that is indeed who he is looking for, but more to ask why. Before he has a chance to confirm or further explain, Brea moves into our space, joining the conversation.

"Is there anyone else you know who would fit that description?" Her question, no doubt meant to be sarcastic, fills me with agitation. Why am I the only one that sees what a problem we have here? Ezera would never travel through miles and miles of ocean if there wasn't a very good reason.

But I realize then that Ezera is a species that they do not fancy. *Human.* And we are not. They don't know him like I do. They don't care for him as I do. His traveling all this way to seemingly deliver a very important message doesn't matter to them. The only reason Marina seems to look as worried as I am is because she cares for me. It turns my stomach to think that these merfolk might need a reminder that up until several weeks ago, I too was a human.

"Ezera." I hold his hands in mine. "What is going on?"

For a long moment, he stares at me intently, his kaleidoscope eyes searching mine, then broadens his stare to the rest of my companions, before settling back to me.

"I heard talk on the docks about a fisherman taking his expecting wife to the endless waters as it is said to bring good health to the child. When I asked where this was, they directed me roughly to the trench, believing that the spot of the ocean has no floor. I knew that had to be how these women were disappearing. I knew I had to take a closer look. But when I arrived just passed the mangroves, she was there. *Calypso.* Dragging an unconscious woman through the water. Her belly swollen."

Bile rises in my throat as shock rolls through my system. The inside of my mouth tingles with disbelief and horror. Marina audibly gasps beside me, but I'm too stunned to move.

"When I realized what she was doing, I tried to stop her. But she's quick and attacked me before I could do any good. Knocked me unconscious and left me for dead." My heart is erratic in its cage as I hear the words leave his lips.

Calypso attacked him.

She harmed all of those women. Each face from the flyers I've collected flashes in my memory. She's been doing this for years.

"I probably would be dead if it weren't for you, Cealene. I remember what you taught me about the taeopaen root near the mangroves, and I eventually made my way there after nearly drowning. I wasn't sure it would work, but I figured it couldn't hurt. As soon as I could, I packed up the *Juliette* and set sail. I didn't know if I would make it in time, but I had to try."

As his declaration hits the group, silence fills the air around us. The words settle like dust, leaving only the story standing in its place. Whole and horrific. Only our thoughts roaring in our heads at his recount. We look around at one another for an explanation. An answer as to what this all means. Betrayal fills my chest.

"Calypso is not who she says she is." As if sensing we needed it spoken aloud, Ezera does the honors, further cementing the truth into our minds.

"No . . ." Marina's voice barely a whisper of disbelief. My mind thinks back to revealing my discovery to Calypso, to taking her to the trench, her concern and anger that she carried with her. The shock that she feigned as she searched the bodies as if she'd never seen them before. As if she was unaware that they lay there, forgotten and abandoned. Oh, how she must have felt when I came to her with such a discovery. How she must have reveled in putting on such an act of leadership, of heroism in taking further investigation with such severity.

"My sister is a foul creature. My sister has always been good at trickery of all kinds." Alana was right. Somehow, she knew. She wasn't just referring to some displaced sibling rivalry but of Calypso's true nature. She knew there was something she was hiding that would show her true colors.

There was no investigation with the other pods. There was no mystery for her to discover. It was only her and her lies. But why? She can't possibly hate humans so much as to kill innocent women, to end a life before it even began. Calypso, of all people, should understand what a miracle a baby is. What a cherished thing it is to be a mother. To raise another. How could this be?

A palpable tension fills the air as movement catches Ezera's attention behind us. His eyes fill with rage as he steps past me raising the steel machete. Before I turn my head, I already know what I will see. The silver flowing hair of Calypso, her dark scales a stark contrast against the pale trail of sand.

"You," Ezera growls, his voice ravaged with loathing. As if time slowed to a snail's pace, I turn to confirm her appearance. As do the others. One by one, she looks at each of us, ferocity in her eyes. As if the next words that come from her mouth won't be of denial, but of unapologetic truth. Before she speaks, I already know she feels no remorse. Once the shock of Ezera's presence passes, only conviction shows in her eyes.

"They had it coming," is all she says, as if that is enough of an explanation for such a violent and vile act. As if that is all that is needed from her for us to understand her motives. Marina moves forward with anger bending her brows.

"They had it coming? They—"Her voice shakes with emotion as she tries to speak. "By *they* you mean the women who were on their way to becoming mothers, or do you mean the innocent lives growing within them?" Her voice rises like the tide as she continues, "Which 'they' do you refer to as you try to justify your actions?" In all the time I've known Marina, I have never once heard her speak this way to Calypso. Never has she been anything but respectful to our leader.

"They sail in our waters hoping that the sea, *our* sea, will protect and provide for them. As if they deserve as much." She spits the words at us, her mouth full of spite. "Why should they get to have the very thing that was ripped from us? Ripped from my flesh? A freedom that is ingrained in all beings, to keep our species thriving? Why should they continue to grow and live on when they are the sole reason we haven't seen new life in our seas in generations? Humans believe us to be evil and unworthy of creating new life . . . Maybe they should take a look at what they've done. Maybe they should remember who threw the first stone. *Maybe I should give them a reason to hate us, truly. Less humans means safer seas.*" Her conviction fills the air around us, charging the tension with something more. Anger fills this island as she releases her truth, laying it bare for us to see.

"A life for a life. For every fallen mercreature that died by their hands will be repaid twice over."

With those words, I nearly collapse. There are simply no words to counter this female's thoughts. There is nothing that will save her from herself. She will only see this as leveling the field, as righting a wrong. She will never see it for what it truly is, and for that, my heart aches. Aches for those women who will never come home. Aches for those babies that will never feel the waves lap at their feet, aches for the wounds that will never heal.

"How can you not understand this does nothing for our kind? Nothing but prove the humans might be right." The words taste like sand in my mouth.

"Unfortunate that others must pay the price for their ancestor's wrongdoings."

With that, I nearly lose it. I can no longer sit here and listen to her try and justify her actions. I cannot look at her as she tries to tell us why revenge is the answer she seeks. Those were my people.

I pull Atargatis from behind me and raise it high in the sky, ready to spear her to this earth. Rage fills my veins and I see red. My body shakes with a wrath so deep, it may as well be hell. Those women were my people, carrying the future of Aqualasia within them. For weeks I studied those posters trying to figure out where these women were, how they were disappearing like smoke. I poured over them every day, asking my father to further investigate.

Marina and Brea dart back at my sudden movement. Kai and Okiro's hands shoot to their weapons in response. Ezera grabs my free arm, attempting to pull me back, but I'm beyond reason as I stare down the devil incarnate.

"Cealene, no!"

TWENTY-SEVEN

Rage fills my every bone as I advance forward towards Calypso. She sends a strike of water my way, attempting to disarm me, but I don't give an inch. She takes a defensive position against me, arms out, claws at the ready. The spiked tip of her tail stares me down like a serpent's head, ready to strike. She bares her teeth at me like the animal she is, and I do not cower from her power.

Ezera's calloused hand slips from my arm as I yank free of his grasp. He lets me go, despite his worry. He knows there's no stopping me now. Kai moves beside me as I advance towards Calypso. Brea shoots in front of me ready to tackle Calypso to the ground, her swift move creating a wind that carries my hair across my face. Her body is a blur of dark flesh and shamrock-colored scales, but before she hits her target, she's thrown aside by Calypso's brutal tail. Blood seeps from her head as her body lies in the sand, unmoving.

Fear begins to claw its way through me as I stare at Brea. Marina rushes to her side, immediately assessing the damage and confirming her rising chest.

I aim Atargatis towards Calypso's heart, my grip on the shaft tight. The engraved metal leaves a print on my palm, marking my harpoon as an extension of me. I see my target in my mind's eye, keeping my focus sharp, but as I pull my arm forward, letting the harpoon leave my grasp, a rush of water pummels me into the sand, taking Ezera along with it. We tumble through the water as it carries us in a spiral and spits us out onto the sand, my body draped over his.

Disoriented as the water settles and finds its path of least resistance to its home, I jolt up, wet sand clinging to the side of my face, and realize Calypso manipulated the water nearby to knock us out of her way. The efforts of such magic are barely visible as she continues to hold her stance.

Before she can strike again, Okiro and Kai are on her in an instant as Ezera and I find our bearings. Ezera's face is a mess of wet golden strands and sand. His saturated eyes find mine immediately. "Are you okay?"

I nod brushing the sand with the back of my arm, feeling its grit slide across my cheek in the process. He gets to his feet, machete raised in defense as he drags a strand of hair away from my face.

Even in a moment of distress, he finds a way to care for me.

Calypso summons the water once again, creating water nymphs from the ocean, but the two sea warriors block each blow that is unleashed in their direction. The water acts as her shield and her weapon as she uses it to protect herself and ambush us with dizzying blows. Every time a translucent water nymph is stricken down by a blow, its form losing shape and blending back into the sea, it comes right back up fully formed and relentless.

Despite her being outnumbered, Calypso is too strong. A force to be reckoned with. Kai and Okiro move in tandem with one another taking turns striking in a dance of battle. All the while, that sadistic smile never leaves her face. It takes me a moment to realize what they have planned.

Slowly, they push her back to the water. They know that once they hit a certain depth, she will be no match for them. Her water maneuvers won't be as effective if they are submerged. Or if they can manipulate it just as she can. They may not have mastered water manipulation as she has, or have as much power as she does, but they do know how to fight.

Vaguely, I hear Brea's voice and know she has regained consciousness. Hearing her strikes something within me and at the same moment, Ezera and I rush towards the water to help Kai and Okiro in their plan. Ezera must have seen what I did only moments ago because he wastes no time in striking Calypso any moment he can, dodging the pelting water, and playing offense. He moves quickly in the sand, and for a moment I miss my legs. I miss the freedom of movement on land.

Ezera, Kai, Okiro, and I work as one battling Calypso's water nymph, and her tail strikes, pushing her farther and farther into the sea. With the movements of her wrist, the water nymphs appear out of the sea-like creatures, fully formed and lethal. Their clear bodies bend and move just as a living being would, but no amount of fighting them off will kill them. They just reform with every strike, controlled by Calypso's power.

Every inch of water we gain, the more mobile we become, sliding and slicing through the water, circling Calypso as we move, surrounding her from all sides. But one thing I didn't anticipate is that although we might have more of an advantage in the water, so does she. Calypso summons the water surrounding us and knocks me off balance once again. I tumble through the waves, kicking up sand that blurs my vision once again. I break through the wave and find Ezera is losing his advantage as the water now laps his middle. He is no match for Calypso once she hits water. Now she is in her element.

Suddenly, Kai strikes Calypso in the side with his dagger, and she cries out as blood mixes with water, spilling from her. Relentlessly he strikes again, but not before Calypso tears her talons along his chest, leaving crimson lines running down his flesh. The waves and quick motions of battle make it almost impossible to have an advantage, or to even get a clear visual of the scene at hand.

Okiro holds up his gleaming trident as he's pummeled by a wall of water that knocks him into the sea. He swirls for a moment before kicking his tail out and finding leverage once again.

At some point Calypso sees she is losing the battle and attempts to head closer to land, knowing that is her only advantage against three sea creatures. Get them out of the water. Inch by inch, she gains more ground, pulling us back up with her, closer to Ezera.

As Okiro and Kai battle against the water nymphs that swirl and whip above Calypso's head, clear water made into a weapon, I summon my power and hold the water with my mind, gathering up as much as I can.

She's not the only one with the power to manipulate the sea.

I keep the water flowing naturally, undetected as I gain control over every drop. When we get close enough to shore, I muster up all my power and concentrate on moving it, bending it to my will. It's heavy and full and wild as any beast, but I summon a swell and push it over Calypso in a wave that carries her to shore, spitting her out onto the wet sand. Her silver hair is like silk splayed out on the beach while she's momentarily disoriented. I don't waste my shot. I am on her in an instant.

With Atargatis in hand, I know what I must do. She will never let any of us leave this island. There is no scenario where we would both leave this island alive. Without a moment to spare, I aim the tip of my harpoon at the center of her chest and lean into the shaft, spearing Calypso through her center, feeling the resistance of the blade as it passes through her chest and into the sandy ground below.

Immediately the water she held power over calms as her blood begins to spread around us in a pool of red before being swept up in a lapping wave and taken back out to sea, only for more to flow in its place. She looks down at her chest in disbelief as her hands settle on the shaft of the weapon. But it's no use, she isn't going anywhere now.

When she drops her head back down to the wet sand, she lets out a vicious laugh that makes my skin crawl. Blood bubbles behind her fangs and trickles down the sides of her smiling mouth, silencing the wicked laughter. She coughs up crimson as she says in her smooth, syrupy voice, "Thank you," before her chest stills and her eyes fix on a point in the sky. Unmoving.

An icy cool breeze blasts out from her body, and something in my blood tells me it is the magic leaving her, dispersing into the atmosphere once again.

The three males join around me as we watch the blood flow from the killer of the sea. Never again will she take an innocent life from this earth. Never again will she harm my people of Aqualasia. We stay there in silence as we watch her body disintegrate into sea foam, each wave taking a bit more of her away with it.

Something deep within my chest struggles to feel grief or relief for what I did. Never before have I killed anything. Although Calypso had a reason for what she did, it doesn't make it right. And her final words, *thank you*, it's like she knew her days were numbered. As if she knew she didn't deserve to live. But it didn't stop her from putting up a fight. It didn't stop her from wanting to take us down first.

Maybe the pain she felt from the years of sorrow and despair was eating her from the inside. Whatever her reasoning, the world is safer without her in it. I don't believe she felt a bit of remorse. Her conscience did not weigh heavily with guilt. She did not mourn the countless lives she stole. Her grief from the past clouded her judgment.

She was beyond reason.

Because of that, there was only one way of stopping her. Ending her.

Brea seems to have recovered as she and Marina move slowly towards us, towards the lapping waves on the shore. Their arms laced in one another as Marina helps Brea along.

"Are you alright?" My voice quivers with emotion. Too much has happened too quickly, and the shock of it all is catching up with me. The blood from Brea's head has dried and crusted over. I leave Calypso's foaming remains to help clean Brea's wound, using the water to wash the blood away.

"I'll be fine. Just wish I could have helped." I almost laugh at her response. Typical Brea to worry more about the challenge in front of her than her own well-being. "But from what I saw, you lot had it handled."

"That we did," Kai counters, now waist-deep in the water, cleaning off his weapon.

"How will we manage this without her?" I worry aloud. "Can it be done?"

"I don't see why not. Calypso was behind the research, but you are the key to this whole thing." Water droplets trickle down Okiro's dark skin as the waves crash around him, splashing off his solid figure. I look over to Ezera who appears as if he's just seen the sky fall. I don't blame him in the slightest. I've never seen a body dissolve into sea foam before either. But for Ezera, there is so much more he's been exposed to in the last hour than I've been in the last month. As soon as our eyes meet, he strides towards me with determination.

"I am in awe of you," he says, threading his fingers through my damp curls. Heat fills my insides as I look up at him in search of any hint of falsity. But I find none. What I did hasn't changed a thing. Or maybe it has but not in the negative way I was worried about. He doesn't see blood on my hands, or a soulless creature. He only sees me, just as he did before. And I couldn't be more relieved, because what transpired here on the beach has left me less than stable.

But I cannot allow that. Not now. I need to get my head on straight for what is to come. I made a promise to my people and I will not break it. After all they've endured, they deserve their freedom. They deserve to have their ties cut from a curse that should never have been created in the first place.

"I hate to ask, but . . . how do we get up there without Calypso to guide us?" Marina's hesitant voice sobers me as I follow her gaze up the rising crater. To the vast opening of the volcano.

"The power of water isn't hers alone," Brea speaks with conviction as she raises her arms, summoning a stream of water to rise from the surf and snake around our tails, lifting us up from the ground. It takes me a moment to find my balance in the strange water, but once I do, I almost feel as if I'm floating on land as I idle within the water's hold.

"Damn, Brea. Since when did you get the power to summon an entire ocean?" Okiro isn't the only one who is wide-eyed with admiration. Kai raises his arms and looks around his waist that's wrapped in water, suspending him above ground. Marina giggles with excitement as she swishes her tail in the snaking river of water connecting us all. All but Ezera of course, who stands in amazement just outside of the stream.

"Oh, you know. I've been dabbling in water manipulations ever since I knew it was possible to summon more than a few drops," she muses. "On occasion, I may tamper with a few ships carrying cargo across seas." I imagine the looks of wary sea merchants as they grab for purchase when caught in a rouge riptide or a misplaced wave appearing from nowhere. Of course Brea enjoys teasing sailors who think the sea belongs to them.

"This is incredible." Hesitantly, Ezera reaches his hand out to the flowing water and brushes his fingers through. If I didn't know any better, I'd say Ezera was under the impression he was caught in some sort of warped dream.

"You coming with us, sailor?" We all wait for his response to my invitation, accepting Ezera as part of this group on a quest to break a curse. He did sail all this way, after all. He might as well stay for the big finale. His smile tells me enough.

"As if I would be foolish enough to pass this up." He chuckles as he secures his weapon on his belt and ties his locks back into a knot. He walks beside us, but Brea extends the water to capture him as well, surrounding him from the waist down in suspension. His eyes are bright with wonder as we begin to ascend up the mountainous rock.

As we make our way up the volcano's side, I can't help but wonder how much power and strength it must take to not only carry a stream of water up such a far distance but to carry passengers within the water too. And not just any passengers. The three males traveling with us are twice the size of Brea, if not more.

I watch her closely as the jungle below gets smaller and smaller with each stretch of the journey, thinking that at any moment I might drop to the rock, water trailing back down the hill. But Brea's hold doesn't break, despite her injury. It doesn't even so much as quiver as we make our way to the top. It is for this reason alone that I don't offer my help. I don't want to rattle her confidence or question her abilities. That must be why the others haven't offered to assist her either. She's enjoying every moment of this. Pride is written all over her striking face.

I look to Marina, noting her prolonged silence as the sun sinks lower to the horizon, creating a violet sky.

"You okay?" I whisper to her from behind. She turns to nod at me, but her eyes don't bring me much reassurance.

"Just nervous."

"You don't think we can do this?"

"No. It's not that. I just . . . I have this feeling. Like something is about to go wrong. Like Calypso didn't tell us the whole truth." Her words strike me right in the gut, causing the dark tendrils of fear to creep in. "Who is to say that the cost of breaking this curse isn't the one wielding it?"

"You think I'm in danger." Understanding her worry, I see the unease line her eyes as she nods.

"Well, it's a good thing I have you as my anchor to keep me where I need to be." The truth is, I'm worried too. What Marina says is entirely possible. Calypso would have done anything if it meant breaking this curse. Even if the cost was me. But I won't back out now. That's not who I am. I will pay the price.

When we make it to the top, the sky is dark and Brea spreads us out around the mouth of the crater and everyone holds their own orb of water in place, except me. Brea will continue to support me as I begin the incantation, knowing I won't have enough control to do both. Ezera stands beside me, ready to fend off any dangers that arise. But if anything threatens my life up here, it won't be something he can battle against. I look around at the group with their faces aglow from the burning contents within the volcano, at the strong souls around me, and pray that I can handle this.

With the moon casting its light upon us, I pull the shell that holds the ring from the pouch on my harness holding Atargatis in place and gently open it up. The ring sits within the bed of the shell, looking as if it were any old piece of jewelry. But I can feel the hum of raw power.

I will my hand not to tremble as I place the ring on my finger, sliding it down to the webbing. It takes everything in me to hold down the fear within me. To keep it under wraps. If I let it go for even a second, I know I won't be able to reign it back in.

I look to Marina who flanks my other side and she hands me the dagger, hilt first. I grab it in silence and turn back to the steaming pit in front of me and begin.

TWENTY-EIGHT

I look up to the moon, wondering if my mother is doing the same. If she's sitting on her balcony, a glass of red in her hand, as she scours the moon's face for answers. Something tells me she is. That she is looking at the same moon as I am and wondering about me.

The pit below heats my face to an uncomfortable temperature. If it weren't for the water that surrounds my tail keeping me cool, I might worry for our safety. The yellow and orange glow that swells and bubbles is mesmerizing, like I'm watching liquid fire. Such contrast to the glowing light coming from above.

Cool white stars twinkle silently amongst the Full Celestia. An entire cycle has come and gone, leaving another glowing face in the sky. Okiro watches above for when the moon is entirely and truly at its fullest for me to begin. Waiting for its blurred edges to sharpen against the midnight sky.

The sound of the waves crashing below lulls me enough to function and keep my wits about me while I wait. Somehow that roaring sound has the power to calm and center me at once. Ring donned and dagger in hand, I practice the words of the incantation in my head, as I have the entire trip here. I've committed it to memory long before we left our waters, but I can't help but recite them once more as if to rehearse for a performance. A performance to the Mother, to give back the merfolk's freedom.

The whites of Okiro's eyes glow from the lava below as he nods at me, sending chills down my spine.

This is it. The final act.

I feel Ezera place a feather-light kiss on my bare shoulder before stepping away, giving me space to work. One last time I look up to the Full Celestia and offer up a silent prayer to the Mother, to anyone who's listening. The hilt of the dagger is now warm in my hand from the heat of the lava, creeping up from the shining metal end.

Marina removes my diadem from the braids that hold it in place and gently hands it to me. I watch the moon's reflection in the many faces of the gems, giving a silent apology to all of the queens that wore this jeweled piece, before tossing it into the molten lava below.

As the heirloom leaves my fingertips, my heart tightens at the loss. Without a sound, it disappears into the glowing orange heat, forever lost to the elements. I hold out my arm over the mouth of the volcano, the ring reflecting its many faces as I turn my palm up.

Pressing the tip of the dagger to my wrist, I draw a long slow line up to the crook of my arm, the blade slicing like butter. A gasp escapes my lips as pain sears through me, burning white hot, like a shock to my system.

I keep the blade steady as I continue on. My blood pours from my arm into the molten lava below, and when the first few drops meet the bubbling orange of the earth's core, I begin reciting the incantation in the unfamiliar tongue of the old language.

As the words flow from my lips, my blood flows into the vast crater. I feel a tug from the ring wrapped around my finger. That familiar hum is strong now, almost as if I can pull on it. Like it is a real living thing connecting me to the moon up above and the earth below. Pebbles dance and the ground beneath us begins to rumble, shaking the entire island. Yellow light shoots up from the depths of the volcano up towards the open sky, and I nearly jolt back from the shock.

I hear gasps from the others, but I continue reciting the incantation as my blood continues to pour. My body feels charged with something strong, like the magic coursing through, and it feels alive with a buzz of electricity. Something so foreign to me.

As the world seems to come alive around me, I continue to let the magic work in whatever way it should, knowing an entire species is counting on me. Calypso said everything will begin to settle when the curse is finally broken. That is how I should know it is done. By every-thing, I see she now referred to the light and the earthquake.

A little notice would have been nice.

My head begins to lighten as the minutes tick by, feeling like enormous trees are growing right from my skull, and I know it's from the blood loss. I know the signs; dizziness, disorientation, pale skin. Sometimes clammy. But in my current state, I can't be sure if the same symptoms apply. I pray I have enough blood in me to break this damned curse. I pray it doesn't kill me in the process because—wait.

Liquid life pays the price. The ring. It was trying to tell me the true cost of breaking the curse was my blood. *All* of my blood.

Even if I wanted to stop now, the magic has its hold on me, and I can't stop what has already begun. Whatever magic this is has its claws deep in me, and it is greedy. It will take all that it needs from me, and now I know how much that is.

Blotches of black and white blur my vision, and I try to blink them away out of instinct. I try to clear my head and keep my wits in check as I begin to shake with fear. I cannot lose consciousness if this is to work.

I need to continue reciting the ancient words while the moon and earth are connected by me.

I breathe deeply through my nose as I continue the words, but I suddenly feel slack, like a wilting flower in a drought. Marina's warm hands cup my shoulders, stabilizing me physically and mentally, and maybe emotionally too.

As soon as her hands connect with my body, I can feel her strength pour into me, giving me life. Bringing me clarity when I can no longer see, hear or even think straight. Magic passes through me at an accelerated rate, causing a disorientation of where I am. Or maybe it's the lack of blood, I can't be sure.

I try to focus on Marina's petite hands resting on my shoulders, giving me something to hang onto as the magic pulls me every which way. But the world around me is muffled now and I can no longer hear my words clearly. I can no longer sense the roar of the waves in the background. For all I know, my voice has become a mere whisper, but still, I continue to recite it, even if it's only in my head. All I see is white. Nothing makes sense and I'm not even quite sure I am upright anymore. I'm losing all of my senses. I'm losing control.

Vaguely I hear shouting in the distance but I can't make out what is being said. I try again to focus on Marina's hands, on her connection to me like a fraying rope, but I can barely register it. Too lost in the power of the magic that courses through me. All I see is pain, all I feel is cold. And I think this is it.

This is the end.

This is the part of the curse-breaking that Calypso didn't want me to know about. This is why my parents hid this from me. Because they knew, just as Calypso did, that breaking this curse was a death sentence. That breaking this curse would be the beginning of a new life for the merfolk, but the end for me. They must have seen my life diminish in the prophecy. That was the price that needed to be paid. Not just my blood, but my entire being.

My soul.

My life.

Never will I get to see my parents again or Angelina. Never will I take my place on the throne. Never will I know what it's like to truly be with Ezera. Never will I know what it is to become a mother. Never again will I live wild and free.

If my sacrifice gives life to countless others, I will endure. I will accept my fate—as what I was meant to do.

I attempt to let go of the tether pulling me—

Blackness. Complete and utter blackness. I see nothing. Hear nothing. Feel nothing. But my thoughts do not stop flowing. Like a dream of consciousness. Or subconsciousness. Is this death? Is this what it feels like?

"*Cealene.*" Ezera's voice fills the empty space, and my heart swells in my chest.

A yellow light dies, and I realize it's from the volcano. I only see shadows and the faint presence of glowing orange. The shaking subsides and someone tugs at my body. Someone grabs my arm and wraps it tightly. I feel small pebbles that litter the mouth of the volcano digging into my flesh, and I begin to understand I'm flat on my back.

Slowly, my senses return one by one. I see the stars above me twinkling, undisturbed by the events of the night. I also see Marina and Ezera hovering over me, their mouths moving frantically. I feel the spatial awareness of my arms and tail as if I've become whole again. Finally, words begin to form in my mind as I hear them more clearly. Like I've just surfaced from the ocean to hear crystal-clear sounds once more.

"Cealene . . . can you hear me?" Ezera's face is aged with worry like he's been kept awake for days on end. The rims of his reddened eyes glisten with tears.

"She's okay, Ezera. Give her a minute to reorient herself." Marina's voice is a comfort to me when I hear her. "You did everything you could. Just give her time." I try to sit up but Marina pushes my shoulders back down, "Oh no you don't. Stay put." Ezera shifts behind me and cradles me between his outstretched legs as I rest my head on his warm chest.

Once the world dies down and my senses return, silence fills the air. I look around at everyone and—

Fire.

Immense pain floods my senses. My muscles seize and I hear the others drop to the ground. Ezera is shouting my name, grabbing my cheeks. I look at Marina convulsing on the ground but I squeeze my eyes in pain as another wave of fire hits me. It feels as if someone is tearing my tail in two. Pain erodes my ribs like someone is tearing at my skin. I grip the loose dirt as fire shudders through me, and I see the scales begin to disappear. I watch as the claws retract and my webbing subsides. I'm . . . shifting. Into human form.

Ezera hovers over me now, still holding my face in his hands. "Cealene, talk to me. Are you alright?"

"Cealene—" His voice is a distance echo through the fire searing through my blood. My tail splits in two and look down to see the damage, almost too afraid to look. I glance at Ezera, who is pale as the moon, eyes like saucers. My fins have turned to sea foam and skin is forming where scales once lived. I begin to feel the sensation of legs once again, after so long without them.

My mind spins searching for answers. Calypso never said anything about the curse breaking any restrictions on transforming. She never even mentioned anything about shifting beyond the moon's cycle. But the proof is right here, on this volcano. It's in my inflamed nerves and my sea foam fins. Can we now shift at will? Is the restriction gone?

I sit up once the pain subsides and look around. Marina is curled on her side, Kai crawling towards her on all fours. Each and every one of us with two legs instead of a tail. No gills, no scales, no pointed ears. Immediately I reach up, feeling for the stones, and huff a sigh of relief to know they're still there, and haven't vanished with the rest of my body parts. I look to Ezera, who has grabbed my shoulders in his hands. "Cealene, you're—"

"Human," I whisper in disbelief.

Twenty-Nine

Nothing makes sense. We missed the window to shift into our human forms. The waning of the moon has already begun, the slightest edge of the moon's crest, fuzzy with black night. We shouldn't be this way. I might have been on the fence about where tonight would take me but the others didn't want this. How can this be?

"What is happening?" Marina asks, losing any sense of calm that she once had. Still recovering from the painful process of shifting.

"The curse." Brea curses aloud. "Before the Sea Wars, our kind could transform at any time, without restriction. Since then, none of us had any desire to visit land so the restriction was all but forgotten as the years went on." She extends her legs in front of her, kicking and bending.

"Why didn't Calypso mention any of this?" I glide my hands along my legs.

"I really don't know. Maybe she wanted us kept in the dark." Brea attempts to walk over the rocky terrain with her bare feet, her dark legs resembling a baby fawn's. Marina is marveling at her toes stretched out in front of her, while Kai and Okiro stride and stretch their newly formed legs, somehow just as muscular as their tails.

The naked body means nothing to the merfolk, but as I was raised human, I try to avert my eyes out of respect as they round our area of the slanted hill. Ezera, raised to view nudity as all humans are, personal and private, tugs off his shirt and slips it over my head, the hem falling just below my bottom.

"Shall we make the descent back down to the beach?"

"Yes." Brea drawls, "I need to get back into the water. These legs feel all wrong." She hurries back to the beach, not wanting to waste another minute.

"Couldn't agree more. This is unnatural." Kai strides down the rocky trail, and I try not to laugh at their strange gait. "How do you two live like this? Everything is so . . . dry."

"And heavy," Marina adds, sensing the constant pull of gravity, and the lack of buoyancy. At that, Ezera and I laugh at the thought of finding the human form cumbersome and strange.

"When it's all you know, it seems pretty practical actually." Ezera scoops me up into his arms and follows behind Marina, stepping through the patchy terrain of rock and sand. "You shouldn't be exerting too much energy. You've lost a lot of blood and have just undergone a tremendous amount of physical stress." He explains his actions before I even have a chance to retort the gesture like he knew I would soon protest. But any retort dies on my lips, knowing he is right. I can still feel the weakness in my bones like lead, and I wonder how much of it is due to the curse breaking and how much of it is a result of shifting.

As soon as we hit the sand, Brea, Kai, and Okiro rush to the frothy-tipped waves, and dive right into the surf, disappearing beneath the dark waters. I know it will take only moments for the shift to complete.

My skin chills at the thought of going through the pains of shifting again, especially so soon after enduring it already, the tearing of flesh and bone, the fusing of tissues, and the reformation of the skeleton. The fire that runs through our veins when our make-up changes from one species to an entirely different one. The literal rearrangement of our entire bodies is a process you don't want to endure often.

But I suppose, for them, the thought of living in this form for a moment longer is more painful to them than the transformation itself. These creatures aren't meant to be human, to live on land. Not only is it unnatural to them, it's unwanted. These souls belong in the sea. Just as mine does. But unlike me, these creatures don't have ties to the land and its people. They weren't raised from birth to rule a kingdom. They weren't primed to lead the lands of Aqualasia.

Marina begins to step into the black surf, the water rushing around her ankles when she turns back to me, noticing my reluctance. "Cealene? Are you coming?"

The wide-eyed, unguarded look on her petite face breaks my heart, not wanting to blindside her with what will come next.

"Actually . . . I'm going to sail home with Ezera." I lace my fingers in his as I look up at him, finding his eyes in the darkness of the night. "If that's alright with you."

His smirk sends waves of heat to my core as his gaze simmers. "I wouldn't want it any other way."

"But it's dangerous, two humans sailing home in just a small boat. Something could happen." The gang hovering in the water looks to me in the dark. My heart swells at the concern my new family has shown.

"We'll be alright. We know these waters," Ezera confirms. "I would never let anything happen to you." He turns to me again and I try not to melt in front of my friends. Tearing my eyes away from his gaze, I look to Kai, Brea, and Okiro idling just beyond the curling waves.

"If we run into any trouble, I can always shift if needed." The group looks to one another considering this new freedom and nods in agreement. After what we've all been through tonight, they trust Ezera and they trust my capabilities. Marina leaves the surf and approaches me, wrapping her chilled bare arms around me in a gentle embrace.

"Please be careful. If you two don't return when expected, I'm coming after you myself." My chest fills with pride to have someone as fierce as Marina in my corner.

"I would expect nothing less." I wink at her with a grin, knowing that this fierce soul is my anchor in every sense of the word.

Hand in hand, we watch as Marina dives into the dark waters, bubbles forming around her beneath the sea. Minutes later, she emerges near the group beyond the surf, their silhouettes just small figures against the vast midnight sea. Kai waves his webbed hand high in the air in farewell before diving below the surface, his fluke spraying salt water into the night sky like glitter. The others follow after him, disappearing from sight in the darkness. Leaving Ezera and I alone on this quiet island.

"Ready to set sail?" He asks, those impossible eyes glowing in the night.

"Lead the way."

Thirty

Watching Ezera get ready to set sail, I am mesmerized by his quick movements. It's second nature to him, no doubt ingrained in him from a young age. Without much knowledge about sailing myself, I find his practiced moves enchanting. He glides across the boat with such ease that I believe if I were to blindfold him, he could still set sail without issue.

As we push off into the open sea, I find that I miss my enhanced vision in the night. Endless black surrounds us up ahead as the hulking form of the island gets smaller and smaller in our wake. Only the bright moon and stars illuminate our night. That, and the glowing yellow lamps scattering the deck of the *Juliette*.

Ezera marks the stars above, double-checking his coordinates before settling down next to me on a small woven blanket he laid out for us.

He pulls the cork from the bottle of rum he procured earlier from the small hatch near the stern and pours the amber liquid into two short glasses. He hands me a glass and before taking a sip, he clinks his drink to mine, "To breaking curses."

"To starry nights," I counter. We sip in silence and I marvel at the heat the liquor provides when it goes down, warming my chilled skin. Another unfortunate trait of being in this form is my sensitivity to temperature. The cool breeze of the open water bites into my skin, causing a constant chill on my arms. I hug the second blanket tighter around my shoulders, trying to hold in the heat.

Sensing my discomfort, Ezera pulls me to his chest, warming my body with his. He brushes the pad of his thumb along my bandaged arm. My finger still tingles from where the ring once was. When the curse was broken, I vaguely remember Marina tearing it off my finger and flinging it into the volcano before the pain of the shift took hold. I assume it was best to bury it in a volcano, lost to the world. Unable to be used again.

"How are you feeling?" His question brings me pause as I truly consider my answer. How am I feeling? After the battle with Calypso, the curse breaking, nearly dying, and then shifting back into my human form, I truly don't know if there is even an answer for how I am feeling.

"I'm . . . really not sure." I consider. "Relieved? Tired? Strange?" His low chuckle against my ear sends an electric current down my spine.

"I honestly thought I was dying. I *felt* like I was dying."

"I thought . . ." Ezera pauses. His voice is thick with emotion. "I thought for a moment that I was going to lose you." I rest my head against his chest, looking up at the stars. "It was the hardest thing I've ever done to watch you suffer and not be able to do anything about it. I tried to. But they wouldn't let me stop it.

"If it weren't for Okiro, I truly don't know if you would be here with me right now."

"What do you mean?"

"You were losing so much blood, I offered to give you mine. Okiro used his water magic to transfer my blood to you. He spun my blood with water like a mini tornado, altering it before sending it to you." He shows me the wound on his arm where they must have siphoned his blood from. "I guess he learned how to do it during the Sea Wars. Said it saved countless lives during battle."

Speechless, I grab hold of his arm, not believing my ears. If it weren't for Ezera's blood, I would be dead right now. Not lounging on a boat under the stars. Sailing home with a beautiful man who saved my life, and solved the mystery of the missing women that has plagued me for months.

"I'm sorry . . ." My words die out as I turn to stare up at him. Before I can thank him, he grabs my chin with his fingers and stares into my eyes with an all-consuming intensity. I stare back at him, lost in his gaze. I cannot seem to tear my eyes away. He leans towards me and my stomach flips.

"Don't ever be sorry, Cealene." His scent is intoxicating. Like sea salt and cedar. Sunshine and freedom. He glances down at my lips, parted but unmoving, and back up to my eyes, our noses only a breath apart.

Our lips meet for the first time as equals, and I nearly melt with desire. I deepen the kiss as his hand trails across my jaw and his fingers find their way into my hair, pulling me closer. Our tongues collide in a dance as I become feverish with greed, needing more. Flowers bloom within my chest as I turn my body towards his.

His lips are soft, and his mouth is warm. My body is no longer cold from the night, but heating from within, like a burning flame. All at once, I taste sunshine, hope, rum, and desire. This kiss . . . it's like nothing I have ever felt before. Nothing else seems to matter except for this, his mouth on mine, his hand on the back of my neck, his fingers in my hair.

The rush of this kiss courses through my veins and I never want this feeling to end, gluttonous for every bit of him. Like he is oxygen and I'm deprived. I reach around his torso, feeling the ripple of his muscles under his rumpled cotton shirt. I glide my fingers up his back and down again, my hand memorizing every inch of him.

He kisses me with purpose, with desire, making me burn all over. My skin is on fire, delicious heat licking at my skin. Such a difference from the burn of shifting. I run my hands down his chest, feeling the small mountains of muscle along the way.

When I reach his hips I roll on top of him with the help of his hands. His fingers travel my skin with feverish intent, and I feel every touch like a brand. His tongue is warm and soft as it grazes my teeth. My mind is shooting stars off to somewhere in space. Before I know it, I am on my back facing the stars that sparkle around, his features aglow from the lamplight.

"I think I've been falling for you since the first day I met you." His conviction swells my heart.

Ezera's eyes swirl with desire and the look on his face is hunger. He takes too much time lifting my borrowed shirt up over my head. Agonizingly slow as the soft material drags up my skin, leaving me completely naked under the moonlight. The fire that burns from within has counteracted the chill from the night.

"You stop my breath," he purrs, looking at me with a hint of a smile. My eyes roam his body, trying to memorize every inch of him. His light tousled hair, the bulk of his shoulders, the smooth skin of his chest. The deeply cut lines of his muscled torso.

He leans down, hovering over me, kissing every inch of my flesh. Marking my skin with each touch of his lips. Traveling down my neck to my chest and past my belly button, each kiss heightens my senses and causes bursts of colors behind my eyes. My insides are molten and I pull his face back up to mine kissing him with a thirst for more. His hands roam down my torso to my hips, sending chills up my spine. My body pulses. He pulls back again to look at me, and my body reels with sensation.

Ezera leans over me once again as his hands travel up my freshly formed leg, up my side, and gets lost in my hair. He kisses my collarbone and I feel him take a shaky breath when he pulls away.

"I need you," I whisper to him as I run my hands down his back. With that, he melts. His ocean eyes are set on fire. His expression intensifies and he dives into me, crashing into the waves of my body. And I am lost. Utterly lost. In space. In time. In *him*.

For the first time in too many days, I finally know what tomorrow will hold.

THIRTY-ONE

As the drums boom over the island in rhythm with my heart, my nerves fray in anticipation of seeing my parents. I tell myself to loosen my grip on Ezera's hand, but it seems my body has stopped taking advice from my mind. My other hand holds the small mermaid figurine Marina made for me when I told her I was heading back to the palace, its icy surface keeping me calm as I walk towards my home. The flowing tail is an exact replica of my own, to remind me of my other home. To remind me of my other family deep within the sea.

Still in Ezera's rumpled shirt and a pair of pants found near the docks and Atargatis proudly strapped to my back, I try to brush out the wrinkles, even though I know the effort is futile. It doesn't matter what I wear. My parents will see my dark, bouncing curls approach and know I've finally come home. Not that the palace guards would have allowed us to make it this far down the path if they weren't positive of my identity.

The sound of the drums marks my return from my supposed trip to a neighboring land, but I know my parents are waiting at the entrance of the palace to welcome me. I'm vaguely curious what they will tell the guards as to my haphazard state, but that is a problem for another day.

The cobblestones of the smoothed pavement that leads up to the palace gates brush on my bare feet, warmed from the sun. The royal flags flying high snap in the breeze.

"You nervous?" Ezera asks, and I almost slug him for asking a question he clearly knows the answer to as he squeezes my white-knuckled hand. My mind reels back to the Prince of Tudeland and the betrothal he spoke of. Without knowing if it was just talk or something signed in blood, I will face it head-on. I will decide my fate.

"Are you?" I counter. "You're about to meet the King and Queen of Aqualasia." His face drops as the words hit him, and I almost feel sorry for frightening him as we near the palace doors.

"Are you sure they are going to be okay with this? You and me?" I watch as the sun bounces off his white-tipped hair and know there's no denying my feelings for this man.

"I mean a princess and a fisherman cannot be a match your parents want." As much as I wish his concerns were superficial, I know they're not. Showing up at the steps of Pearle Castle with Ezera on my arm after being gone for weeks speaks volumes. I'm not expecting them to take this news lying down. But they know I wouldn't waste time bringing just anyone to them. And so publicly. But he isn't just anyone. Not to me.

"If my parents believe in me enough to one day rule the island, I think they can trust in my decision to bring you to the palace. They know my values and they will know I do not make this decision lightly." Again, I look up at him and meet his gaze, the sun peeking out from behind his frame. "Plus, you're quite charming if I'm being honest."

That gets a chuckle out of him, which is exactly what I was going for. His smile brightens his whole face as he tilts his head to the skies. His free spirit fits right in line with mine, and those of the sea. No wonder he's so drawn to it.

Last night I decided that my life is my own and mine alone. That I can live up to my name without losing a part of myself in the process. I've faced death and won. If court life is not what I need it to be, I have the power to change it. I can be the heiress to the throne *and* live wild and free. If I decided to give up a part of myself, I would no longer be me anymore. I would lose a part of myself that would change who I truly am. If I decided to deny the part of me that yearns for the sea, I wouldn't be fit to rule my people. Just as I wouldn't be whole if I gave up my life on land. I have proven to myself time and time again that I can handle more than I give myself credit for. I broke an ancient curse and lived a life in the sea, fending for myself and learning what it truly means to be me.

Upon returning home, the people will learn the true histories of our kind and of what lives beneath our waters. I have to believe that the king and queen as well as our council will see the future that I do. That they will understand there is no longer a way to ignore the reality of merpeople living amongst us. And if they don't, I will make them see. The faults of our ancestors shouldn't define our future. Our kingdom will view the people of the sea as equals and will be protected under the royal crest. A royal decree will be issued stating that the merfolk will be welcome to our lands and can call it their own if they so wish. If any harm comes to them as it once did, there will be grave consequences.

If land and sea once lived in harmony, we can do so again.

As we near the castle, the pearl accents come into view giving the palace a dreamy feel. The guards line the path, armor polished to a shine, as we ascend the wide sprawling steps. My parents await at the gates, tears streaking my mother's cheeks.

Before I know it, my steps quicken as I remember how my mother knelt below my willow. She bursts forward and we rush to one another. I barely feel Ezera's warm hand leave mine as I hurry into my mother's arms and weep. Weep for all that has happened to me, to her, to our people. From both land and sea. I weep for frightening her with my sudden disappearance. For not fully understanding what they tried to protect me from. For the threat that Calypso posed to her just moments after she gave birth in a storm. For everything.

As old as you grow, I don't know if anyone ever truly won't find comfort in their mother. As we embrace each other under the beaming sun, I feel my father's arms encircle us. He plants a kiss in my hair and I smell his signature scent of leather and cinnamon.

I pull away too soon, knowing there are things that need to be addressed. Like the strapping fisherman standing behind me, who no doubt feels out of place right about now.

"Mama. Daddy." I look directly into their eyes as I speak, head held high, "This is Ezera Calder. He's a fisherman from the docks . . . and he . . ." Suddenly I find it hard to speak. "He saved my life." I reach my hand out to him and he smiles as he takes it, walking forward as I tug him near. When he approaches my parents, he bows low.

"It is an absolute honor, Your Majesties."

"Rise, dear boy. I am quite familiar with your father, Harrison. He is a respectable man and has been of quite assistance on the docks for years. Your boat has recently been marked with the royal crest if I'm not mistaken."

"That's right, Your Majesty. I thank you for the opportunity to provide your family with what the sea has to offer."

My mother cups my face in her slender hand and smiles, glancing at Ezera. "Come. We have much to discuss."

With Ezera at my side, we walk with the king and queen into Pearle Palace. Into a brighter future.

Epilogue

The wisps of clouds pass by overhead through the canopy of green vines that dance in the breeze. My legs rest along the trunk of the willow as I lie in my favorite spot. Dark curls dangle from the branch as I turn to watch Ezera lap the vibrant pool below. His tanned skin shines in the sun as the muscles in his back ripple with his movements.

Upon arriving home, I learned that meetings had been held in my absence about teaching our people the truth of our histories and how the king and queen plan to go about handling this. Apparently, when their daughter disappeared the night of a full moon, they knew it was time to come clean. To my delight, the Full Celestia celebrations have come to an end and I can now view the full moon from the quiet of my balcony along with Ezera and Angelina, who took a liking to each other quickly. Or maybe I will spend the night under the full moon out on the water, with my pod near the grotto. No matter what I plan to do, it will be my decision and it will be true. No longer will my life be decided based on lies or deceit or due to anyone else's desires but my own.

Upon coming home, at the first opportunity, I came to visit my willow, searching for Alana. I wanted to inform her of her sister's death and what it would mean for her captivity. I wanted to tell her that even though Calypso was gone, that I wouldn't give up on finding a way to free her. But when she didn't respond to my calls, I dove into the sparkling blue pool in search of her, my legs shifting to a tail, but she was nowhere to be found.

Instead, I found her jeweled crown lying on the sandy base of the willow with one word etched into the sand. *Thanks.*

Somehow, when Calypso died, or maybe when the curse was broken, Alana was freed from her prison. Maybe I will see her again in the sea, but if I don't, I can't blame her for wanting to swim as far away from here as possible. To start her life anew.

"You ready?" Ezera stands waist-deep in the water, sun rays bouncing off his glistening skin. I jump down from the arm of the willow as he walks out from the water, his strides sending him higher and higher onto the mossy grass. I meet him halfway and wrap my arms around his neck, kissing his sea-salted lips. When he wraps his arms around my waist, pulling me in, I squeal feeling the cool water seep through my lilac dress.

"Not anymore, now that my outfit is soiled!" I scold him playfully. But instead of replying, he hoists me up, threatening to toss me into the sparkling pool.

"I don't think a group of mermaids will care if your frilly dress is wet with seawater." His accusation isn't lost on me as he raises an eyebrow. A challenge of sorts.

"I just want to look nice for them! For the baby." When Marina sent word that she was with child, I nearly dropped to my knees and wept with joy. I knew it wouldn't take long. Her desire to mother one of her own was something she never thought she'd get a chance to do. And she's not the only one. Many mermaids have conceived successfully since the curse has been broken, and soon our waters will be filled with tiny tails learning the wonders of the sea. The amount of aquamarine gems Brea has sent to me on behalf of others is now laughable. I understand that the merpeople are grateful for my role in breaking the curse, but to me, it just feels like something I needed to do. Something I was meant to do.

"Come on, Princess. Your chariot awaits." Ezera's hand extends to me, palm up towards the sky, and I grab it following him out of the forest and to the docks so we can sail the *Juliette* to the Blue Grotto. As much as my heart yearns to dive into the sea and swim out to visit my friends, I have business to attend to here on land that is essential to the lives of both humans and merfolk.

My father has requested another meeting amongst the Aqualasian council to finalize the new law allowing peace and harmony to be extended to our neighbors who live in our surrounding waters. Merfolk will now be protected by the royal crest and are welcome on our lands. Anyone who threatens harm to the merfolk will be dealt with swiftly. Tomorrow the new laws will go into effect, starting a new chapter for Aqualasia Islands. There will be bumps in the road and some resistance, but we will take it in stride.

Soon I will have time to shift once again, trading my legs for fins, and live beneath the surface with my people of the sea. Brea has since taken the role of leading our pod in the rock caves, giving structure to an already well-oiled machine. She was the obvious choice, already knowing much of Calypso's role from her status as her second. I'm proud of her, having always seen Brea as a leader. She's strong, sure, and has the wits to accomplish anything she desires.

When I introduced her to Angelina during a visit on the *Juliette*, she said Brea might be her sister from another species. The two hit it off immediately when Angelina suggested that Brea teach her how to sneak into her father's wine cellar without getting caught. Brea promised to teach her stealthy ways if she promised to return the favor in wine.

Upon my return home, Angelina and I spent an entire day catching up on everything and devouring pastries with tea on my balcony overlooking the sea. I told her all about that night of the Full Celestia, about Ezera, Calypso, and the curse. I told her how it felt to live in the sea and how I almost lost my life on Ember Island. She told me about court life while I was gone, and how loathsome it was without me. Something about her admission of missing me made my heart swell with love.

It's nice to be missed. To have someone who notices when your presence is no longer there. I missed her too. I missed the connection to someone who knows me inside and out. Who knows my life at the palace. I looked at her as she stuffed her mouth with a sweet cinnamon puff, sugar dusting her slender nose, and knew that I could never live my life without her in it, would never want to.

As Ezera sails the *Juliette* out to the Blue Grotto to meet Marina and the gang, I think about how dramatically my life has changed over the past six months and wonder where I would be right now if I never leaped off that ledge. If I resisted the pull that brought me to the ocean that night. I wonder if I would do it all again if given the chance. And I would. I honestly would. I would go through the pain, the heartache, the grief. I would do it all again because it wasn't all painful, and it wasn't all heartache. Most of it was filled with joy, with discovery, with adventure.

I experienced love, friendship, and the discovery of my own strength. I found myself in a way that I didn't even know I was missing. In a way that makes me feel whole now. My willow will always be my place, but I don't need it now like I used to. I don't need it to get through my days as I once did. Now I wake up knowing I can handle whatever life throws at me. Whatever riptide it sends my way.

And I'm ready.

ACKNOWLEDGEMENTS

There are so many people that helped me along this journey, and I cherish each and every one of them. First, to my husband. Thank you for all of the support you've provided while I figured out my story and how I was going to present it to the world. You gave me the time I needed to pursue this dream of mine and I will never forget that.

To my best friend and beta reader, Jess Tudela. You have been my cheerleader, my number one fan, and my confidant through it all. You were there for me every step of the way and I cannot thank you enough for your friendship and support. I literally couldn't have done this without you. I love you, Bun. To my other beta readers, Taeopae Wetterman and Jacki Miulli, thank you for allowing me to give you homework and for your insight as avid readers and lovers of story. To my fabulous critique partner, Jackie Bridges, who was my only other friend pursuing the same goal as me, thank you for your wonderful critiques and continuing on this journey with me. You have been a beacon of hope and willpower through it all and your emails have brought me to tears on more than one occasion.

To my editor, Becky Wallace, you are a lifesaver. Your expertise and wisdom went beyond anything I could have imagined. I cannot thank you enough for not only dealing with my worst habits, but also giving insight to the story. You helped me polish something into a real book I am proud of. Thank you.

To my design artist, Hampton Lamoureux, you helped my vision become a reality with this beautiful cover. Something that I have envisioned since day one is now in print and I owe that to you. Thank you for taking the time to create this work of art.

To my parents, who raised me to be confident in myself and my abilities, who showed me the world and allowed me to take it with both hands. I owe you my life.

To any and all of my friends and family who have encouraged me along the way and have shown such enthusiasm in getting your hands on my work, thank you for never letting me give up. You made me accountable.

And, finally, thank you to my readers for picking up this book about the sea and supporting me. For allowing me to gush about the glories and mystery of the ocean while weaving it into Cealene's journey. I hope my words spoke to you and you will continue on this journey with me. Thank you for letting me live my dream and obsess over mermaids in a story.

ABOUT THE AUTHOR

Tara Gabrys was born and raised in the suburbs of Chicago, Illinois and graduated from Elmhurst University. She was raised with a passion for telling story through dance all the way into her adulthood. She has since found that telling story through writing is much like a dance of words. She is most happy when surrounded by nature or near the sea. UNDER A VIOLET MOON is her debut novel with more to come. In her downtime, if she isn't ravenously reading, she is spending time with her husband, children, and chocolate lab. You can find updates on the latest via Instagram @tarangabrys

www.ingramcontent.com/pod-product-compliance
Lightning Source LLC
Chambersburg PA
CBHW021230310726
48971CB00006B/1763